"Cal, I'm telling you he's on to us!"

Andrea paused in the act of knocking on Len Daggett's door. The sound of his voice came through clearly, and she froze in place. He was speaking on the phone to her boss, Calvin Slattery. She leaned closer to the door.

"We're only asking for trouble if we mess with McLaren," Len continued. "He has to know it's us. Someone's been tailing me...the girl's room was searched and the papers have been looked through. So what does that mean to you?"

Andrea reeled in shock from what she was hearing. What was Len talking about? And who was McLaren?

Then fear assaulted her, and she spun on her heel and fled silently down the hallway.

ABOUT THE AUTHOR

Like her heroine Andrea, Marti Laven has worked as a headhunter, although her raids "weren't nearly so exciting." A longtime resident of Pasadena, California, Marti currently sells display advertising for a daily newspaper. She shares a house with two neurotic cats and enjoys travel, thrillers, Southwestern history and walks on the beach.

A MATTER OF REVENGE

MARTI LAVEN

Harlequin Books

TORONTO • NEW YORK • LONDON
AMSTERDAM • PARIS • SYDNEY • HAMBURG
STOCKHOLM • ATHENS • TOKYO • MILAN

To Kay,
for all her encouragement
in the beginning,
and to Margaret,
for her help along the way.

———————————◀———————————

Harlequin Intrigue edition published July 1985

ISBN 0-373-22022-7

Chapter One

The flight from Atlanta to Los Angeles had been tiring, the previous week's recruiting raid exhausting. Andrea Barrie was glad to be home.

The petite blonde hoisted the heavy travel bag higher on her shoulder, gripped her attaché case more firmly and stepped off the escalator into the holiday throng of the L.A.X. terminal. She paused, ignoring the rush of passengers bumping past her. A tension headache furrowed the pale skin of her forehead. There was no explaining it, but Andrea could always feel her boss's presence. As her sapphire-blue eyes swept around the terminal in tired resignation, she sighed deeply and wondered what would prompt Cal to meet her at the airport on a Sunday afternoon. Wary, she continued searching. Then she saw him, briefcase in hand, barreling his way toward her, the crowd parting like the Red Sea before Moses.

Calvin Slattery had that effect on people. While of only average height and build, Cal was a dominating presence. The shock of thick graying hair, worn fashionably long, and sharp hazel eyes were the first things a person noticed about him. After that came an awareness of money, the flaunting of it: solid gold watch, flashy gem-and-gold rings, heavy gold chain bracelet, finely tailored suit. The ready smile and the gregarious personality were for making money—selling bodies, as Cal always put it, to his customers. Watching him, the young woman shivered from a tiny trickle of fear.

Weary from too many nights of too little sleep in Atlanta, Andrea felt gritty and unattractive and wished that she had been able to freshen up before meeting Cal. He was very particular about her appearance when she was out representing the company. She might wear T-shirts and jeans to the office, but on the road, she dressed in fashionable good taste. At the moment, though, she almost couldn't have cared less about ComSearch, the engineer recruiting firm that Cal owned. Andrea wanted only to feel the soothing effects of a long, hot shower and the crisp, clean sheets on a comfy bed, neither of which she suspected she would be able to indulge herself with for several more hours.

As Cal strode toward her, his shrewd eyes reflected his approval of her traveling outfit, a soft blue wool suit worn with a white silk blouse. The tailored clothing emphasized her slender build, and her makeup, as always, accented the delicate transparency of her coloring. Yet the polished professional image was tarnished by a wisp of ash-blond hair that had strayed from its smooth twist. A judgmental smirk appeared on Cal's crooked mouth as he halted in front of her.

"How was the trip, Andi?" The man's raspy, booming voice assaulted Andrea's senses and made her headache pound furiously.

"Things went very well." She cringed as another hurrying traveler nearly knocked her off her feet. "Do you mind if we move out of this area? I feel as if I'm in the roller derby."

"Sure. Let's get a cup of coffee." Cal snatched the travel bag from her shoulder, spun on his heel and marched off, leaving Andrea to follow in his wake. As she trailed behind, her irritation at his domineering manner increased the jackhammer assault of her headache. Andrea wondered why she still worked for the man when there was so much about him that she didn't like.

He turned around in the coffee shop doorway, his penetrating gaze flowing over her. Once again, Andrea was acutely aware of the rumors that circulated the office—that she had her job only because of Cal's favor, a favor won through a discreet affair unknown to his wife. Lies, all lies. But how could she refute them when his eyes moved over her in that odd, caressing way? Of course, everyone believed the rumors. If she had been someone else, she would have believed them, too.

After Cal had returned to their table from the buffet line with their coffee, Andrea decided to get the bad news. She tucked the stray strand of hair behind her ear and smiled ruefully. "Now, I know you didn't fight the holiday airport traffic just to welcome me home. So, what's up?"

Cal's boisterous but unusually tight laugh rang out. "That's what I like about you, Andi. Bottom line. Always bottom line." From the bulging briefcase he pulled out a thick expansion cardboard file. When he spoke again, his voice was twenty decibels lower. "You're going to Seattle."

Dismayed, Andrea protested, "Cal, you must be joking!" Her normally soft, melodic voice dropped in pitch and became brisk when she asked, "When?"

"This evening." He held out the file. "Your tickets and all the trip information are in here, along with all the recruiting cards."

Her bright blue eyes hardened. "I just got back from a very long week in Atlanta. You can't expect me to fly to Seattle—not just like that."

"'Fraid so, Andi. The customer wants to do a raid on the companies up there. Especially the biggie. They landed an important government contract while you were gone, and we've been recruiting like hell this past week."

"Cal, I can't afford to go to Seattle. I'm beat. There's all my wrap-up work to do on this Atlanta trip." Andrea shook her head and said firmly, "Someone else can go."

"No." Cal swallowed a mouthful of steaming black liquid that looked to Andrea as if it could fuel a space-shuttle rocket. He glanced surreptitiously around the crowded coffee shop. "I need you there, to finish up loose ends and make sure everything goes smoothly. This Seattle raid is important." His next words were vehement. "You make the trip."

The frown etching Andrea's forehead deepened. Of course Cal wanted her in Seattle. With all of his recruiters to choose from, he never picked anyone else to make these trips. Andrea knew the reason that she was always the one to go. It wasn't because she was the most capable head-hunter in the firm, which she was, but because Cal liked to send the twenty-eight-year-old woman along as window dressing. Having an attractive recruiter run interference for the customers boosted his reputation. Of course, acting as liaison and hostess for engineers scouting for talent to steal away from unsuspecting companies often required Andrea to run her own interference. Right now she was too fatigued from the difficult assignment she had just completed even to contemplate another. Yet despite her tiredness, Cal's uncharacteristically brittle tone caught her attention.

Leaning her elbows on the table, Andrea gently massaged her throbbing temples with her fingertips. She closed her eyes for a moment and debated the wisdom of trying to pry for the reason behind Calvin Slattery's uptight manner. While the man was an arrogant, aggressive manipulator, he rarely betrayed his feelings—and even more infrequently shared any explanations. Andrea decided she would only antagonize him by expressing concern, but she didn't bother to keep her annoyance out of her voice when she stated, "I suppose I don't even have time to go home and shower."

Cal's tense belly laugh roared again. "Sorry, your flight leaves in forty minutes."

Andrea glanced at her wristwatch. It was 5:20 P.M. "I don't have any clean clothes." She glared forlornly at the carryon travel bag draped over a chair. It had been sparingly packed for a week's stay and now bore nothing but a load of laundry.

"Send them out when you get to the hotel." Cal shoved his coffee cup aside. "The Atlanta files?"

Andrea picked up her attaché case and laid it on the table. Flicking the catches open, she said, "It was a good raid. The Nordon crew was happy. It looks as if we may get some hires out of the trip." She passed an expansion file to Cal and tossed the one he had handed her in the case. "Any offers?"

"Six that I know of. And from the engineers' responses, it looks as if we have a chance to land two. Mitton and Geary. They were turned on to the work Nordon's doing. And the pay they're bound to be offered, even with the cost-of-living difference, should be good enough to tempt them." Andrea finished her bottom-line summary with more of an upbeat tone in her voice than she felt. She switched her attention to spooning sugar into her muddy coffee.

"Good."

Cal didn't sound enthusiastic, which was surprising, because when money was involved, he was always enthusiastic. Andrea wondered what was on his mind to cause that lackadaisical attitude. Sighing, she suspected that she'd find out soon enough. She usually did. And usually regretted it.

Once again the fleeting question raced through her mind: How on earth had she ever become a headhunter? After all, she had no technical training for her job as an engineer recruiter. But then, considering the way Cal ran his operation, all a person needed was the ability to learn key phrases and the quick mind that knew what question to ask next when the right answer had been given. Andrea had always thought a well-trained parrot could do most of her job. It was the interviews and raids that used her sales skills. And the badly needed money she had earned during the past two years made it worthwhile for her not to think about her choice of occupations, which she had fallen into totally by accident and ignorance. If she had to do it all over again, if her circumstances could be different, Andrea would have run for her life, knowing now what her profession meant.

"How long am I to stay in Seattle?"

Cal leaned back in the plastic chair and lit an expensive, foul-smelling cigar. "Five days. I want you to finish recruiting out of the groups that are in the files and set up all of the appropriate people for interviews." Heavy smoke exploded toward the ceiling in bursts of puffing. "The Tectron crew will fly up Thursday afternoon. Interviewing will start that night. You will all fly out Friday afternoon."

Andrea's dispirited gaze strayed from her boss to roam the nearby tables. A pair of love-struck college students huddled close, their paper cups forgotten. A trio of bored, suit-clad businessmen sat in silence, their briefcases, cigarette-butt-filled ashtrays and wrinkled overcoats declaring their airport layover. A large group of twittering gray-haired tourists were trying to pull enough tables and chairs together to seat everyone. A lone man three tables away ignored the tourists next to him and watched Andrea over the top of his raised Styrofoam cup. Andrea returned the man's blatant, dark-eyed stare, noticing nothing about him except the intensity in his magnetic eyes. Then, feeling uncomfortable, she forced herself to look away.

"It's a pure and simple raid," Cal was saying. "In and out. I don't want those Seattle companies coming down on my neck like three years ago. I don't like being threatened."

Andrea felt a cold dread spread through her. Yes, she knew exactly how Cal reacted to threats. He was a belligerent man. A threat was a challenge to be met. He was also a sore loser—so sore a loser that he rarely lost. Calvin Slattery retained one of the finest lawyers in southern California to do his fighting for him.

Cal was now talking about the last raid he'd carried out in Seattle. So far, Andrea had been spared the problems of companies threatening her boss because of her recruiting activities within them. The thought of having a VP with some aerospace company calling Cal and threatening him out of righteous anger was unnerving. She'd overheard those kinds of phone calls before and had seen the aftermath. Sometimes Cal simply laughed with bravado. Other times he ordered the entire firm to cut back on calls to that particular company. There had also been a few rare instances when a section manager had been called into Cal's office behind closed doors, only to emerge shaken and usually livid with anger. She was sure Cal wouldn't absorb all that heat, not even for her, his top headhunter.

Andrea had tangled with him over suspected misdealings in the past and knew what it was like to come face-to-face with him in tactical warfare. Despite her china-doll appearance and little-girl voice, Andrea was, to quote Cal, tough. A born survivor who knew how to fight in a man's world—and win. Yet, unknown to anyone, she was afraid of her boss for all the reasons that others feared him. But, always prudent, she did not allow her fear to show.

Cal quickly skimmed her notes on the Atlanta trip, and a gloating smile appeared on his face. "Looks like you did a great job again. Oswald called me this morning, raving about the assistance you gave him."

Andrea could just imagine what the Nordon personnel rep had said to hide his anger. The evening she had spent shaking off his roaming hands was still too fresh in her mind. Oswald had not taken her rejection well, and in the end he'd been nasty. The only thing that had worked for her was the man's position with his company and her thinly veiled threats of what would happen if he didn't behave himself.

Diplomatically, she said, "Ken's a sharp guy. He did a great job of screening our applicants."

As she sipped her cooling coffee, Andrea wondered if Cal really believed she was a ready playmate for the engineers who made these trips with her. Thinking back over their relationship for the past two years, she couldn't imagine that Cal thought she was such a person. Andrea hoped he gave her credit for having more character than that. But Cal was a master games player, so who was to know what he actually thought about anything?

"Keep up the good work, Andi. Have to run. Ed Rees is expecting me at the plant. Even he's been putting in seven-day workweeks lately." Cal slipped the Atlanta file into his briefcase and grinned smugly. "He's supposed to have buttoned down twenty-five new openings for us this weekend. Don't want to keep him waiting."

"No, of course not."

"Try to get a good night's sleep for a change. You look terrible. I want you bright-eyed and bushy-tailed tomorrow morning." Cal glanced at the file lying in her open attaché case. "You'll find a new company in there to be recruited. Go after it. I want to see at least ten resulting interviews from that company."

"Ten? And you expect me to be able to find the time to sleep?" Andrea glared at her boss. "Come on, Cal. Give me a break."

Cal pushed his chair back and stood up. "I will. When you return. Ten's the magic number. Ten." Stepping away, he turned back for a moment. "Have a good trip."

Andrea shoved the cup of cold coffee to one side and sagged dejectedly in her chair. The expression in her eyes was murderous as she watched Cal disappear through the restaurant doorway into the terminal crowd. Leaning her elbow on the table, she buried her chin in her fist and stared unseeingly at the scratched Formica top. Her eyes began to mist, and she fought down the feelings of anger and frustration that were about to explode into a great sob.

She felt drained, unable to give any more to the job that had received all of her attention and energy since the breakup of her romance a year earlier. Always required to be "on" and on top of everything in an extremely detail-oriented job, headhunters were frequent victims of burnout. Andrea, a reserved and private person, was burning out fast from the high-pressure situations in which Cal kept placing her.

After drawing several deep breaths, she felt in control again and resigned herself to another long night. Not only was there the two-hour flight to Seattle, but, knowing Cal, there would be three to four hours' worth of work to be done once she reached the hotel. Andrea slipped the elastic cord from around the file folder and rummaged through its contents until she found the envelope with her plane tickets. Oh, well, she thought ruefully, here was another seventy-five dollars per diem.

Wearily, Andrea hitched her travel bag back onto a sore shoulder, threw her coat over an arm and hefted her attaché case. Edging her way between the closely packed tables, she consoled herself by thinking, *I only feel this way because I'm so tired. I need a vacation. I'll ask for one after this trip; Cal owes it to me.* Yet as she lugged everything toward the ladies' room, she knew that Cal would want her there every day, seeing things through to the bitter end, or, preferably, to the commission she'd earn for herself and the handsome fee she'd earn for ComSearch. It could be months before the Atlanta and Seattle trip files were closed. And then there were always future trips to complete. That thought did not brighten her waning attitude.

She had only a few minutes to freshen up. The cold water felt good on her skin as she splashed her face and patted the back of her neck with a wet paper towel. She'd removed her makeup, and as she stared at her reflection in the wide mirror, her frown returned. Cal might be cutting, but he was right: she did look terrible. She was pale and had faint circles under her large eyes. Well, pots of makeup could hide the signs of too little sleep. Unfortunately, she didn't have time, so she contented herself with a few strokes of blusher, a glimmer of lip gloss and a spray of her favorite fragrance.

Pulling a brush from the makeup kit she carried in her attaché case, she yanked out the hairpins that held the classic twist in place and shook her shoulder-length hair loose. She brushed it vigorously for a minute, then smoothed her bangs forward and flipped the ends in loose curls. The thick, shiny mass of moonlight-blond hair softened the strain on her face.

Andrea smiled briefly at her reflection, just to prove to herself that she could still make those muscles work. Then she quickly gathered her belongings for the long trudge to the boarding gate.

The DC-10 to Seattle was filling up rapidly. Andrea slid her attaché case under her seat and leaned back. Swiveling her gaze around the business section, she saw nothing to pique her interest and turned her eyes to the window.

Despite being a seasoned traveler, Andrea never tired of views from thirty thousand feet and always chose a window seat. But with the darkness outside, there would be little to be seen. Just as well; she needed to sleep. The blanket and pillow she had pulled from the overhead rack rested on the middle seat to her right. The aisle seat was, so far, unclaimed. Momentarily eyeing that seat, Andrea knew, from the number of passengers already on board, that the plane was too heavily booked for her to have the luxury of two empty seats next to her. If she were lucky that evening, the center seat would remain empty, which would at least give her some elbow room.

Turning her gaze back to the window, Andrea fastened her seat belt and watched a PSA 727 next to the DC-10 pull away from the boarding gate. As the smile painted below the 727's cockpit faded in the darkness, she closed her eyes and again felt the exhaustion that was numbing her senses.

The din in the cabin subsided to a steady drone in her mind. This trip to Seattle was one too many. Next time out, someone else would go. For once, she would refuse the per-diem pay, weather Cal's wrath and smile knowingly when the unfortunate soul who went in her place returned, frustrated and swearing never to go again. Everyone in the office thought she had a marvelous time on these trips. It was about time for one of them to go and come back agreeing with her that raids were an exciting aspect of a headhunter's job. And definitely on the list of calamities to be avoided.

A faint smile touched Andrea's lips as she thought of the people she worked with. ComSearch was a collection of unusual individuals, all witty, daffy, offbeat. Her co-workers were writers, musicians, interior decorators and others who were quick studies and simply needed money—money quickly made—to survive while they pursued their true vocations on the side. Few stayed at ComSearch for any length of time, finding headhunting difficult and high-pressured work. Andrea had been there the longest of all employees, present and past.

As sleep blurred her mind, Andrea's thoughts wandered from ComSearch. Chris. *Oh, Chris! I forgot to call her. Must do that as soon as I get to the hotel. Less than three weeks to Christmas. Must get started on shopping.* Will we get the week between Christmas and New Year's off again?

Cal's conniving face flashed through her mind, jolting sleep a little further away. Two years. It seemed as if she had arrived only the day before, the new kid on the block. She remembered those days vividly; of being scantily trained and quickly thrown on her own to see if she'd survive in the unusual profession. Andrea had watched many come and go at ComSearch. She often wondered why she had succeeded when others who were so much sharper or more talented or more tenacious had failed.

Even Cal admitted that he'd never thought she had what it took to make it in the business when he hired her. Now, half a million dollars richer because of her success, Cal only said he was glad he had listened to his "headhunter's instinct," which she had prompted him to hire her against all logic. Andrea had proved to be the most successful woman in the aerospace engineer recruiting business, and Cal held on to her with a life-crushing grip.

He was afraid of losing her, and she knew it. She had tried to assure him that, if she were ever to leave Com-Search, she wouldn't remain in the field. Cal really believed she would go into competition with him. If she did, she would be a major threat—at least within his own market in southern California. What he didn't realize was that Andrea knew her limitations—or thought she did. Andrea felt that she lacked a strong business sense and could never survive in business for herself.

Cal's reactions to threats echoed hazily through the mazes of her mind, sleep not far away. But a commotion above her head roused her. Curious, she forced the mists of sleep back.

While her lashes fluttered open slowly, her seatmate finished stowing his trench coat in the overhead storage compartment and snapped the door closed. As he eased into the aisle seat, his dark, nearly black eyes captured and held Andrea's bleary gaze.

"I'm sorry. I didn't realize you were asleep." His voice was a quiet, rich baritone, soothing in the clamor surrounding them. "Sorry I woke you."

Andrea stirred and sat up straighter, trying mentally to shake the cobwebs of drowsiness from her mind. As if hypnotized, she stared into the fathomless depths of those lush-lashed eyes, oblivious to everything around her. Andrea's earnest gaze was returned for several long, disquieting seconds. Then the dark eyes that she had seen before flicked away for a moment, breaking the spell that the man had unwittingly cast upon her.

Then his eyes returned to hers, accompanied this time by a gentle smile that sketched the lines of his full, masculine lips. Andrea liked his smile—the way it dimpled one cheek and caused the corners of his eyes to crinkle.

It was definitely a smile worth staying awake for.

Chapter Two

Blinking back sleep and the mild confusion she felt, Andrea exclaimed, "Oh, I wasn't asleep. Just thinking." She tried to hide a large yawn behind a small, delicate hand. Her seatmate laughed, and she added hastily, "Really, I was thinking."

Amusement danced in the man's dark eyes. He stretched his long legs in front of him as much as the cramped airline seating would allow. His clothing— brown tweed jacket, fisherman-knit sweater, tan corduroy jeans—was totally casual, totally unbusinesslike. He struck her as an artist, perhaps a writer, certainly someone much different from the engineers who inhabited her world. But from the way his jacket was tailored to fit his broad shoulders and chest, and the jeans his narrow hips and long legs, Andrea knew the casual effect was expensive. It didn't take a glimpse of his highly polished leather boots for Andrea to realize he was a man who sought the best.

Again his nearly black eyes met and held her gaze without flickering. Their expression was mildly curious now, slightly puzzled. Andrea took in the curling lashes that framed the magnetic eyes, the straight nose, the square, stubborn jawline. Even the thick, dark auburn hair whose waves had been styled into obedience projected a defiant air. The man was handsome, in an individualistic sort of way, Andrea thought. She guessed him to be in his middle or late thirties.

"Cat got your tongue?" One heavy eyebrow arched as his gaze flowed over her in a friendly, inquisitive study.

"No." Andrea paused, feeling a spark of humor and something else ignite in a hollow place inside. She smiled with mock modesty. "It's just that my mother taught me never to speak to strangers."

"That was wise of her." His tone was teasing. "But then, I suspect that she also told you never to share lollipops or play spin the bottle because both are very germy pastimes." His voice, low-pitched and bordering on husky, was distinctly seductive.

A tiny shiver of agitation coursed through her, and she wasn't certain if he was aware of the effect he was having on her. The fact that he was causing her nerves to flutter in delightful abandon was unexpected and distressing. But this was only a flight to Seattle, and Andrea decided to enjoy it.

"As a matter of fact, Mother did." Responding to his playful expression, she asked, "Out of idle curiosity: Do boys' mothers tell them the same things?"

His gaze pivoted toward the cabin ceiling while a solemn look molded his angular features. "To be perfectly honest, I don't remember." He glanced back at Andrea, his eyes caressing her face. "But I never did listen to my mother. I don't think most boys do."

A flight attendant tapped the man on the shoulder and reminded him to fasten his seat belt. As she moved forward, he turned back to Andrea. The same gentle, warm smile touched his lips. "I'm Gage," he said casually.

"First or last name?"

"First."

Andrea automatically stored that information in the back of her mind and then wondered why she had bothered, except that asking questions and filing away answers had become second nature to her. She decided not to build a mental file on this man; it was only a two-hour flight. Since he hadn't offered his last name, she responded in kind. "I'm Andrea."

Gage nodded formally at her, a thin, almost roguish smile on his lips. When the flight attendants began preparing the passengers for takeoff, with instructions on the use of emergency equipment, he turned to face the front of the cabin. Andrea noted dourly that it seemed as if he had never heard the patter before, considering the undivided attention he paid the head attendant, a lovely, long-legged redhead. Feeling unreasonably irritated with Gage and even more so with herself for reacting in such a manner, Andrea turned her gaze to the window.

There were two jets ahead of them on the taxiway, their landing lights blazing in the dark. The first was gathering speed as it left the head of the runway. Within minutes, the second jet was on its way. Then the DC-10 bound for Seattle was at the top of the runway. The engines roared to full power, and soon the buildings and aircraft of L.A.X. fell beneath as the jumbo jet lifted effortlessly into the night sky. This was the most exciting moment of any trip to Andrea. She leaned closer to the window, her pale hair falling softly over her shoulder. The lights of the city below twinkled like those on a tiny Christmas tree. Then an angel-hair layer of clouds threaded between airplane and earth, blurring the scene. The tightness of excitement was in her throat, and she swallowed in an attempt to clear the feeling away. Soon the wispy clouds turned into a sea of darkness, hiding both land and ocean.

Andrea settled back in her seat, a pleased smile softening the strain on her face. Eventually she felt Gage's observant eyes upon her. Swiveling her gaze to meet his, she carefully kept all expression from her face.

He said quietly, "Thrilling, isn't it? Even after all the thousands of miles I've flown, I still get a charge at takeoff. I haven't decided if it's because of the kick of feeling the power in those engines or if it's because one of those engines might quit and it just might be my last few moments in this world."

Andrea gasped, unable to hide her surprise at his verbalizing such a morbid thought. "That was an awful thing to say!"

Gage laughed. "But true, you have to admit."

"I don't think I'll be able to sleep after a comment like that."

"I'm sorry." His tone was apologetic, yet there was something else in Gage's voice. "I never sleep on planes, always waiting for the moment my feet get back on terra firma. I'm a devoted believer that if God had intended man to fly, He would have given us wings...."

Andrea started to laugh, then noticed how tightly his hands were gripping the armrests. Taken aback, she exclaimed, "You're afraid of flying!"

Gage muttered uncomfortably, "It's not something I readily admit." He paused, then explained, "I simply hate flying. Particularly takeoffs."

Andrea shook her head as she leaned toward him. "You should have said something before we took off." Her smile was warm, and her blue eyes sparkled with sincerity. "The worst is over." Seeing one dark eyebrow rise in skepticism, she said, "Of course you've heard all about how much safer it is flying in a plane than driving a car?"

"Several times."

"Right. Well...it's true." Andrea shrugged her slender shoulders. "You can take my word for it, if that's any comfort."

Gage's calm, easygoing nature seemed to be regaining control. He grinned sheepishly and relaxed his grip on the armrests. "If you say so." He paused as the flight attendant came by and asked if they would like anything to drink. Andrea shook her head. Gage ordered a scotch with ice. Turning back to Andrea, he said, "When I sat down, you seemed upset."

"Did I?" Andrea laughed offhandedly. "Well, I guess I was. I was wondering if there was any way to kill my boss and get away with it."

"Is your boss the man you were sitting with in the coffee shop?"

She glanced at Gage in surprise, momentarily having forgotten seeing him during her meeting with Cal. The intensity that had been in Gage's dark eyes then perked Andrea's curiosity for a moment. Yet that intensity was not in his eyes now, and she chose to ignore the memory of the discomfort she had felt in the coffee shop.

"So what's the motivation?" Gage prompted.

Andrea sighed deeply. "He's beginning to think L.A. is only a place for me to change planes. I fly in from Atlanta and go out on a plane for Seattle. Feels as if I haven't seen home for weeks." She leaned her elbow on the armrest and propped her chin on her fist.

"Where do you live?" Gage swirled his drink in the plastic tumbler, watching the ice carefully.

"Santa Monica." She tilted her head to the side and asked, "What about you? Is Seattle home for you?"

His friendly attitude retreated somewhat as he answered cautiously, "Not anymore. L.A.'s where I hang my hat."

"Are you flying up on business?"

This time the reservation in his voice was pronounced. "Unfortunately, yes." Gage sipped at his drink and withdrew into silence.

Andrea sensed she had brought up a poor subject and decided not to pursue it. Lack of sleep was catching up with her, making it hard for her to concentrate on even a simple conversation. Her eyes felt as if they had been rolled in sand, and the headache she'd landed with in L.A. was beginning to pound again. She took the pillow and blanket from the middle seat and settled down for a nap. Gage was stirring in his seat; soon she heard what sounded like the rustle of magazine pages. Then, with exhaustion overpowering her senses, sleep came within minutes.

AND IT WAS IN SLEEP that he came to her. Again it was that lovely fall day. A hot October sun burned down on the pair as they stood on the pier in Malibu. Andrea felt the cool Pacific breeze fan her face and swirl her hair into her eyes. The coastline of the Los Angeles basin stretched south before them, but tears blurred her vision. Blinking them back, she turned to face David. David, her gentle, sweet lover. David, the fast-rising star, an actor who did not understand her love for him, her need of him. David, the man she had given her being to, the man who could not feel love for anyone.

Only his face appeared in her dream: smooth, patrician features with a hint of toughness in the jawline. Dove-gray eyes peered at her, the gentleness that had been in them in the past replaced by a callous glare. Over and over, his cruel words echoed in her mind, humiliating phrases meant to destroy her love for him. As his wounding utterances continued, a soft moan escaped from Andrea's throat. David's harangue began again, and as his face dimmed through her tears, Andrea felt a hand on her shoulder. It was a tender touch that separated itself from her dream. Her long lashes flickered open, and her eyes moved to focus on the strong, tanned hand resting lightly on her shoulder. Again it gave her a gentle shake.

As her sleep-shrouded eyes edged to his face, Gage saw the pain that darkened them. Her pale complexion had blanched to a deathly white. Concern tinged his voice. "Are you all right?"

Andrea stared at him, her mind still magnetically drawn to her dream. For a moment, David's face superimposed itself over Gage's. Then, slowly, sleep lifted its net from her senses, and Andrea saw the worry in the dark eyes that watched her so closely.

Embarrassed, she nodded. "I'm fine. Really." Her smile was tremulous. "It was simply a bad dream. I haven't gotten much sleep lately. Guess it's starting to tell."

Gage withdrew his hand hesitantly and nodded. "You do look a touch worn."

"Oh, thanks," Andrea grumbled. She pulled the pillow from behind her head with a yank and tossed it, along with the blanket, into the empty seat between them. Sounding more like herself, she added, "But thanks for waking me."

A broad smile etched itself on Gage's angular features. "Anytime." Again, several long seconds hung in eternity as Andrea and Gage exchanged silent glances. Then, reluctantly, he returned his attention to the small loose-leaf notebook spread open on his knee.

A hint of a smile still lurked at the corner of his mouth, and Andrea idly wondered what it would be like to kiss him. Probably quite exciting. That thought jarred her tired mind fully into the present, and a faint blush crept up from her neck. A workaholic who focused all her energies on the job that she hated, Andrea was unaccustomed to fantasizing about strange men. She blinked, unsure why she had thought that, and looked away to stare out into the darkness beyond the plane. Yet, slowly, her gaze returned to the man beside her.

As Gage jotted notes in the binder, Andrea watched him, thinking the tiny scrawl incongruous with the large, masculine hand that scribbled it. Realizing that he was using a form of notescript, she asked, "Are you a writer?"

"A writer?" Gage's tone was incredulous. "Whatever would make you think that?"

"You look the part. The way you dress. The way you look, even. All you need is a pipe. Then you'd look like some crazy Irish poet." She smiled as she said this.

Gage laughed heartily. "As a matter of fact, I once smoked a pipe. But I never realized I had an image like that." He studied her face, its soft curves, the pixie nose that looked as if it might have once been broken, the pert mouth. "What are you doing in Seattle?"

"Working."

His dark eyes flicked over her again, making her feel self-conscious. "Working at what?"

Andrea straightened in her seat. "Just work."

"Okay," he drawled. "What about after work?"

In spite of her runaway thoughts of passionate kisses, this minor flirtation was to end when the plane touched down. As much as Andrea enjoyed Gage's company, she was going to Seattle on business. And business left her no time for a private life. She answered coolly, "That's all I'll be doing—working."

The no-smoking sign flashed on as the plane began its descent. Gage closed the notebook and slipped it into the breast pocket of his jacket. "Let's start over." His smile was inviting. "Would you care to go to dinner this evening?"

"Can't. I'm working." As his friendliness faded, Andrea shrugged apologetically. "Really I am. Thanks for the invite, though, but I've at least two hours of work ahead of me." And that didn't include all of the hand washing she had to do, she thought ruefully.

His tone was reserved when he asked, "What hotel are you staying in?"

Hesitating a moment, Andrea saw no reason why she shouldn't tell him. "The North Winds."

A peculiar smile touched the corner of his mouth. "So am I." At her raised eyebrow, Gage added, "I've stayed there several times since it opened last spring. Kind of my home away from home. Have you been there before?"

"No, I haven't." Andrea wondered if Gage was telling her the truth or if he had simply decided to play games. "You fly up here often, I take it."

The look Gage shot her was sharp. "Hell, no! Usually I know far enough in advance so I can take Amtrak. I don't fly if I can get out of it."

Andrea remembered his reaction earlier to her question about his work. "But you couldn't get out of it this time."

Gage regarded her for a long moment, then admitted grudgingly, "No, not this time. There have been a number of, uh, accidents at my company recently. Had a bad one this morning."

"An accident?" Glancing up from tightening her seat belt, Andrea found that the disturbing intensity had returned to Gage's eyes. "I hope no one was hurt."

Gage noted the concerned but impersonal expression on her face and slowly shook his head. A brief smile touched his lips. "No. Fortunately, no one was injured."

After a long pause, he added, "I'm going to take care of the problem this time."

The constraint in Gage's voice was glaring, and his easygoing manner had vanished when he talked about his company. Andrea felt the tension within the man and decided not to pursue the subject. When she didn't speak, Gage glanced at her, then fell silent himself.

Almost as quickly as it had appeared, the tension faded. As the comfortable quiet lingered between them, Andrea wished she had time to spend with Gage while she was in Seattle, but it would be impossible with her work load. Especially with the recruiting she would have to do to set up ten interviews. Sighing softly, Andrea bit her lower lip and momentarily regretted everything—her dismal job, her financial dependence upon that job, meeting Gage.

As Gage tightened his seat belt for the landing, he glanced her way and said drolly, "You'll like the North Winds. It's quite a palace—opulent but homey in a strange sort of way." Then he retreated into another detached silence.

Puzzled by his withdrawal, Andrea turned her attention to the window as the plane continued its descent.

A chill cut through her as she stared out into the darkness. Crossing her arms tightly against another shiver, she was disturbed by her aroused emotions. Was her reaction due to the dream? She had successfully ignored the memory of her relationship with David. That bitter afternoon a year earlier haunted her only in sleep. But the desperation she had felt on the pier that day was back now. After having refused to acknowledge it for so long, Andrea was nearly overwhelmed by it. Intellectually, she knew that the breakup of her three-year romance was not her fault. But she had been so devastated emotionally by the unexpectedness of David's cruel words that she couldn't listen to her mind, only to her heart. Why was she feeling the pain now? Was it because she was so exhausted that her conscious mind couldn't keep those memories buried?

Or was it because—Andrea's eyes strayed to the man in the aisle seat—was it because the excitement she'd felt around David had edged back? Glancing again at Gage, Andrea fought the tension that was arousing her senses. No, it was not going to happen again. What had happened with David was a lesson that she needed to learn only once. She would not submit to the sensation that now flickered in the pit of her stomach. She certainly would not get involved, however briefly, with the man who sat next to her; her instincts told her that he was a man who got whatever he wanted and who was secure in his ability to break away and move on when it suited him. David had taught her well. She would rather fight the loneliness than suffer the pain.

The jet bumped onto the rain-slick pavement, and Andrea watched the building lights flow past, blurry in the night. She heard Gage let out a deep sigh of relief and unfasten his seat belt. Now that he was safely back on the ground, Andrea assumed that his quiet, easygoing manner would change to one of aggressive self-confidence; he seemed that type of man. With the little flame still warming that hollow place inside, she had no desire to be faced with having to refuse a second invitation from Gage. She didn't want to have to deal with the confusion that would create in her tired brain.

When the other passengers started to line up to exit, Andrea finally pulled her gaze from the window. Retrieving her attaché case from under her seat, she devoted her attention to finding the directions that Cal had written on a slip of paper tucked inside the plane ticket envelope.

Gage thoughtfully studied the woman who sat by him, her head bent, moonlight-blond hair hiding her face. His expression was sober, but an amused and slightly wicked smile played on his lips. "May I offer you a lift to the hotel?"

Looking up from the paper in her hands, Andrea shook her head. "Oh, thank you, but no, thank you. I have some things to attend to and I wouldn't want to hold you up," she lied pleasantly.

Gage stood up and pulled his trench coat from the overhead compartment. While the smile remained, a strange glint darkened his eyes. "Have an enjoyable stay in Seattle, Andrea. Perhaps we'll meet again."

Andrea felt a tightening in her chest as she looked up at him. He was taller than she had guessed, well over six feet. And despite her cool look, she thought she was probably an absolute fool for turning him down. "Thank you. I hope yours is a good stay also and that you solve that problem with your company." The smile she flashed him was sincere. "It was nice meeting you. Good-bye."

Gage nodded, hesitated a moment, then turned toward the exit. Not seeing the directions she was staring at, Andrea firmly resolved to avoid the man in the future. She didn't like the way she had no control over that little warm feeling deep inside. She simply didn't have the energy to devote to any type of romance; there were too many bills to be paid, too much money that had to be earned before she could grant herself the luxury of thinking about the future. And she wasn't certain she'd be able to say goodbye to Gage many more times, if indeed she could again.

Yet while Andrea rode the escalators into the main terminal of SeaTac Airport, she idly wondered if she would see him again. After all, they were staying in the same hotel. Even though she knew she almost never stepped out-

side her room during these trips, Andrea thought she
might possibly run into him in a hotel restaurant or the
lobby. Anything was possible. Then she reminded herself
that her interest in him was purely as a pleasant diversion
during a hectic business trip. *You know very well that there
just isn't any time for love or anything else along similar
lines.* And at that thought, her frown returned.

Stepping off the escalator, Andrea readjusted her load
of luggage and looked around the uncrowded terminal.
SeaTac, like L.A.X., was ultramodern; this evening,
however, it lacked the always-present scurrying crowds of
Los Angeles International. Andrea searched for the exit
signs. Across the expanse of the terminal she saw Gage
leaving the baggage-claim area with his overcoat and
suitcase in hand. Slowing her pace and hoping that he
wouldn't see her, she watched him closely. If he was really
staying at the North Winds, she did not want to ride to the
hotel in the same courtesy airport limousine with him. She
would stop off for a light supper in the terminal coffee
shop.

To her relief, only a moment later a small, wiry man
strode toward Gage, hailing him with a wave. The two men
stopped in the center of the terminal. A smile touched
Andrea's lips as she watched the animated red-haired man
talk. Gage seemed amused himself, a suppressed smile
lurking at one corner of his mouth while he gave the man
his undivided attention. Then they moved toward an exit
to the parking area. As the glass doors closed behind them,
Andrea surmised that Gage would not be taking the hotel
limo after all. She continued on to find the courtesy van's
pickup point.

The ride to the downtown hotel—Seattle's newest and,
if publicity could have its way, the finest in the city—was
uneventful. There were four other passengers in the van,

all eagerly making plans for their spare time while attending a national sheriffs' convention at the hotel. One of the men in the group asked Andrea what she was doing in Seattle and if she'd care to join them for a drink after settling into the hotel. She declined with a polite smile and no explanation, which was readily accepted by the group from Colorado. During the remainder of the ride, Andrea was left alone to muse and stare out blankly at the cold heavy rain soaking the city.

She came to life as the van turned into the driveway of the North Winds. The travelers climbed out and headed for the registration desk. As Andrea trailed after the foursome, she fleetingly wondered if she would run into Gage in this gigantic hotel. She stood beside one of the many elevators and looked around the huge lobby, taking in its multilevels, which provided numerous alcoves for sitting. By the main lobby door stood a beautifully adorned Christmas tree that rose from a platform to pass a second-floor skywalk. It was the largest cut tree she had ever seen, and she marveled at it. The entrance to the coffee shop was nearly hidden by the tree, but when Andrea spotted it, she realized how hungry she was. Her last meal had been breakfast in Atlanta; both plane flights had been used for sleep. The sooner she checked in, the sooner she could order room service.

A few minutes later, she tipped the bellhop and closed the door to her room behind him. Leaning against the door, Andrea surveyed her home for the next five days. It was fastidiously decorated in blues and greens, restful and soothing. Across from her, a window the width of the oversized room beckoned with its view of downtown Seattle, whose nighttime lights were dimmed by the steady rain.

She slipped out of her coat, tossed it on the king-size bed and crossed to stand next to the table and two armchairs that occupied a space in front of the window. Windblown rivulets etched the glass. Andrea put her hand on the window and could feel the winter chill outside. She looked forward to morning and what she would see in daylight from twenty-two stories up. If the weather were clear, would she be able to see Mount Rainier? Andrea had no idea in which direction her room faced or what might lie between the hotel and the famous peak, but she thought it would be the highlight of her trip to see the mountain looming above the city in the distance.

After pulling the geometric-print drapes shut against the cold coming through the glass, Andrea turned to gaze longingly at the bed. To be able to crawl under the covers and sleep for twenty-four hours was her idea of heaven right now. What a fantasy that was! There was work to do and laundry to wash, and neither was going to get done with her standing there staring at the king-size bed. She sighed deeply and crossed to the luggage stand where her travel bag lay.

With a start, she remembered that her sister had expected her home that afternoon and was unaware of the trip to Seattle. Andrea checked her watch. It was 9:15 P.M. Chris would be home at this time on a Sunday evening and would probably be worrying about her absent sibling. Andrea smiled, knowing what a worrier Christine was. She perched herself on the side of the bed and picked up the telephone receiver.

Christine's voice, cheery and lively, came on the line after three rings. "Merry Christmas! And what can I do for you?"

"Pour me a glass of wine."

"Andi!" Christine screeched. "Where are you? I've got dinner in the oven!"

Andrea said sorrowfully, "Invite the neighbors for supper. I'm in Seattle."

"I thought you went to Atlanta."

Andrea filled her half sister in on the afternoon's events, ending with, "So I won't be home till Friday night sometime. Late, I think."

"Jeez, that's rotten of Cal. When are you going to quit that hideous job?" Concern tinged Christine's voice. "You sound depressed to the max."

"No. Just tired. Bone-tired." And missing home. "What's the news on the local scene?"

She could hear the hesitation in Christine's split-second pause. "Well...you've had some phone calls."

"Any that I should return?"

"It depends on how much of a masochist you want to be."

The sarcasm in Christine's voice told Andrea exactly who had called. There was no one else in Andrea's life who brought such comments from her seventeen-year-old sister. "Oh, no! Don't tell me that The Masher called again!" She cringed, remembering the man she had met at a party recently and, in a moment of weakness, had agreed to date. That had been one evening well worth forgetting.

"Yes. But don't worry, I told the jerk you'd gone off to some oil-rich foreign land with a wealthy project engineer. The Masher definitely will not be calling again."

Andrea's laugh mirrored her relief. "Chris, there's no such animal as a wealthy project engineer—well-paid, perhaps, but never wealthy. Not in the way you mean wealthy."

"What do I know? I'm just a dumb archaeology student." Christine, the tomboy, was a freshman at UCLA, getting the education she needed to "go off into the wilds of the Southwest and delve into the mysteries of Chaco Canyon."

Andrea was always amazed when she thought of the differences between herself and Christine, who each seemed to take after the mother who had borne her. Andrea was sedate and realistic. Christine was a worrier and an incurable romantic-optimist. Their father had given them their names and very little else.

"Hey, I got the applications to go on the dig at Chaco this summer!" Christine announced.

"You know that we discussed this already. I think you are too young to go off to New Mexico for an entire summer, in the middle of the desert in the middle of nowhere."

"For heaven's sake, it's not like I'll be alone! There'll be fifteen or so in the group." A whine was edging into Christine's voice. "Besides, I'll be of age then and I can do what I want."

"Not when I'm helping put you through college—especially UCLA. Your scholarship isn't exactly paying all the expenses, you know. And then there are all your hospital bills."

"But, Andi—"

"Chris, I'm not up to arguing about this long-distance. And certainly not tonight. I'm too tired. We'll discuss it this weekend."

"You sound just like Daddy."

But Daddy and Christine's mother were dead, victims of an automobile accident on Interstate 5 two years earlier, an accident that had also severely injured Christine. The winter's first snowstorm at the Grapevine north of Los Angeles had iced the highway, and there had been a multicar pileup. Andrea had been Christine's guardian since that day, a duty she took seriously. She had also inherited the staggering bills that had been incurred during her sister's six-month hospitalization and subsequent care.

Yet it was a compliment to be compared with her father, and it cheered Andrea a bit. She had loved him dearly, faults and all, the only natural parent she had known. Andrea's mother had deserted her husband and infant daughter to disappear somewhere in Europe, seeking something she felt her life had lacked. For years now, since Andrea was a teenager, she had believed her mother was dead. She had never known her, but the loss she felt was eased by the thought of the woman's death.

Andrea's loneliness echoed in her voice. "Any other news?"

"No-o-o-o. Say, you sure you're okay? You sound funny."

Her laugh was strained. "I just miss my own bed, that's all."

A sharp snort thundered through the receiver. "I bet! What you need is a nice man."

"Chris!"

"'Fess up. Aren't I right? You've got this god-awful job. Every masher in the world hits on you—both on the road and at home. Now, what you need is—"

"Christine Barrie!"

There was a moment's silence before Christine mumbled, "You know I'm right. You're too young to be an old maid."

"Um." Andrea paused, wanting to lighten the load of guilt she knew her sister felt because of their financial situation. "I did meet a man on the flight up I think you would approve of."

"Really?" Christine's voice perked up. "Well, tell all!"

"It'll wait until I get home. I just wanted to let you know where I was in case you needed me."

Christine laughed and recited the North Winds' address and phone number. "Got it. Now you get some rest, and I'll have the apartment cleaned before you get back."

"You'd better! I don't want to come home to two weeks' worth of your mess!"

"Say good night, Andi."

"Good night, and take care."

"You, too."

The glow of affection she felt for her sister warmed Andrea as she placed the receiver in its cradle. She wished that she were home, eating, the dinner in the oven and arguing about the trip to New Mexico that Christine wanted to take so badly. It was less than three weeks before Christmas, but she wasn't yet into the spirit of the season that she loved so dearly. Well, Friday night she would be home, and she promised herself that Cal would not rout her out of Los Angeles until after New Year's. She would be firm on that issue. She was looking forward to the peace and joy that the holidays always brought her.

An hour later, Andrea had showered and washed all the clothes she could by hand, leaving them to drip-dry from every towel rack in the bathroom. A bucket of ice and two cans of soda were on the built-in desk across the room from the bed. The color television set was tuned to the latest hit sitcom, its dialogue and canned laughter providing the background noise that made the hotel room seem more like an office. Dressed in her velour robe, Andrea sat cross-legged in the center of the bed and reached for her attaché case.

She spread her working materials around her, everything within easy reach. The kraft expansion folder she saved for last. Then, finally and none too eagerly, she slipped the elastic cord from around it. The file held company telephone directories from all the aerospace firms in the Seattle area—none of which ComSearch, or Andrea, could have in its possession legally—and paper-clipped piles of group work sheets. In the bottom of the folder was a rubber-banded set of recruiting cards, numbering fifty or sixty, she guessed. On top of these cards were those indicating the applicants who had already been scheduled for interviews. Andrea separated the five-by-eight-inch cards into two piles and counted those with yellow interview slips stapled to their corners. Thirteen so far. She shuffled through papers to find the interview roster. Thirteen interviews for the Tectron crew.

A sigh of relief eased from her. For the first time since she had seen Cal at L.A.X., Andrea felt this trip might not be as bad as she had believed. The standard practice was to schedule as many interviews as possible—that meant twenty or more—and keep the cancellation rate low. That was Andrea's main function on the trip—to keep the interviewees coming in and not let them back out for any reason short of death. If Cal wanted ten resulting interviews from the new company he had talked about, all she had to do was schedule two more from the big company, refuse to allow any cancellations, then recruit the new company. So simple in theory for a crack headhunter, and nothing but hard work in reality.

What a bizarre way to make a living, Andrea mused once again. Pull a name and a phone number out of a company directory. Call up the usually happily employed, unsuspecting individual, introduce herself, and get that person to discuss his or her current job, previous background and future employment goals. When Andrea hit pay dirt with a recruit that matched a customer's requirements for an open position, she would talk the applicant into an interview and work it through, hopefully, to a job placement and a big commission. What always amazed her was that no technical knowledge was needed for her job, only a memorized understanding of terms and phrases and an agile salesperson's mind. It would probably horrify everyone she recruited to know that a lifetime career had been placed in the hands of a woman whose working knowledge of electronics extended only as far as pushing the buttons on her microwave oven.

Flipping through the smaller company directories, Andrea frowned. She had recruited most of these companies before, to bring people down to Los Angeles to interview. Which was the new one?

She found the directory at the bottom of the pile. There was no note from Cal to specify this was the company he had been talking about; he obviously expected her to know which one it was from her own experience of the Seattle firms. This directory was the smallest of the lot and only twenty pages thick. Andrea thumbed through it, glaring at the tiny print. She'd get eyestrain trying to work from it that evening. That chore could definitely wait until morning, after she'd had a good night's sleep.

Tossing the book aside, Andrea looked for the interview roster again. The names of the applicants meant nothing to her, but the Tectron names did. Knowing each of the men who interviewed for Tectron helped her to determine what types of people she should look for in scheduling and even which groups in the aerospace companies to recruit from. Andrea went over the Tectron crew names again: Ed Rees, the man Cal had been on the run to meet that evening, who was head of software engineering; George Nazareth, a Tectron recruiter who handled its personnel end of things on trips; and Kipp Cross, a bright young engineer in communications software.

Andrea smiled, thinking of Kipp. Of all the Tectron engineers she had dealt with both on trips and at home, Kipp was her favorite. Three years younger than she and absolutely brilliant, he reminded her of a Saint Bernard puppy: big, clumsy and totally lovable. A huge man, he was never without a face-splitting grin and a joke on his lips. Kipp Cross could be a merciless tease, and Andrea looked forward to seeing him again. If nothing else, he could save this trip from drudgery and dullness.

Andrea had met Rees only twice before and knew him to be a quiet, reserved man who was all business and nothing more. There would be no hassle from either Kipp or Ed. They'd leave her alone to do her job. Andrea's only worry came from George Nazareth, Tectron's personnel man. She had never been on a trip with him before, but her conversations on the phone with him several times a week warned Andrea that she needed to be careful around George. The one luncheon she had had with him—to talk strategy about getting a high-priced mechanical engineer to accept George's offer—also confirmed her instinct that he was a man whose words did not contain idle flirting.

Laying the roster on the geometric-print bedspread, Andrea crawled off the bed and stretched her tired muscles. She stepped to the desk and filled a glass with melting ice. While she slowly poured the can of soda, she tuned in to the comedy on the television set. Parent and child were arguing in typical generation-gap style. Once again, Christine's summer trip to New Mexico confronted her. Was it possible that she was holding the reins too tightly, she wondered. Perhaps she should give Christine more freedom. Yet she felt uncomfortable with the idea of her sister's spending the entire summer there when she had never been away from home before. David had accused Andrea of being an overprotective parent after the accident. At the time, she had attributed his comments to possessiveness and jealousy at having to share her with Christine. Now, she wasn't certain. It was possible that David had been right.

A knock on the door jolted her from reverie. Andrea glanced at her travel alarm clock on one of the nightstands. It was 10:05 P.M., nearly a half hour since she had called room service to order quiche, salad and hot tea. Setting the glass of soda on the desk, she straightened her robe and opened the door.

Gage stood in the hallway, smiling benignly as mischief danced in his dark eyes.

Andrea stared at him, her emotions whirling from anger to pleasure at seeing him again. With a note of irritation in her voice that she could not tamp down, she asked, "What are you doing here?"

Gage leaned a shoulder against the jamb, standing just outside the half-open doorway. He folded his arms across his broad chest and continued to smile, now somewhat crookedly. "Good evening." His dark eyes flowed from the blond hair piled on top of her head, wisps of it straying loose about her face and neck, to the pale blue velour robe that ended inches above her knees, to her bare feet, pink-painted toenails scrunching into the royal-blue carpet. "I dare say they did a much better job of matching the color scheme of your room to you than they did for me."

"Pardon?" Andrea blinked in confusion while trying to sort through her feelings.

He laughed, a warming sound. "Never mind. Just thinking aloud."

Regaining her composure, Andrea asked, "How did you get here?"

"Here? A friend gave me a lift." Gage's eyes lingered on the V-necked throat of her robe.

"That's not what I meant. I mean, how did you find out what room I was in?"

"Actually, it was quite simple. I merely asked one of the young men at the desk when you checked in." He noticed the firm hold her hand had taken on the edge of the door. "A brief description of you is enough to jar any man's memory. You are very lovely." He paused, sincerity reflected in his expression.

A reluctant smile found its way to her lips. Andrea breathed deeply, then said, "Thank you."

"It took me all of approximately twenty seconds to learn your room number." A quick grin skipped across his face.

"I see. Well, I'm sure it cost you something for that information, so what can I do for you?" Andrea's head tilted to one side as she studied the man who stood so casually a foot from her.

"I thought you might be finished with your work by now and would reconsider my invitation. Perhaps you would like to join me for a drink?"

From the lingering smell of liquor and cigarette smoke on his clothing, Andrea suspected that he had already had that drink, and she said so.

"That was business. You see, I also had things to take care of this evening. But that's squared away, and…I enjoy your company." The eyes that held her uncertain gaze captive were calm, yet enticing. And once again, his quiet, husky voice was having its disturbing effect on her.

As she stood so close to Gage, Andrea had trouble breathing normally. The senses numbed so long ago by pain and regret were awakening and responding to his presence, making her feel frightened. Not of him, but of herself. The fact that she wanted to be with him only added to her consternation.

She struggled to fight the alarm going off inside her and glanced over her shoulder at the papers and books spread out on the rumpled bedcovers. "I'm sorry, but I've only just gotten started." She forced herself to face him. "Thank you for your offer, but I can't. In fact, I'm waiting for my dinner to be brought up right now. I thought you were room service," Andrea finished with an apologetic smile that barely touched her lips.

Gage looked past her into the room, curiosity flickering in his eyes for a moment. Then he shrugged, raking a hand through his thick hair. "Looks as if this just isn't my night."

Andrea bit her lower lip and nodded wordlessly. Gage straightened and dropped his hands to his sides, watching her. He took a step back and grinned. "If you give me a chance, you'll find I'm a very remarkable guy. A really pleasant cuss most of the time."

His guileless comment drew a halfhearted laugh from Andrea, and she shook her head in disbelief at the situation. "I'm sure you are."

"Then have breakfast with me tomorrow."

She felt the force of his persistence. "Don't you ever give up?"

His grin was cheerful and his reply honest. "Not usually."

Andrea sagged against the door, laughing. She shook her head wearily and asked, "Has anyone ever told you you're incorrigible?"

"Several have."

"And they were all correct." Surprisingly, Andrea discovered that she was in full control of her emotions again and gained courage from that.

"Surely breakfast won't interfere with your work schedule." Gage shoved his hands into the back pockets of his jeans and raised an eyebrow in speculation.

Slowly, Andrea said, "You do have a one-track mind."

"Guilty as charged."

Releasing the door, Andrea crossed her arms. "I still have a lot of work to do tonight." She paused as Gage leaned against the doorjamb again. "You seem to be a nice man." Indeed, Christine would heartily approve of him, she thought. "But the truth is, I'm not sure I want to get to know you any better."

One cheek dimpled with unoffended humor. "That's honest."

When Gage said nothing else, Andrea searched the dark eyes for a clue to what he was thinking. The usually expressive eyes were carefully guarded, and Andrea thought that, for all of his friendliness, he was a man who could be very difficult to know. Moments from the flight flashed through her mind. How his apparent friendliness had quickly disappeared into a cautious reserve; how he had withdrawn from her. Instinct told her that he was looking for only a pleasant fling with no commitments. If she were to get involved with anyone, she knew there had to be a hope of something lasting longer than a night or two, or the resultant pain would not be worth it.

A glimmer of understanding lifted the mask from his eyes. Gage's nod was nearly imperceptible as he straightened, but his smile was tender. "Well, it's getting late. Been a long day." The noise of the elevator doors sliding open and the sound of a rattling cart caught his attention.

"And I think your dinner has arrived, so I'll let you get back to work."

Andrea nodded and watched Gage step toward the elevators.

With his back to her, he paused a moment, then turned. "Don't work too hard, Andrea. Remember, there's more to life than work." The flicker of sadness in her blue eyes didn't escape him. "Have some fun while you're up here. Seattle's a beautiful city."

The melancholy and confusion she was feeling found their way into her smile. She murmured, "I will. You do the same."

The enchanting dark eyes flowed over her once again, returning slowly to focus on her face. Andrea's poignant gaze dropped to stare at the hallway carpet. She wanted desperately to be with the man, yet her silly fears would not allow her to accept his invitation. Furious with herself for feeling as she did, Andrea knew that the inevitable had happened. She had lost the ability to hide from the past. Now she would have to deal with it—as well as with the present. She didn't want to, but she had to. And doing so meant that she would have to make some changes.

Andrea didn't look up until the cart had clattered to a stop in front of her. When she glanced surreptitiously down the hall, Gage was gone.

Chapter Three

The heavy mist that hung in the brittle morning air gathered on her lashes as Andrea jogged through the empty streets of predawn Seattle. The steady rain of the night before had changed to a low-lying fog that shrouded the tops of the buildings of the uptown area. It was just beginning to grow light when Andrea ran past the small triangular park with its huge green statue of John H. McGraw, second governor of the state of Washington.

Glancing at the statue that loomed over her in the near-light, Andrea shivered and reached her red-mittened hands up to pull the red-and-white knit ski cap farther down over her ears. She increased her speed slightly, hoping she'd warm up some more. The two T-shirts she wore under the faded green hooded sweatshirt were not enough to withstand the biting cold wind blowing in off the bay. Atlanta in the throes of its first cold snap of the season had been Palm Springs, compared with Seattle.

Her breath hung before her, crystals on the wind, as she puffed toward the towering Washington Plaza Hotel. Half of the forty-story cylindrical building was invisible as the fog crept lower to the ground. She wished her three miles were up. A glance at her wristwatch confirmed what she had already guessed: she had about a mile left. Normally it took her forty-five minutes to run her customary three miles a day, and she had been jogging only a half hour. An out-of-service taxi splashed past her. It was the fourth vehicle she had seen that morning. At a quarter of six, uptown Seattle was a dead city.

As one foot slapped in front of the other on the sidewalk, Andrea once again wondered why Cal had been acting so peculiarly the previous evening. She had thought she'd seen him in every mood he would betray, but obviously she had been wrong. She had never before seen Cal in a state of—of what? Nervousness. That was the word that whispered in her mind. But what would make him nervous? The last raid he'd conducted in Seattle? Evidently it had resulted in many angry threats from the local aerospace firms either to lay off recruiting their employees or to face legal action. Andrea wasn't certain what legal action could be taken, but she had heard from others in the industry that shutting down a headhunting operation could be an easy and quick revenge for stealing employees. Since Cal's recruiters were bringing in over two million dollars a year in commissions, Andrea guessed that fear of retaliatory revenge was sufficient cause for nervousness. But still, it was so uncharacteristic of Cal, who seemed to fear nothing. The man loved winning any type of battle; that was why he retained that top-notch lawyer.

Convinced that things weren't making much sense, Andrea turned her mind to the "happy times" to which she devoted most of her running schedule. Jogging was her way of relaxing, of forgetting everything connected to her high-pressured world. Happy thoughts free-floated through her mind. Christmas. The upcoming weekend at home. Going to the movies and seeing the new hit comedy everyone was raving about. All thoughts of the long, draining days in Atlanta were pushed out of her consciousness.

She became aware of the sound of another runner's stride far behind her. Turning right on Sixth Avenue, into the long stretch back to Freeway Park and the nearby North Winds, Andrea was unconcerned about the footsteps that were growing ever closer. The company of another jogger would be pleasant. Despite her increased speed, the runner was rapidly gaining on her. From the footfalls she guessed it was a man; certainly the length of the stride sounded like that of a man. Andrea continued on, settled in her pace. The runner drew close and, with only a few strides, pulled alongside Andrea. Only then did she glance his way.

A look of surprised recognition flashed across Gage's face. As his eyes took in the wary expression Andrea wore, his smile was hesitant. "I should have known that tiny figure in the middle of the sidewalk was you. What are you doing out here? Don't you realize it's dangerous to be running alone when it's hardly light?"

The sharp concern in his voice didn't go unnoticed. Andrea smiled pleasantly. "So what are *you* doing out here?"

"It's a bit different for me."

"Oh?" Andrea unconsciously slowed her pace. Gage matched it. "In what way?"

"One reason is I'm more capable of taking care of myself."

Andrea's eyes flicked over him. He was wearing a baggy, faded burgundy sweat suit. "Perhaps. But I do okay for myself. I have a black belt in karate."

Gage laughed in disbelief. "Sure."

Challenge rose in her voice. "Perhaps you'd like a demonstration?"

Meeting her frosty gaze, Gage said, "Not particularly." He paused, then added, "My ego couldn't handle it today if you were to throw me."

Andrea's laugh turned warm and friendly. "Well, just between you and me, I wouldn't be able to." She caught his glance and explained. "I lied. I don't have a black belt in karate. I don't even know any karate. But you'd be surprised how effective that line is in tight situations."

He grinned. "Yes, I would. I bought it. After the demonstration bit, that is."

"See what I mean?" Andrea was pleased that Gage was still talking to her after her rebuff of the previous night. She knew he had gotten the message to leave her alone.

They jogged a few blocks in companionable silence. Then Gage said, "I'd never guess that a dainty little thing like you would be into running. Do you run a lot?"

"A minimum of three miles a day, more if I'm training for a race. How 'bout you?"

"Five miles. Almost every day. So you race. In what?"

Andrea was beginning to puff, unused to carrying on a conversation while running. "Mostly 10-K. Do you compete?"

Gage shook his head and shortened his strike to slow down for Andrea. "No, that sort of competition isn't my thing. I run to...well, relax. Meditate, if you will. It's the only time I have to think of things otherworldly."

"Ah. A transcendental runner. I've heard about the breed, but you're the first specimen I've met."

They were running alongside Freeway Park now. The sound of the park's waterfall was thunderous in the early morning quiet. Designed to drown out the sound of highway traffic in the canyon under the park, the waterfall was a stylized imitation of a cascade and seemed definitely otherworldly in the fog-darkened dawn.

With their hotel only a few blocks away, Andrea realized that she didn't want the run to end. But if she pushed her distance, she would be even more tired than when she had awakened at a quarter of five. Right now she felt invigorated, alive and happy. And she didn't want that to change. Without thinking, she asked, "Does your offer of breakfast still stand?"

There was no mistaking the surprise that lighted Gage's eyes for a brief moment. When he spoke, his voice was expressionless. "Of course. When would you like to get together?"

"This morning. I'm starved!"

"What happened to dinner last night?"

Andrea laughed and admitted sheepishly, "I fell asleep before I ate a bite of it."

Gage chuckled. "Hope you got a good night's sleep."

"Oh, I did. I feel great today." They came to the hotel, and Andrea said, "This is the end of my run."

"I've got a ways to go yet." Gage looked at his watch. "Why don't we meet in the first-floor coffee shop—say, in an hour?"

"You're on." Andrea turned into the North Winds driveway and called back over her shoulder, "See you then."

The lobby was empty as she walked through it with a spring in her step. The desk clerk smiled vacantly and agreed to have room service deliver a carafe of coffee and the morning paper to her room. Only minutes after she had stopped by the desk, there was a tap on her door. Leaving the hot water running in the shower, Andrea retrieved the tray and newspaper from the hallway. A cursory glance at the front page told her that no earthshaking developments in the world scene had occurred. She tossed the *Times* onto the table and poured a cup of steaming liquid from the carafe. Idly emptying a packet of sugar into the coffee, Andrea wondered what she should wear for her breakfast with Gage.

With a start, she realized that she had actually made a date with the man and that it had been her idea. What had possessed her to do such a thing? She gulped down a mouthful of the strong brew and decided that the joy and relaxation of the morning's run had definitely affected her better judgment. Just eight hours earlier, she had made it clear to Gage that she wanted to be left alone. No wonder he had seemed surprised and a bit remote when she had asked about breakfast. Smiling ruefully, Andrea figured she'd probably get stood up that morning, and she wouldn't be able to blame Gage.

The steamy bathroom was a cocoon that she didn't want to leave. As Andrea lathered a bar of soap, she leaned her shoulder against the warm tiles of the shower and let the fine needles of hot water massage the remaining tension from her body. A good night's sleep—short as it was—and the run had put her in a better frame of mind than she'd been in for weeks. Hopefully, the long day ahead would not dim her cheerfulness. Perhaps she would even find time to sneak in a nap during the afternoon's recruiting. Smoothing the soapy washcloth over her arms, Andrea thought she should take care to do a couple of things for her own well-being. As she stood under the shower head to rinse off, she realized that accepting Gage's previous offer of breakfast was one way of doing something for herself.

She dressed in navy wool slacks and a gray-and-navy paisley blouse, checked her light makeup and fluffed her still-damp hair. When she slipped on navy pumps, she was dismayed to feel a tightening of her stomach muscles.

Knowing the reason, she tried to will her nerves into stillness but failed.

After placing a call to the housekeeper and requesting
that her room be cleaned while she was at breakfast, Andrea picked up her leather clutch and room key. Glancing
upward, she whispered, "Give me strength!"

The first-level coffee shop was crowded. Andrea wondered if all the men in the restaurant were attending the
national sheriffs' convention at the hotel. There was only
one other woman present.

Gage sat in the far corner, perusing a menu. While she
hesitantly approached his table, Andrea tried once again
to still the nerves that were causing her stomach to feel as
if a flock of butterflies were trying to find their way free.

Gage smiled warmly when he saw her and rose, pulling
a chair out. "Good morning."

Andrea nodded and slipped into the chair. Suddenly
unable to think of anything witty or brilliant to say, she
murmured, "'Morning."

"Coffee?"

"Please." While Gage poured her a cup of the steaming, black liquid from the carafe on the table, Andrea
scanned the menu. After she had decided what she
wanted, she held her cup in both hands and studied Gage
through the steam wafting from the coffee.

He was dressed in a business suit, the dark gray pinstripe and silk tie giving him an ultraconservative appearance. His wavy auburn hair was styled into order.
Gold cuff links shone dully, as did the watch he was wearing. Andrea found herself once again assessing the value
of his wardrobe, and once again she realized he was a man
who could afford anything he wanted. Thinking back to
their run, Andrea smiled at the memory of the faded and
baggy sweat suit he'd been wearing. The custom-made

running shoes had been new, but the sweats must have been years old.

While Andrea stared into her coffee cup, Gage leaned back in the barrel chair, rested an elbow on its arm and propped his chin onto a tan hand. "You do look as if you got a good rest last night."

"Yes, thank you." Andrea kept her eyes focused on her cup, wondering why she was so reticent. She was a reserved person, but her caution had never made her introverted. Of course...there was Gage's apparent interest in her. And her own disquieting reactions to him.

"I didn't expect you to show."

Andrea looked up. "No? Why not?"

"Despite the turnaround this morning, I'd gotten the impression that you were a bit afraid of me—in spite of my efforts to be nonthreatening." There was a disarming smile on his lips, but the expression in his eyes was serious.

Andrea's laugh was strained. "Well, I wouldn't say that I am exactly afraid of you."

"Then what—exactly—are you?"

She sipped at the warming coffee, her eyes retreating to study the linen tablecloth. "Nervous."

Gage chuckled under his breath. "At least you're honest. What about me makes you nervous?"

Andrea was trying to form an answer when the waitress stopped by to take their orders. As the woman left, Gage prompted, "You were about to say?"

Unable to decide on a reason that would not embarrass her, Andrea shook her hair back over her shoulders and met his disquieting gaze. "Now if I knew what it was, then I wouldn't be nervous, would I?"

"Only if you could do something about whatever it is that is making you nervous," Gage commented quietly. "You do look lovely this morning, Andrea, and I'm glad that you reconsidered." A gentle smile lingered on his lips while he waited for her response.

Strangely, Andrea found that her nerves were calming down. "Thank you for the compliment. And I'm glad I did, too." A pert smile erased the shyness from her face.

"What does your day hold in store for you?"

Andrea laughed. "What else but work?"

Gage poured himself another cup of coffee. "What is it you do?"

Andrea hedged, not wanting to take the time or the effort usually required to explain just what she did for a living. Every time she told someone she was a headhunter, she received an amused wink of the eye and a line that usually went something like: "Oh, modern-day Zuluism, huh?" Then she'd get a nudge in the ribs from an elbow, followed by, "Come on, tell me what you *really* do for a living."

No, she wasn't up to anything like that this morning. She merely said, "I'm a talent scout."

His raised eyebrow was skeptical. "In Seattle?"

She laughed. "You find talent everywhere." And that included talented engineers, she thought.

There was a curious glint in his dark eyes as Gage regarded her over the top of his cup. "What type of talent?"

Andrea sighed, wanting to forget her job just for a while. "Oh, this and that. All types, really. Nothing too particular."

"You mentioned that this is your first trip to Seattle?"

"Yes, it is." Andrea paused while their breakfast was set before them. "You said on the plane that you've been here several times. 'Home away from home,' if I recall correctly." As she sipped her orange juice, Andrea watched Gage prod the rare steak with his fork before he finally turned his attention to his tomato juice. "Bloody Mary?" she asked.

"What? Oh, no. I wish it were, though. I could do with some hair of the dog."

"I thought as much. You seemed fairly jovial last night."

He paused, fork midway to his mouth. "I don't do that very often."

"What? Drink?"

"Heavens, no. I drink all the time. No, I don't normally ask ladies out while they're standing around in their bathrobes." There was a wicked gleam in his eyes. "You did look bewitching, though, dressed in nothing but velour and hair ribbons."

Trying to appear blasé, Andrea asked, "What made you think it was only velour and hair ribbons?"

A lazy grin spread across his face, and the dark eyes stared into hers. "Eat your breakfast. I'm not about to answer that one. I'd hate to get slapped in front of this crowd of virile he-man cops."

Andrea suppressed a smile and tasted her Spanish omelet. "You aren't attending the sheriffs' convention, then?"

"Do I look like a cop?" Gage sounded offended.

Andrea drawled, "No." After a brief pause, she added, "Oh, that's right. You mentioned something about accidents at your company and taking care of them."

Gage put his knife and fork down and leaned back, studying her closely. "Right."

"What type of business is it? Industrial? Do you know what's causing the accidents?"

"You could say it's industrial." Gage's eyes narrowed. "And yes, I do know what's causing the accidents."

Feeling the tension behind his succinct comment, Andrea realized that once again she had brought up what appeared to be a touchy subject. She nodded vaguely and returned to her omelet.

Gage evidently didn't care to continue discussing work. After a few awkward moments, he pursued a different topic. Their conversation picked up again, idly ranging from the weather to the restaurant's cuisine to getting back to Los Angeles.

Finally Gage looked at his watch. "It's time that I run. I'm expected shortly."

Andrea patted her lips and laid her napkin down. "What time is it?"

"Eight-thirty."

"Really? Time has flown! I must get to work. But—" she smiled sweetly "—I have enjoyed breakfast very much."

"So have I. It certainly brightened what promises to be a dismal day—in more than one way."

"What in more than one way—brightened or dismal?" Andrea teased.

They had reached the cashier's counter. Gage, busy paying the check, only glanced at her a moment. "What?" Pausing, he added, "Both, actually." He took Andrea's elbow and guided her toward the exit.

As they stepped out into the huge lobby, now bustling with activity, Gage grasped her arm gently and pulled her to the side by the sweet-scented Christmas tree. Looking down into her sapphire eyes, he smiled warmly. "Thank you again." His quiet, seductive voice dropped to a near-whisper. "You are a lovely person to be with on such a gray morning. It would be very nice if we both didn't have work to do."

The nerves that had been quiescent during most of the meal exploded into action again. Andrea forced a calmness into her voice that was strained. "But if it weren't for our work, we wouldn't have met in the first place, would we?"

"You're probably right. Unless fate has something to do with it."

A man after Christine's own heart, Andrea thought. "Not knowing what the gods have in mind, I can't quibble with that."

She was just barely keeping in touch with her sanity. Why had he pulled her so close? Didn't he realize what he was doing to her? Andrea tried to quiet the erratic thumping of her heart, certain that Gage could hear it. If only he didn't have this effect on her! She really should listen to herself when she knew she should be avoiding the man. There wasn't time for romantic interludes.

"I must get back upstairs," she said, her voice quavering. "I'm expecting a phone call from my boss. If I'm not there...I don't want to face his anger. He expects me to have my nose constantly to the grindstone on these trips."

"All right, pretty lady. I'll let you get to work—again. But I promise you, you won't be so lucky next time!"

As he stared into her eyes with that incredible magnetic intensity, Andrea felt a warmth spread through her, and all thoughts of pulling away from him vanished. She stood motionless, Gage's hands upon her shoulders. The disarming smile on his mouth faded, and he bent toward her. When his lips brushed hers with a warm caress, the commotion about them dissolved. The tingle of surprise Andrea felt was overcome by the spark of pleasure his kiss kindled. Gage's lips brushed hers again slowly.

Alarmed and yet thrilled, Andrea struggled with her warring emotions. Feeling the light pressure of his fingers on her shoulders, she met his questioning smile with one of her own. Then, wavering, she took a step back, forcing Gage to release her. Despite the whirling thoughts in her mind, one was dominant. She had no doubt that Gage was totally aware of the effect he had on her; his seductive kiss had just confirmed it.

Feeling insecure and confused by what was happening, Andrea murmured, "I'd better get upstairs for that phone call." Faced with his silent scrutiny, she added, "Thanks again for breakfast."

Then she spun on her heel and walked quickly to the elevators.

Chapter Four

Her morning was uneventful. By noon she had recruited selectively from the group work sheets Cal had given her and set up an additional five interviews. After confirming a previously made interview appointment, Andrea set the phone back on the nightstand and crawled off the bed. She stood on her toes, enjoying the softness of the thick shag carpet, and stretched toward the ceiling. Then, room key, ice bucket and change in hand, she waltzed out into the hall.

The ice and soda machines were in an alcove at the far end of the hotel wing. Andrea strode down the corridor, a tuneless whistle on her lips. She smiled at a maid and continued on; her hair, caught up in a ponytail, swung with each step. Dressed in faded blue jeans and a dark magenta T-shirt, she looked like a college girl on vacation. Yet there was a determination reflected in her eyes that came from experience and developed character. At the moment, much of that determination was derived from the inner war she was fighting in regard to Gage.

Work had kept her mind occupied since breakfast, and she had not thought of him once. But now, during this short break, the events of the morning demanded her attention. As she scooped the cardboard bucket into the ice machine bin, Andrea frowned and bit her lower lip. Why did she have to meet this man in the first place? And for heaven's sake, why hadn't she kept her resolution to avoid him? Admittedly, she was attracted to him in a way that was fascinating and—she searched for the right word— yes, mysterious.

Gage was handsome, but not *that* handsome. He was charming, but not *that* charming. Andrea fed quarters into the soda machine and punched a button. And yes, he was seductive. Remembering his kiss, she nodded to herself. Seductive, yes. But that wasn't it, either.

As she strolled back to her room with the ice bucket and a can of soda, Andrea admitted to herself that the attraction to Gage was, to use the old cliché, pure chemistry. She'd never been able to avoid the magic of that special attraction. And she wasn't certain that she wanted to this time. But there were things about the man that kept her reluctance to get involved at a rather high level. First, there was his vacillating friendliness; cool detachment never seemed far away with Gage, particularly when she was trying to learn something personal about him. Then— what was the other thing? His charming pursuit of her this morning had ended in a kiss that was designed to arouse and—and what? Andrea sighed. She guessed the first answer to that last question was fairly obvious. Yet, for some reason, she didn't feel that getting her into bed was his only intent.

The telephone was ringing when she reached her door. Andrea set the can and ice bucket on the carpet, fumbled with the key and sprinted for the phone. "Hello?"

"Where have you been?" Cal demanded.

"Oh, it's you." With a start, Andrea realized that she had been hoping Gage would call. "Just down the hall getting some soda. Hang on. I've got to close the door."

After rescuing her soda and ice from the hallway, Andrea snatched up the receiver she had tossed on the pillows. "I'm back. What's up?"

"How's it going?"

"Fine. We've got six interviews set for Friday morning." Andrea perched on the edge of the bed, next to all of the papers, cards and directories. "That just about fills up the schedule."

"Good." There was a pause, and Andrea wondered what was on Cal's mind. The usual bluster was missing from his voice. "Have you hit the new company yet?"

"Stratcom?"

"Yes."

"No, I was going to pull a group after lunch and work it this afternoon. I wanted to get the big companies out of the way first, interview-wise. Why?"

If she hadn't known Cal so well, she would have missed the wariness in his voice. "Just wondered if you'd gotten a few good leads out of that book."

"That reason doesn't wash, Cal. What's the real one?"

The belly laugh boomed halfheartedly through the receiver. "Sharp girl. Be careful when you're recruiting Stratcom. The head honcho there has a deep-seated hatred for headhunters. I'm likely to get a phone call from him if you stir things up."

Andrea felt cold. "Uh, Cal, you'd better level with me. I'm up here all alone. Whom should I avoid while I'm calling around Stratcom? Just so you don't get any threatening phone calls and so no one shows up at my hotel."

"Let's put it this way." Andrea knew that phrase spoke ill of the situation. "When you recruit there, use the name Ann Baird. Don't use your real name. Baird is close enough to Barrie so that when your interviewees ask for you at the desk, they'll get through to you. The hotel personnel will think they got your name wrong."

Ann Baird. The same name Cal had her use when he had forced her to do some rather illegal telephoning a few months back. A name that was not her own, harder to trace to ComSearch, but close enough to hers that it would incriminate her in any legal proceedings. Cal had a habit of setting up employees to appear as the guilty party if something went amiss with his schemes.

Andrea wound the telephone cord around her finger. "What's so special about Stratcom? I took a look at their phone book. They must be a tiny outfit. Why would Tectron be interested in any talent a hole-in-the-wall company might have?"

"Because any company in the country would pay a hefty fee for the talent they've got. Stratcom employs the top three-percentile scientists and engineers in the nation."

Andrea tried to keep her skepticism from her voice. "Why haven't I heard of them before now?"

"Because until Tectron received that new government contract, they didn't have any need for the type of talent Stratcom has. When it comes to analysts, Stratcom's got an esoteric group, highly specialized."

"And very high-priced."

"You got it. But now Tectron has the money to go after one or two of their best, so see what you can do about lining up the interviews."

"Will do. Anything else?"

"Yes. Tomorrow morning a friend of mine is flying up to Seattle. He'll be staying at your hotel, and I want you to show him the ropes. His name is Len Daggett—an old engineering buddy of mine whose company experienced a big layoff with the loss of the F40A contract. Len's decided to give headhunting a try. He's spent the last week in the office here, and I'd like him to see you at work on one of these raids. Show him how you operate, Andi, and what it takes to pull a raid off.''

Her anger flooded over the phone line. "Cal, you know I don't have time to do anything like that—and keep everything from falling apart! I simply cannot baby-sit one of your buddies.'' Andrea glared at her toes burrowing into the carpet.

There was a long silence on Cal's end of the line. When he spoke again, his words were carefully chosen, his tone deliberate and chilling. "You will find that Len knows all of the headhunting basics. He has an extensive engineering background to draw on, and he might even prove helpful to you in working the Stratcom groups. What he needs to pick up from you is finesse. You will find him a quick study and a gentleman.''

Andrea had trouble believing that any old friend of Cal's could be a "gentleman,'' but she had her orders and knew that protesting further would be futile. Her voice was frosty. "Okay, fine. Do I need to pick him up at the airport?''

"No, Len will take the limo. He'll check in and take you to lunch. You two can get to know each other and compare notes on what you've done so far and what remains to be done.''

"Anything else?''

"Don't antagonize him.'' Cal's tone was patriarchal. "Remember you're representing ComSearch.''

When the line clicked dead, Andrea slammed the receiver into its cradle. Jumping up from the bed, she stormed to the window and stared out into the cold, gray day. Rain still blurred the city skyline, as it had done since she'd returned from breakfast. Only now, gusty winds blew it in swirls. Why did Cal do things like this to her? Raids were difficult enough without the handicap of working with a novice.

Needing to burn off her angry energy before she could face an afternoon of recruiting out of Stratcom, Andrea pulled on socks and jogging shoes and grabbed her room key. One nice thing about staying in a huge hotel, she thought while glaring disdainfully over her shoulder at her working materials spread out on top of the bedspread, there was always something to explore. She yanked the door open and slammed it shut behind her.

BY THE TIME Andrea returned to her hotel room an hour later, most of the anger she felt toward Cal and the situation as it was developing in Seattle had diffused. As much as she didn't like what was happening, there certainly wasn't anything that she could do about it, short of quitting. And quitting was not an option right now. Closing the door behind her, Andrea leaned against it and closed her eyes.

No matter what Cal was up to with this Seattle raid, she prayed that she wouldn't get caught in the middle of a backfiring plan. The only employee who could be considered part of ComSearch's "inner circle," Andrea knew very little of Cal's dealings in the business world. And of what she was aware of, she wished she had retained complete ignorance. Cal was a schemer, a man who played both ends against the middle and the middle against the ends. She had witnessed the lopping of high-placed heads at companies Cal had recruited for, the firings and forced resignations part of the manipulating Cal could do within those firms. The power the man grasped hold of and used was staggering to Andrea's imagination. The lack of ethics exercised behind that power was dire.

Sighing softly, she pushed herself away from the door. One day—soon, she hoped—she would be able to resign and turn to a more normal, honorable profession. What that was, she had no idea, but she was open to almost any suggestion.

She dropped her room key on the desk and nudged her jogging shoes off with her toes. Studying the materials on the bed, Andrea knew she couldn't put off calling the Stratcom engineers any longer. It was time to get back to work.

But as she nestled into the pillows propped up against the bed's headboard and reached for a blank group sheet, a pencil and the Stratcom telephone directory, she paused, her eyes flicking over the piles of cards, sheets and directories. Something wasn't right.

Muttering to herself, Andrea said, "Now that's not where I left that. It's way out of reach." Still sitting cross-legged against the pillows, she stretched toward the stack of directories. It was a foot beyond her fingertips' touch. She leaned back a moment, pursed her lips and frowned. Scooting over far enough to grasp the stack, she dragged the directories into her lap and flipped through them. The small Stratcom directory was in the middle of the pile. She could have sworn she had left it on top.

Setting the directories aside, Andrea picked up the group of cards scheduled for interviews and thumbed through them. They were out of order. She was a person who couldn't function in a disorderly environment; she had her own system of sorting and handling all the various cards and papers she dealt with on a daily basis. The frown cut deeper across her forehead. The cards in her right hand were not as she had left them after setting up that last interview. Her worried eyes swept the room.

Tossing the cards down, Andrea leapt off the bed and scrambled for the travel bag that hung behind the closed closet door. Sliding the door panel aside, she quickly felt the outside pocket of the bag, then unzipped it and pulled out the small, flat case in which she carried her jewelry. When her trembling hands opened the brown velvet case, Andrea breathed, "Oh, thank you!" Snapping the case shut, she looked around the room again but couldn't spot anything missing. Other than her few items of jewelry, which were all intact, she carried nothing else of value when she traveled.

Unless she was losing her mind from lack of sleep, Andrea was certain someone had been in her hotel room. But why hadn't the intruder taken anything? It seemed such a risk to break into a room and then not make the risk worthwhile. She had always been warned of the dangers of having her hotel or motel room burglarized. It was such a common occurrence, she considered herself lucky that it hadn't happened before now.

Andrea shrugged her shoulders philosophically, replaced the case in the travel bag and zipped the pocket shut. Perhaps her burglar had more expensive tastes than her own modest jewelry could offer. Giggling, she said aloud, "Bet you were surprised to find such low-ticket items in such a grand hotel!" Crawling back on top of her bed, she added, "Better luck next time."

After her moment of excitement, the afternoon passed slowly, the recruiting from Stratcom going badly. By four-thirty, Stratcom's quitting time, Andrea was tired and depressed. She slumped in the armchair, massaged her temples with her fingertips, and tried to figure out what she was doing wrong with this company. Engineers rarely took a headhunter seriously until an offer was made. Andrea's experience had made her believe that her sex was a plus—male engineers tended to be more willing to talk to a female recruiter simply because women headhunters were such a novelty.

Of course, she knew that none of the engineers saw her as a threat, a person who could come along and upset the routine of their lives. But many had found, usually quite abruptly, that Andrea could not only talk them into telling her about themselves but also con them into going for a job interview at Tectron or one of her other customers when they were already happily employed. The biggest shock to an engineer who dealt with her was how tough, competent and tenacious the sweet-sounding young woman really was.

But this tough and tenacious young woman had gotten nowhere with the personnel of Stratcom. Only one man had been willing to talk to her—and she had called over fifty. She should have been able to talk with forty or forty-five, using her standard recruit-to-call ratio. Andrea couldn't understand it. Was there something out of the ordinary about this elite group of brains at Stratcom that made the fact that she was a woman a liability instead of an asset? It was possible, she thought.

Dusk was falling, and the city lights twinkled through the drizzle. After a week of hotel rooms, she wanted to get out and about, even if it meant getting cold and wet. The hotel laundry services had returned all of her clothes an hour earlier, so she had a clean, if limited, wardrobe again. While trying to decide what to wear on her excursion, Andrea turned on the television set and tuned in a five o'clock news program.

As she put her working materials away in a drawer, Andrea realized that Cal would accuse her of shirking and not earning her per-diem pay. Still irritated that her duties would be interrupted, not to mention heavily hampered, by the nursemaiding of a headhunting rookie, she scooped up the last of the papers from the bed and dumped them unceremoniously in the drawer. Slamming it shut, Andrea symbolically dusted her hands of her duties and poured herself a glass of soda.

The hour-long news program was half over. Andrea had finished her drink, decided what to wear and was about to take a quick shower when there was a soft knock on the door. Immediately, her heart started fluttering—much to her dismay, but not to her surprise.

Gage stood in the hallway. He was still wearing the pinstripe suit, but his tie was loosened and the collar unbuttoned. The gentle smile that had warmed Andrea's thoughts periodically throughout the day touched the corner of his mouth but stopped there. The dark eyes that caressed her face were disturbed.

Andrea wondered what had distressed him and what sort of mood he was in. "Hello," she said cautiously.

Was it relief that flickered in those dark eyes? Andrea wasn't certain. But Gage's smile grew, and his voice held the husky tones that she found so captivating. "Hi. Have you had dinner yet?"

Andrea tried to ignore the unsteady thumping of her heart. "No, I haven't."

The humor that had lurked in the corners of his eyes the night before had been replaced by lines of strain. Gage straightened, shoving his hands into his trouser pockets. "Well, my day turned out more dismal than I expected. It's been a real dog. And I've got a good case of the doldrums." He smiled tightly. "After breakfast this morning, I don't know how you feel about me. But on the way back to the hotel I was thinking that if anyone could cheer me up, it would be you. It's been a bad day. I could use the company. And I promise I'll try to be the pleasant cuss I told you I was.''

''Oh, I think you're pleasant enough.'' Andrea paused, running her finger along the edge of the door and telling herself that dinner with this man didn't mean a life of romantic entanglements. ''But you have to promise me one thing.''

He hesitated before answering. ''If I can. What is it?''

''Get me out of this hotel! I'm going absolutely stir-crazy!''

Gage's laugh was tense but genial. ''You've got it. How long will it take you to get ready?''

''Half an hour?''

''Done. I'll be back in thirty minutes. Dress casually and warmly.''

The smile Gage flashed her was genuine, and as his gaze held hers, Andrea felt weak inside and wondered why her resolve kept disappearing. Her smile was a faint imitation of his, her mind whirling once again from a wide array of conflicting emotions and rationalizations. A strange expression crossed Gage's face before it closed in a mask of calm self-assurance. He reached his hand out, tucked a stray lock of hair behind her ear and traced the line of her jaw lightly. Then he stepped back.

As Andrea remained motionless, her hand gripping the edge of the door, Gage smiled again. ''A half hour.'' He turned abruptly and strode down the hallway to the elevators.

Consternation fought with happiness as Andrea closed the door. She had a half hour to get ready, and she could barely pull her thoughts together into a coherent string. Wishing she were more rational, more her usual in-control self, she moved toward the bathroom in a trancelike state.

The rain had stopped by the time Gage returned. He smiled approvingly as she stood in the doorway, dressed in charcoal wool culottes, a pearl-gray mohair sweater and burgundy suede boots. Her shiny hair was pinned up, held by an antique silver barrette that had belonged to her maternal grandmother. It was her most prized possession, and she was thankful her afternoon burglar had left it behind.

Gage's eyes lingered over a second inspection. "You're certainly worth cheering up for."

"Why, thank you, sir." Noticing his return to sweater, corduroy jeans and sport jacket, she asked, "Is this casual enough? I could change into slacks."

Gage slung his trench coat over his shoulder. "You're fine." He brushed a kiss on her cheek and murmured, "That's enticing perfume."

Gage had showered and shaved and was wearing an earthy musk scent. "You don't exactly smell like an old sock, either," she told him.

He laughed warmly. "I'm glad I decided you were the one person who could cheer me up. Tonight will be a night to remember!"

She turned to collect her coat and clutch purse from the bed, sneaking a few deep breaths to calm her trembling rebellious interior. "Where are we going?" she asked.

Gage pulled the door shut after Andrea had stepped into the hallway. "The rain's quit, and it looks as if this storm has blown over. I thought we'd stop in the second-floor lounge and have a drink, if you'd like, then hop the Monorail over to the Space Needle for dinner."

Slipping his arm loosely around her shoulders, he drew her gently to his side and guided her to the elevators. His leg grazed her hip with each stride, and at first she wanted to pull away. But walking with him this way, their bodies touching so briefly and naturally, was oddly comforting.

"You'll get a bird's-eye view of Seattle," he continued. "It's a dazzling sight at night."

Glancing up at his rugged profile, Andrea said, "Dinner sounds great, but personally, I could skip the drink."

"Don't tell me you're a teetotaler?" A bushy eyebrow arched in curiosity.

Her laugh was soft. "No, I do drink, but to tell you the truth, I'm starving."

"No lunch, huh?"

"No lunch."

"Then dinner first, sight-seeing afterward."

It was half a block's walk from the North Winds to the Monorail station. While they waited on the elevated Westlake Mall platform for the next train, Andrea looked down the concrete guideway and said sheepishly, "You know, this will be the first train I've ever ridden."

Gage shrugged on his overcoat in the brisk breeze. "You mean you've never ridden the monorail at Disneyland?"

Andrea's smile was pert. "No, I haven't." She slipped her bare hands into her coat pockets. "Never been on Amtrak, either."

The incoming train's headlight grew larger in the night, and Gage stepped to Andrea's side. "Get ready for a quick trip. Seattle Center's just over a mile north of here."

The electric train coasted to a stop, and the pair stepped inside. Gage sat Andrea next to the window so she could easily see the view of nighttime downtown Seattle. He placed his arm on the back of the seat and leaned close. When the Monorail began its silent commute, he said, "This is the way to beat the parking crunch. Seattle never completely got it together to solve the Center's traffic problem.''

Andrea turned her gaze from the window. "How long does the trip take?''

Her sapphire-blue eyes had darkened as she met his glance. Watching the flicker of emotions that darted in the lush-lashed eyes, Gage answered, "Ninety seconds, give or take one.'' He smiled and pointed a finger toward the window. "Better look quick or you'll miss all the sights.''

Gage was right; within a minute and a half, they had arrived at Seattle Center. As they exited the Monorail station beside the Space Needle, Andrea looked up at the graceful, soaring structure that commanded the night sky. "I've seen pictures but never realized just how big and tall it really is.''

Gage once again slipped his arm around her shoulders, pulling her close to his side. Andrea tensed for a moment, then relaxed in the circle of his arm. If he had noticed that moment of anxiety, she couldn't tell. He commented lazily, "You can't see the actual tip from here, of course, but the Needle is 607 feet tall. The restaurant's at five hundred feet, and as I said, the view's great.''

The Monorail trip had been fun, but Andrea thoroughly enjoyed the glass-elevator ride to the restaurant. Even more, she delighted in the window table with the dazzling view Gage had promised.

After dinner she sipped at a glass of sherry and thought back over the evening. She already knew that Gage was a tranquil, easygoing man who fluctuated between periods of companionable conversation and an almost remote silence. She wasn't certain if he was as withdrawn as he seemed. Andrea had slowly realized that the only time he became detached was when she sought to learn more about him on a deeper personal level. Questions of work and family were obviously taboo. But Andrea was coming to enjoy those long moments, even minutes, in which neither felt compelled to fill the calm between them with idle chitchat. The only thing that bothered her was the flash of intensity that would darken his eyes or toughen his jawline when she had asked too personal a question. After she had stopped inquiring, the easy rapport between them had grown.

Sitting across from him, Andrea felt strangely comfortable. It was the same feeling she had experienced when they had walked to the hotel elevator. They had met only twenty-four hours earlier. Yet after the long, leisurely dinner, she felt as if she had known him for a very long time.

Gage was watching the city slowly revolve, its lights twinkling below them and along the shores of Lake Washington. Andrea followed his gaze. The rain had stayed away, as Gage had said it would, and the lights of Seattle were like millions of tiny diamonds scattered on a midnight-blue velvet cloth. It was an enchanting view, one Gage seemed to find particularly captivating.

Andrea set her wineglass down on the red linen tablecloth, smoothed the fabric under her hand, then leaned back in her chair. "Penny for your thoughts."

Gage pulled his eyes away from the view below. As his gaze focused on her face, soft and gentle in the dim lighting, he chuckled. "With inflation, that should be a quarter."

"Okay. A quarter it is." She smiled impishly.

He sipped at the remaining burgundy in his glass. "I don't think you'd like to hear my thoughts." There was a sly smile on his lips and darkness in his eyes.

"Do they have anything to do with me?" She leaned forward, resting an elbow on the table and propping her chin on her hand.

His answer was slow in coming. "They have everything to do with you."

"Oh, good. For a while there I thought I'd lost out to the view."

Gage laid his hand on top of hers. "Don't ever think that you're number two." His thumb stroked the back of her hand, a featherlight touch, while his eyes burned into hers with an intensity that disturbed Andrea. She looked at her hand cradled in his and pulled away slightly to free it. Gage did not let go of her hand immediately, clasping it tightly for a long moment before he finally gave in to the tug. "What's wrong?" he asked quietly.

"Nothing," Andrea lied.

Nothing? she thought. *Everything's wrong. I shouldn't be here. He shouldn't be looking at me that way. I don't even know what "that way" is, what it means. He's the most private and confusing man I've ever met. And I shouldn't be feeling the way I'm feeling. Happy. Safe. Warm. Hopeful.*

Hopeful? Hopeful for what? Andrea didn't want anything to be between them. She was supposed to be avoiding this man by her own decree, and she was doing everything but. If nothing else, his reticence tended to confirm her guess that he was a married man with a wife and family back in L.A. Why else hadn't he told her his last name or his background? As Andrea gripped her hands under the table, she felt the fool for allowing her emotions to be aroused by him; intellectually, however, she knew it was also his air of mystery that captivated her so.

Gage seemed to accept her answer. "Why don't we take a walk around the Center before we head back to the hotel? I think it's prettiest at night."

Andrea was relieved to find the conversation turning away from them. "That sounds terrific." Her smile was tight. "A great way to work off some of this fabulous dinner."

They left the restaurant, Gage respecting the silence she had retreated into. As they stepped outside into the biting cold wind that was blowing in from Lake Washington, he buttoned his trench coat and glanced at her. She huddled in her coat, strands of her hair coming loose and whipping about in the wind.

"The temperature's dropping. Perhaps we should go back to the hotel."

"Oh, no," Andrea protested, pushing the hair out of her eyes. "Not on my account. I love walks on chilly winter nights."

"And you're crazy."

"That, too." She stopped under a light pole and looked up at Gage, her teasing smile daring him to give her the sight-seeing tour he had promised. "Are you going to renege? You said you'd show me the sights."

"But I didn't promise you a case of pneumonia." Gage shook his head at the expression on her face and laughed. "All right. Have it your way."

They strolled along a walkway lined with bare-limbed trees and headed toward the Pacific Science Center. Five graceful Gothic arches rose above the lighted plaza fountains that cast their watery music on the night wind. Miniature lights adorned the branches of the trees in front of the science center pavilions, and the reflecting pools captured the glow of the scene. Once again Andrea was reminded how close Christmas was and how she wished she were at home.

As she stood staring silently at a fountain, Gage sauntered to her side. "Penny for your thoughts."

Andrea shook her head, not answering him. She didn't know why, but at that moment she was very close to tears.

Standing there, hands shoved deep into coat pockets, Gage studied the woman whose face betrayed her every feeling. Slowly he placed a hand on her shoulder. While her eyes remained fixed on the fountain, he brushed her cold cheek with the backs of his warm fingers. "I don't know about you, but I'm beat. It's been a long day. Do you realize it's almost midnight?"

"Is it really?" Andrea turned toward him as he withdrew his hand. "It's beautiful here." She listened to the sound of the wind and the silence it covered. "It's almost like another world."

Gage shoved his hand back into his pocket. "I thought you'd like it. Anyone who loves nighttime views from airplanes has to love Seattle Center."

A tinkling on the wind caught Andrea's attention. "What's that?" she asked, a touch of excitement in her voice.

Gage cocked his head, listening. Snatches of "Silent Night" were floating on the wind. "The music?"

"Yes."

"That's probably from the International Fountain. It's a type of programmed water-and-music show, over in the center of the park."

"Show me." Andrea's smile was beseeching. "Please."

"I gather you're a Christmas nut."

"Guilty."

Gage slipped his arm around her shoulders and pulled her close. "This way, then."

Despite the cold and the wind, they walked slowly through the park, past the Center House and the Art Museum, cutting between buildings and then strolling through the quad toward the International Fountain. Over two hundred shooting jets of water rose into the air, the multicolored lights playing off the droplets of water in a fascinating array of beauty. Light, water and music synchronized into a Christmas pageant. As "We Three Kings" began to play, Andrea relaxed against Gage, shielded from the wind by his body and secure in the embrace of his arm about her shoulders. They stood like that for several minutes, silently watching the fountain and listening to the music from the excellent sound system. Finally, she tried to stifle a yawn and was unsuccessful.

Gage hugged her and said, "The carriage is going to turn into a pumpkin if we don't get back to the Monorail station, little one."

She nodded reluctantly and allowed him to turn her toward the Center House. "I guess all good things must end. But I've had a great time."

"Good. Work is no fun without a little play to make it worthwhile."

Andrea groaned. "You just ruined a perfect evening by mentioning work."

As they hurried past the children's amusement park, Gage admitted, "I did, didn't I? Well, I'm glad you've had a good time, because you've certainly cheered me up this evening. And I thank you for that."

"Anytime," she said nonchalantly.

A peculiar expression flitted across Gage's face before a grin settled on his lips. "I'll hold you to that promise."

They arrived at the station just as the train slid silently to a stop. The platform was empty, and they had a cabin to themselves for the short ride back to Westlake Mall.

Andrea had to admit to herself that she certainly felt much safer on these dark city streets with Gage by her side than she had felt jogging that morning, or rather, the previous morning.

It was close to 1:00 A.M. when they stepped from the hotel elevator onto Andrea's floor. As they walked down the long hallway, Andrea realized that she was breathing a little faster than normal. She stole a glance at Gage and could tell nothing of his thoughts. The familiar expressionless mask had settled over his features. He stopped outside her door and she unlocked it, just barely pushing the door open. Turning to him, she said in a voice a shade too high-pitched, "Thank you again. I had a marvelous evening."

He rested his strong hands on her shoulders and stared down into the blue eyes darkened slightly by uneasiness. "Anytime, my lovely." Slowly, his lips lowered to hers, brushing them with a warm kiss. He should have withdrawn after that first kiss but didn't.

His breath mingled with hers, and during a single moment's sanity, Andrea hesitantly pulled away. Her gaze focused on a button of his overcoat and her words were a soft murmur. "I don't think I should mislead you."

Gage slipped his hand under her chin and gently tipped her head back. When her eyes finally slid up to meet his, he said, "I knew kissing you this morning was a mistake. How am I going to rectify it?"

As Andrea watched that warm, gentle smile steal over his lips, she felt a fondness for this man whom she barely knew settle somewhere near that pilot light burning deep inside her. Standing on tiptoe, she kissed his cheek and answered cheerfully, "By saying, 'I'll see you tomorrow.'"

Chapter Five

Andrea dropped the receiver into its cradle after yet an-other unsuccessful phone call to a Stratcom engineer. The recruiting raid on Stratcom was still going badly. She had managed to line up two software analysts for interviews the next evening, but she doubted if either would show. The response she was getting from the firm's engineers was puzzling. At first she had thought that perhaps being a woman headhunter was a handicap in working this or-ganization. Now she wasn't so certain that was the problem.

She stood up, stretched and went over to the rain-streaked window. The view of the city was even more blurred than it had been the previous day, with the arrival of a new storm front. The rain was falling harder, and the wind was blowing in off the Puget Sound in galelike gusts. Her breath frosted an uncertain oval on the glass, and she absentmindedly traced its form with her finger.

As they had done so many times that morning, her thoughts turned to Gage. The huskiness of his voice, the fathomless dark eyes, his ingratiating smile—combined with the sexual impact he had on her—were most dis-turbing. She was finding it impossible to resist his dis-arming and seductive charm.

Even more unsettling was her distressing yet definite emotional response to him, which she did not understand. She barely knew him; in fact, she didn't even know his last name. Her reaction to him erased her fears and made her yearn to be with him, while at the same time the uncontrollable effect it had on her resolve not to get involved infuriated her. But wasn't it she who kept opening the door to seeing him again?

Andrea turned her back to the dismal view and paced the room, trying to figure Gage out. She was certain that his charm was totally natural, but a little voice inside kept reminding her of his secretive manner. What was behind those flashes of intensity and uncommunicativeness? Sighing, she bit her lip. Probably a wife and a passel of kids. Knowing that was a definite likelihood, Andrea didn't understand why she kept wanting to see him. She had a firm rule never to date a married man, let alone get involved with one. Gage didn't wear a wedding band— she'd noticed that on the plane—but, of course, that didn't mean he wasn't married. Perhaps...

Perhaps it was that she was certain he would be a gentle lover. The thought of sharing her bed with him made her aware of a deep hunger. It had been a very long time since she had been with a man as tender and strong as Gage. In fact, the last man had been David. And David, she thought, had hurt her much more than Gage ever could.

As Andrea tried to separate the pain of the past from the ache of the present, she returned to the table. Staring at the piles of recruiting cards and directories, she decided to put memories of David and thoughts of Gage out of her mind and concentrate harder on her work.

The next hour was slightly more productive. Andrea managed to recruit three promising Stratcom men who appeared to be exactly what Tectron was looking for:

bright, young, highly technical professionals with four to seven years' experience in all the right fields. She scanned the cards she had written up while talking to each man. If she could get only these three to the interview stage with Tectron, the customer would be happy. She would call each man back the next morning to set up a Thursday evening or Friday morning interview.

While she was jotting a note to herself, she heard a knock on the door and glanced at the travel alarm. It was shortly after one. Cal's friend was arriving right on time. Andrea pushed herself out of her chair and felt a new wave of irritation wash through her. If only Cal had listened to her! She was too weary for the added chore of recruiter training. The smile into which she forced her lips was purely public-relations-oriented. She resigned herself to her fate and opened the door.

The man standing there was below average height and compactly built. As Andrea's inquisitive gaze flowed from his stylishly cut light brown hair to his brown eyes, businesslike smile, conservative blue suit and polished oxfords, he bowed his head slightly. "Andrea Barrie?"

She nodded silently, suddenly feeling ill at ease.

"Len Daggett. I believe Cal told you to expect me today?"

Trying to hide her discomposure, Andrea stepped aside. Her tone was gracious. "Come in, please."

He waved a hand around the room, at the working materials spread out on the bed and the table by the window. "I see you're hard at work."

Andrea closed the door slowly, not certain that she wanted to be alone in the same room with this man. She had no reason for it, but her nerves had prickled instantly. It was as if her female intuition were screaming a warning. It was also ridiculous for her to react this way when she didn't even know him—or so she told herself. She assumed the reason was simply that she so much resented his being there.

Len Daggett turned his astute gaze on her, his smile impersonal. He extended his hand. "It's a pleasure to meet you, Andrea. I'm looking forward to learning the business from you."

His handshake was merely a firm, momentary grip before he released her hand. Andrea noted the dispassionate tone of voice that was so different from Gage's. The unexpected comparison she'd made reflected on her face for a moment. She masked her surprise quickly and said smoothly, "Thank you. I hope your trip was pleasant."

"It was fine, thank you. How are things going?" Len set his briefcase on the floor as he stepped to the table. He picked up a recruiting card. "Having much success?"

"Well..." Andrea's usual come-hither tone was absent, replaced by a capable briskness. It was an attitude she assumed when dealing with people she was uncertain about. Yet she never used it over the telephone, only in in-person situations. "Enough to pay off."

Len seemed unruffled by her aggressive demeanor. "I don't know about you, but I could do with lunch. Let's get to know each other over a salad."

While they waited in the second-floor cocktail lounge for a table in the adjoining restaurant, Andrea learned that getting to know this man would be on a business level only. Cal had not lied to her this time; Len did seem to be a gentleman—in every sense of the word, Andrea thought. He treated her with a refined courtesy that she found very welcome, but it lacked the hidden warmth of Gage's manner. After a companionable lunch, they were back in her room, flipping through recruiting cards and comparing notes on Tectron's needs.

Len had shed his suit coat, loosened his tie, unbuttoned his shirt collar and rolled up his shirt sleeves. Sitting across the small table from him, Andrea watched him scribble notes on the back of a card. He was indeed the professional. From the comments he made, Andrea knew that his engineering background was extensive. She wondered why he had been laid off by his company. Even if they had lost a government contract, Len Daggett seemed to be the type of engineer for whom a company would scrape funds together to keep him on board.

If he were as knowledgeable and talented as she perceived him to be—and she didn't doubt her headhunter's instincts—any firm like Tectron would snap him up off the streets and even toss in a good salary increase over his last job. Knowing that, Andrea wondered why he chose instead to become a headhunter. He didn't strike her as the type to get into such a chancy, offbeat profession. Engineers, on the whole, were a breed of people who tended to be security-minded; that characteristic made them good at their jobs.

Len looked up, catching Andrea deep in observation and thought. The intensity that she had felt upon first meeting him was still there, fortified by a quiet determination. That determination did not show on his even features or in the brown eyes that were so unexpressive. It showed only in his attitude, which was professional, expert, extremely urbane. That bothered her. He was too suave, too genteel to be a recruiter. At least on the surface, he lacked the aggressiveness that the job required for success. Even determination was no adequate substitute for the "killer instinct."

Len pushed a card across the tabletop. "Have you set this man up for an interview?"

Andrea scanned her notes on the back of the card. "No, I haven't."

"Why not?" It was an impersonal, nonchallenging request for information.

"One, he's with Stratcom. They don't like headhunters there. Two, he's had only two years' experience as an analyst." Andrea attempted to hand the card back to Len. "He doesn't meet Tectron's requirements."

Daggett leaned back in his chair and studied her. "With the new government contract, the requirements have changed. They've got more junior openings than they normally have. And I'd guess that his three years at Langley were spent in communications analysis. That would give him the basic five years' background required."

Andrea felt that her ability as a recruiter was being questioned. "Working with the CIA at Langley doesn't necessarily mean that he was an analyst there."

Len shrugged noncommittally. "That's true. What did he say when you asked him where he was employed before he started at Stratcom?"

"Have you ever talked to one of these ex-CIA people?" Andrea laughed. "They are the most paranoid, suspicious types you'll ever recruit."

Len nodded in a vague, neutral manner. "What did he say?"

Mildly irritated, Andrea parroted their conversation. " 'CIA.' I asked, 'Langley?' He said, 'Yes.' I asked, 'Doing what?' He said, 'That's classified.' And his stock in paranoia jumped twenty points that instant."

Len nodded again. "Set him up. He's what they're looking for."

Andrea's pride as a headhunter was ruffled. "What makes you think so?"

Daggett took a pack of cigarettes from the suit coat that hung on the back of his chair and shook one out. "His first job out of college was with the Central Intelligence Agency. He majored in computer programming at MIT. He left the CIA after three years to work for Stratcom as an analyst on a classified communications program. You got that much out of him." He paused to flick open a gold lighter. As a puff of smoke wafted upward, he asked, "Do you know anything about Stratcom?"

"Nothing. Cal said nothing, and I've found out very little from the people who've talked to me. All I know is that they are an esoteric bunch and their head man hates headhunters." She added nervously, "I'm expecting a hostile person to show up here at the hotel any minute now."

Len's businesslike attitude faded into a tight little smile that turned down the corners of his mouth. "I don't think you'd like Stratcom's chairman of the board."

Curious about the man who evidently demanded and received extreme loyalty from his employees, Andrea asked, "Do you know him?"

"Sort of. Anyway, get this guy set up. Tectron will be very happy with him." Len turned his attention to another card."

Andrea found Len's manner highly suspicious for a novice headhunter. She leaned back in her chair and forced indifference into her voice. "Did Cal send you up here to screen the Stratcom recruits?"

Len continued scribbling notes, his head bent. "Cal told me to be helpful in any way I could. He did mention that you could use some help with Stratcom. He knows they're a tough bunch to talk to. He's never succeeded in recruiting a single person out of the company." Len held up the dozen or so Stratcom recruit cards and glanced at her.

"This type of recruiting success in that company is phenomenal. Cal's right—you're a crack headhunter."

Andrea was determined to have her curiosity satisfied. "Just what was your last position—the job on the F40A?"

Len crushed out his cigarette and returned to his note making. "Project leader."

"Project leader?" She stared at the man. That meant he had been one of the top people responsible for the ill-fated F40A, a spy plane that had fallen from favor when the newly elected government had taken office in Washington. The F40A had been an extremely controversial defense project that had also proved to be incredibly costly even by inflated defense budget standards. Involvement with the project had cost many upper-echelon talents their aerospace careers. It explained why Len Daggett, obviously a brilliant engineer, was turning to headhunting to pay the bills. He would be riding out the wave of bureaucratic head-lopping and disfavor for a long time.

Len paused momentarily in his writing to take in Andrea's enlightened expression. "Does that surprise you?"

A faint smile eased some of the defensive aggression from her face. "Not really. But it does answer a lot of my questions."

A quick grin flitted across his mouth before it closed around another cigarette. "Good. Now you can quit sizing me up and we can get down to work."

The candor was unexpected, and Andrea laughed in spite of her uneasiness. She had not intended to be so obvious, yet knowing the man's background made it easier for her to deal with the situation. His impersonal, professional attitude would allow her to concentrate on showing him how she recruited. And being aware of his qualifications would help her to trust his judgment.

Andrea picked up the recruiting card on the Stratcom communications analyst that she had tossed on the table. ''I'll see if I can set him up.''

Len dragged deeply on his cigarette. ''I may not be able to use your approach—Cal warned me that I wouldn't—but I want to learn the tricks of the trade. I'm a willing student.''

As Andrea reached for the telephone, it rang shrilly. She shrugged at Len's questioning look and answered it. ''Hello?''

''Hi, this is Gage.'' His husky voice was even more resonant over the telephone.

Andrea's eyes dropped to the card in her hand. Trying to keep her tone businesslike, she replied, ''Hello. How are you?''

''Just fine. How 'bout you?''

As usual, Gage sounded totally in control. Andrea wished that she could keep her emotions under tight rein, but they seemed to be taking the bit and running away with her. ''Great. Say, I have someone with me right now.''

''Is he loaded with talent?''

Andrea glanced at Len and laughed lightly. ''As a matter of fact, yes. But...''

''Not right for the part.'' Gage paused, then said, ''I'll make this quick. Still up to seeing me tonight?'' There was a note of expectancy in his voice, and it lifted Andrea's spirits.

Despite her attempt to remain businesslike, the tenderness she felt for him crept into her voice. ''Of course.''

''Great. I'll pop around about five-thirty, if that's convenient.''

''Perfect.''

''See you then.'' The gentleness Andrea responded to warmed his voice. ''Bye-bye.''

"Bye." Andrea listened as the line clicked dead. She met Len's curious gaze and offered no explanation. Depressing the receiver button, she said, "Let me start the lesson by saying that if you can see your way through to going to law school, become a lawyer. It's a lot easier than being a headhunter."

"DARRELL SMITH, PLEASE." Andrea doodled on the corner of the recruiting card while she waited for the engineer to come on the line. Across the room, Len Daggett sat on the bed, pillows propped up behind him, the Stratcom telephone directory on his knee. He was busy pulling the names and phone numbers of engineers in a software analysis section. Tomorrow morning Andrea would be calling from the list. But now it was nearly four-thirty, and she was trying to set up one more interview.

"Smith here." Smith was the ex-CIA employee whom she had been trying to reach all afternoon. The sound of his nasal Bostonian accent immediately reminded Andrea of their earlier conversation and the young man's level of paranoia at the end of it. She breathed deeply and plunged into the murky uncertainty of the call.

"This is Ann Baird from ComSearch. I spoke to you earlier today."

"Oh, yes." Smith's voice warmed minutely. "What can I do for you?"

Andrea's laugh was soft, friendly. "I'd say it's more what I might be able to do for you."

"How's that?"

"One of my customers will be in Seattle, interviewing Thursday evening and Friday morning. I've talked to Ed Rees, software development manager for Tectron, about your background, and he would like to get together with you. Ed thinks he has something you would be interested in. He'd like to talk to you about it.''

"Tectron?'' Smith paused. When he spoke again, there was interest in his voice. "That's a communications firm in Los Angeles, isn't it?''

"Yes, in the South Bay. They're a medium-sized advanced communications company looking to double their size over the next three years because of the recent awarding of the ISU contract.'' She had repeated this pitch hundreds of times, but always managed to make it sound as if this was an original sales presentation. "That's one of the programs Ed would like to talk to you about.'' Andrea glanced up. Len had paused in his pulling names from the directory and was idly tapping his pen against his knee. She smiled at him and shrugged. Continuing with her sales pitch, she said, "Tectron will be interviewing at the North Winds. Are you familiar with the hotel?''

"Yeah, I know where it is.''

"Good. Why don't we make it eight o'clock tomorrow night? Ask for me at the desk. I'm in room 2204.''

"I can't make it at eight.'' During his silence, Andrea feared he was refusing the appointment. "Is nine too late?''

She hid her relief, the tone of her voice sounding as if she'd known he could not turn down the invitation. "Nine will be fine. We'll see you then, Darrell.'' Andrea said good-bye and hung up the phone in a glow of triumph.

"That didn't sound too hard,'' Len commented.

"You didn't hear the suspicion in his voice.'' Andrea laughed, shaking her head. "I wouldn't be too surprised if the only reason he's coming is to see just what Tectron is up to in this town.''

Len tossed the directory aside. "You know the old saying, 'Curiosity killed the cat.' As long as they get here.''

He lighted yet another in the endless chain of cigarettes. "Well, it's four-thirty. Quitting time around town. Why don't we knock off until they all go home? I could do with a drink. Want to join me?"

Andrea stretched her tension-knotted arm muscles. "No, thanks. I think I'll rest awhile. I've been at this since seven-thirty this morning. I could do with a nap."

He shrugged into his suit coat and asked, "When do you want me back?"

"I usually make my evening calls between seven and nine. That gives them time to get home and have dinner, yet doesn't drag anyone out of bed later in the evening."

"Okay, chief. See you at seven."

Andrea stared at the door as it shut behind the departing engineer. Then she shook her head in amazement and disbelief. Len Daggett was too good to be true. She was having difficulty believing that the man could be so businesslike. He had remained politely aloof, concentrating on the duties she had assigned him and listening in to her phone calls. Even with such a refreshing demeanor, she still could not relax around him. A few times that afternoon, she had tried to ease her nervousness with a few jokes. The fact that Len had not found them humorous had simply increased her anxiety.

While she cleared their working materials away and stacked them into neat piles, she wondered if Len was married. He wore no wedding band, but he did wear the mantel of devoted and true husband. She guessed that he was somewhere around forty and could easily picture him as the father of a couple of teenagers, a no-nonsense, domineering patriarch. At that thought, Andrea admitted to herself that she did not like the man.

After plumping up the pillows, Andrea stretched out on the bed and breathed a contented sigh for the chance to rest. In less than an hour, Gage would be by. She hadn't told him that she'd be working for a couple of hours that evening, not wanting to let Len know that she was seeing someone. Gage would probably welcome a few hours' rest before she'd be free for dinner. Assuming, of course, that dinner was what he had in mind.

The telephone rang, jarring her out of her reverie. Cal's boisterous voice came over the line. "Andi, how's it going? Did Len make it up there?"

"Everything's moving along smoothly. And yes, Len arrived safe and sound."

"Let me talk to him."

"You just missed him. He left a few minutes ago. Said he needed a drink."

"I trust you didn't let him sit around idle."

"You know me better than that, Cal." Andrea laughed. "I put him to work helping me with Stratcom." Prudently, she neglected to mention that she believed Len's main purpose for being there was to assist her in recruiting Stratcom. Len hadn't had to make a trip to Seattle to learn the headhunting trade.

"How's it going with Stratcom?"

"Better. The word seems to have gotten around that there's a recruiter out there who's interested in them. They must have egos, after all—they're starting to talk to me."

Cal's raucous laugh roared through the receiver. "If anyone could get through to them, I knew it would be you!"

"Thanks for your vote of confidence. Say, you'd better warn Tectron that these Stratcom applicants may not be really serious. I suspect they're simply trying to find out what Tectron is up to. Is Stratcom competing for anything? Any government contracts?"

"Not to my knowledge. Tectron merely needs their talent."

Andrea murmured a sound of skepticism.

"I'll call Len later tonight. Got to go. My private line's ringing."

Andrea frowned. Talking to Cal tended to tire her lately, and after this brief conversation, she realized just how tired she was. She rolled onto her side and tucked her hand under her cheek, taking several deep breaths to ease the tension she felt. Yes, she needed a vacation, and she was determined to take one over the holidays. Little could be done as far as setting up second and third interviews for any applicants; and job offers tended to slow down at this time of the year, since few people were willing to change jobs during the holiday period.

As her eyelids drooped, Andrea realized that if she lay there much longer, she'd fall fast asleep. Crawling off the bed, she decided that taking a quick shower was a better idea than a nap.

The ringing of the telephone minutes later called her out of the steamy bathroom. She wrapped the skimpy bath towel around her, pulled her wet hair over one shoulder and pressed the receiver to her free ear.

"Hi, what are you doing?" Gage quizzed.

"I'm dripping."

"You're what?"

"Dripping. I was in the shower."

He laughed, a tired but cheery sound. "Then I won't keep you."

"You'd better," Andrea taunted. "Or I just got this towel all soapy for nothing."

"Okay. Look, I've gotten hung up here at the office. It doesn't look as if I'm going to be able to break away for at least a couple more hours. I'll probably be here till nine.

It'll be nine-thirty by the time I get back to the hotel. That's rather late to be starting an evening out, so if you'd like to cancel, I'll understand.''

''Don't be so understanding!'' Andrea laughed at the silence that followed her words. She explained, ''The thought of getting out of here tonight has let me keep my sanity all afternoon. I've really been looking forward to seeing you.''

The sincerity in her voice was unmistakable, and Gage sounded pleased to hear it. ''I've missed you, too. Okay, so I guess I'll see you when I get there.''

''And don't worry about being late. I'll be busy with work myself until nine, so anytime after that will be fine. And since I snuck a bit of a rest this afternoon, I'll probably outlast you. You sound beat.''

''I'm okay. I'll see you in a few hours.''

''Take care.'' Andrea lowered the receiver slowly while a small smile played over her lips. She definitely felt a fondness for Gage and, with a start, she realized that things between them were not as detached as she had thought that morning. Unless she was mistaken, Gage's feelings were mutual. She could be wrong; it could just be the man's charm that made him sound as if there was something more there than mere attraction. She could be wrong; perhaps he kissed every woman he met the way he had kissed her.

Remembering those kisses, Andrea felt a knot of tension grow in her stomach and she wondered what would happen that evening.

LEN DAGGETT ARRIVED PROMPTLY at seven, just as Andrea had finished pinning her hair up with the antique silver barrette. While she held the door open, he strolled in, the perpetual cigarette in his hand, the vague smile on his lips. The intensity she had first felt upon meeting him struck her anew. The man simply radiated tension.

As she pushed the door shut, Len commented, "You look good with your hair pinned up. Very classy."

Andrea's hand strayed to touch her hair. "Oh...thank you."

He peered at the barrette. "That's a striking comb. Family heirloom?"

"Yes, as a matter of fact. My grandmother's." She moved to the desk and poured herself a glass of soda. "I understand a gypsy gave it to her when she was a little girl. Or at least that's how the story goes."

"Must be quite valuable by now."

"Evidently not," she said dryly. "My burglar yesterday didn't take it. And I guess I'm really thankful for that!"

Len's eyes narrowed. "You had a burglary? What was taken?"

"Nothing. That's what's so strange about it." Andrea frowned. "Seems whoever it was must have been looking for something more valuable. The only thing I found out of order was the papers." As Len's eyebrows rose in an unasked question, Andrea giggled. "He probably couldn't figure out what all those recruiting cards were about. They were all messed up."

Len obviously missed the humor she saw in the situation. He clamped his mouth around a newly lit cigarette, turned toward the table by the window and mumbled, "It's after seven. Let's get to work."

Andrea found it difficult to concentrate on her work that evening, although Len didn't seem to notice. He made a few recruiting calls on leads he had brought with him from Los Angeles. She listened, offered constructive criticism after each call and even coached him during one or two. Her first suspicions appeared correct; Len did not seem to have the necessary ''killer instinct.'' He tended to be too polite, allowing the other person to control the conversation instead of retaining subtle leadership himself in order to get the answers he was seeking. He might be a brilliant engineer, but Andrea thought he would never succeed as a recruiter.

As Len once again hung up the phone, he noticed her reflective mood. ''Well, it's nine o'clock. I guess we call it quits for the night?''

Andrea stretched her toes toward the carpet. ''Right.'' Sipping on her now-flat soda, she met and held his shrewd gaze.

''What do you think?''

Leery, she asked, ''About what?''

''What are my chances of making it as a headhunter?''

It was at times like this that Andrea wished she smoked; lighting up a cigarette would provide the perfect stall. But she didn't smoke and she had no stall. Andrea answered him honestly. ''Why don't you talk to Ed Rees while he's here? Perhaps Tectron has something going that will interest you.'' Tectron might even overlook his involvement with the F40A project.

''You don't think I can do it.''

''That's right.''

Len exhaled a thin stream of smoke and crushed his cigarette out in the butt-filled ashtray before getting to his feet. ''I tend to agree with you.''

''Then why pursue it?''

He shrugged and straightened his tie. ''Tell me, why are *you* a headhunter?'' As wariness flashed across her face, he added, ''Forget that I know Cal, that I'm a friend of his. Why are you in the business?''

She studied him for a moment, then dropped her eyes to follow the path her finger made as it traced the edge of the table. When she spoke, her voice held a trace of shame and a large portion of defensiveness. "For the money."

"That's as good a reason as any, isn't it?" He slung his suit coat over his shoulder. "Got to pay the bills some way. There's a lot of quick money to be made in headhunting. I'd like to make my share."

"The money's there only if you're good at it. And if you're willing to work very hard and very long hours." She glanced at him uncertainly. "What has Cal said about this? I understand you worked in the office last week. I imagine that he was the one to introduce you to the way we operate."

"Cal has spared my feelings."

Andrea's laugh held a tinge of sarcasm. "That doesn't sound like the Cal I know." When Len only stared at her in that impersonal way of his, she became sober. "I have one suggestion to make—if you're serious about pursuing this. Loosen up. You have to sell these people on the idea of talking to you, listening to you and, ultimately, trusting you. I think the main reason I'm successful is that I talk to every person as if I've known him or her for years. If you're friendly, people are receptive."

Len nodded. "I'll sleep on that. Good night, Andrea."

"'Night."

She watched the door close behind him, then shook her head. The man would never make it in the business. And, whether it was because of Len Daggett himself or simply the way she reacted to him, Andrea had the peculiar feeling that he had not told her the truth about his wanting to be a headhunter.

Chapter Six

She stood beside the door for a long minute, trying to analyze different moments of the afternoon and evening, trying to determine the source of her discomfort. The only thing she could identify was her dislike of Daggett. It wasn't actually dislike, she corrected herself. It was...distrust. Yes, distrust was the word. But why should she distrust him?

Andrea slowly began to clear all the working materials away, shoving them into a drawer as she had done the evening before. Then she busied herself with putting the room in order. Later, she pushed the sliding window open a bit more to get rid of the heavy haze of smoke from Len's cigarettes.

While she stood at the rain-streaked window, breathing in the crisp air, her sense of uneasiness mounted. Something was going on, she was sure of it. Something that had Cal's fingerprints all over it. But what? Nothing she could think of made sense. She could not point to one specific item and say, "That's it!" But her nagging little voice kept telling her there *was* something—she just wasn't looking in the right place. Frustrated with herself, Andrea ordered that little voice to go to sleep for the rest of the night. She didn't want to hear any more comments on Cal, Len or Gage.

Gage. As if on cue, a tap sounded at the door. Andrea smoothed her skirt and tried to calm her fluttering heart. Gage returned her amiable smile as she stood in the half-open doorway, her hand resting on the knob. He was dressed in a dark brown three-piece suit, his tie still neatly knotted. Andrea was glad she had changed into her pale blue silk chemise and navy pumps. As he stood there framed by the doorway, she couldn't decide which she liked more—the offbeat air he projected when dressed in casual clothes or the appearance he gave now of a consummate businessman.

"Got here as soon as I could. Hope you aren't angry."

"Why would I be? I told you to take your time. Come on in."

Andrea closed the door slowly as Gage walked about the room, his hands shoved into the pockets of his trousers. She glanced around. No, she hadn't missed anything. All the glasses had been washed and put back on the desktop. The wrinkles of the bedcovers had been smoothed out, the pillows put back under the spread. The ashtray had been emptied and wiped clean. Only the tell-tale smoke lingered, despite the cold, fresh air coming in through the window. Of course he had noticed the smoke—he knew she was a nonsmoker—but he said nothing.

Andrea stepped to his side at the window. As she linked her arm through his, she said brightly, "Now that the business day is over for both of us, what are we going to do to relax and forget all our worries?"

Gage looked down at the small white hand that rested so lightly on his arm. "What would you like to do?" His dark eyes moved up to her face, studying its sweet expression. For a brief instant, an expression of doubt glinted in those eyes, only to vanish before Andrea realized it had even been there.

"You look as tired as you sounded on the phone," she said, noting the faint circles under his eyes.

A self-derisive smile touched the corner of his mouth. "It's probably the three-martini lunch I had."

"Sure."

Laughing at her skeptical tone, Gage explained, "Business lunches tend to be a curse on me. Did you eat dinner? If not, I know a great little place off Pioneer Square where we can get supper."

"Sounds wonderful to me." Andrea flashed him a quick smile. As Gage helped her into her coat, she asked, "They wouldn't happen to serve cappuccino, would they?"

"A wicked cup that will keep you awake till dawn."

"Terrific!"

Gage slipped his overcoat on, then gently grasped her forearm, pulling her to him. His eyes caressed her face, studying each feature as if for the first time. "Just one thing before we go," he said softly.

Her own eyes grew a little wider, and she breathed, "What's that?"

The moment before his mouth lowered to hers, he whispered, "This."

He tasted her lips in a gentle exploration of their curves, and the hands that had rested so lightly on her shoulders strayed to her back to draw her to him. Andrea followed the gentle pressure, sliding her palms over the smooth fabric of his raincoat to rest on his hips. As his teasing kiss solicited her response, she realized that she had longed for that kiss all afternoon and evening. The tiny pilot light deep inside her blossomed into a small flame of yearning.

But even as she murmured words that were lost in his kiss, a sense of reluctance coming from an unknown source dampened the fire within her. Andrea found her hands slipping between them and pushing against his chest.

Gage's mouth left hers unwillingly, his lingering lips returning once to brush across hers in a gesture of obvious regret. Then he straightened, sliding his hands from her back and shoving them into his pockets. "Yes, we should be moving on. Damn."

Andrea breathed a sigh of confused relief and stepped away. She could think more clearly with some space between them. Buttoning her coat, she felt protected from possible temptation; unreasonably so, she knew. A false calm ruled her voice. "What is the specialty of this place we're going to?"

Gage pulled the door shut behind them. As he stalked to the elevator beside her, he muttered, "Jazz."

THE MAITRE D' of the private club greeted them warmly and spoke with Gage for a brief moment. Andrea could not hear either man distinctly over the lively beat of the jazz quintet's music. She stood close to Gage's side, his arm held loosely about her shoulders, and looked around the small, crowded room. A thick haze of blue smoke hung over the tables and booths. The bar was filled to standing-room-only capacity. Circulating deftly between patrons and tables were formally dressed waiters, all wearing black suits, white shirts and black bow ties.

After their coats had been checked, Andrea and Gage were shown to a table at the front of the long, narrow balcony that ran the width of the club. Gage pulled his chair close to hers and placed his mouth next to her ear. His breath was warm on her skin. "What would you like to drink?"

Andrea tried to make herself heard over the music. "White wine."

Gage nodded and gave their order to the waiter who hovered by his side. A minute later, Andrea was sipping at a glass of splendid wine, watching the band from what was obviously the number-one table. Gage stirred his scotch-and-water in beat to the music. He was studying the pianist, whose solo appeared to captivate the entire audience. No one spoke. Everyone was caught up in the stirring mood of the music. When the set ended, the round of enthusiastic applause followed the band members as they threaded their way through the crowded room and disappeared behind a doorway near the bar.

Much of the restraint Gage had displayed the previous night appeared to have vanished, replaced by a deceiving ease. He turned his attention to Andrea, moving ever so slightly closer to her side. As his knee touched her thigh, Andrea fought to control the tremor of excitement racing through her. She knew Gage was aware of her reaction, but he merely asked, "Well, what do you think of my place?"

"Your place?" Andrea glanced around the floor again, its atmosphere now buzzing with conversation, laughter and the tinkle of ice. "You own this club?"

Gage set his tumbler down and nodded matter-of-factly. "Yes."

Startled by the sudden revelation, she asked, "This is where you've been all day?"

He chuckled, then shook his head. "No, it's not. I may own the club, but this is not work."

"Oh. Well, I like it." She paused, wondering why he was being more open this evening. A tiny giggle escaped from her throat. "But I would never have guessed you were a nightclub owner. You just didn't strike me as the party type."

"Of course not. I struck you as either a wild Irish poet or a gun-toting cop." He grinned. "Do you have to be a party type to like nightclubs?"

"Well, it seems as if that would help—what with all the music and hubbub."

An amused light danced in his dark eyes. "You know, I've never looked at it that way. You might be right." He leaned close again and whispered in her ear, "Are you the party type?"

Her heart began to beat a little too rapidly for her liking. "Only until the witching hour."

Gage looked at his wristwatch. "Well, then, I've got an hour and seventeen minutes. Better make the most of it." As he leaned closer, Andrea glanced upward and smiled impishly. Gage hung his head a moment, sighed softly, then turned to the waiter who had appeared at his elbow. "What's best tonight, Bob?"

"I recommend the Creole gumbo, unless you'd like something heavier, sir."

Gage caught Andrea's nod of approval. "That'll be fine, and we'll have a bottle of wine to go with that. You make the selection, Bob." The waiter departed, and Gage turned his attention back to Andrea. "Have I told you that you look very lovely this evening?"

"No." Andrea had already wished she had more suitable nighttime clothes with her than the silk dress she wore. Fortunately, she had brought her black pearls on the trip and now wore them, knowing that the single strand with its matching stud earrings lent an elegance to her appearance. Smiling demurely, she added, "But thank you."

Gage slipped an arm around her shoulders. "You know, when you pin your hair up like that, it takes a lot of willpower not to unclasp that barrette and have all those silky tresses come cascading down on a man's hand." As Andrea's eyes widened in dismay over the thought that he just might do that in his own nightclub, Gage changed the subject smoothly. "To go with the jazz, we have a genuine New Orleans chef who makes the finest Creole dishes this side of the Mississippi. And we book some of the best bands coming off Bourbon Street."

"I still can't picture you as a nighclub owner, a businessman. You looked so much the reclusive artist on the plane the other day. You really surprise me." Andrea smiled, tilting her head to one side. Her parted lips revealed the tip of her tongue pressed against the small, even white teeth.

Gage could not ignore the unconscious invitation. His lips brushed over hers once, twice, a third time before he leaned back, his eyes still focused on her face. His voice was unsteady. "I think I could have skipped dinner tonight."

"I couldn't," Andrea purred tranquilly. "I'm starving."

Gage grunted and withdrew his arm from her shoulders. "I haven't decided if you're an incredible tease or just plain scared of me." He sounded hurt, and she wasn't certain that his tone of voice was an act.

While he downed half of his drink, Andrea said, "I'm not a tease. No one has ever accused me of being one before, at any rate." Gage muttered something unintelligible. Ignoring his mumblings, she continued. "And despite your cussedness, as to my being afraid of you—no, I'm not. I think you're the most gentle man I've ever met, and I can't imagine you hurting anyone." As his eyes flicked to hers, she added, "So why would I be afraid of you?"

A strangeness lurked in the depths of the eyes that Andrea found so magnetic, and its presence disturbed her.

Still watching her closely, Gage asked, "Are you always so trusting?"

"Trusting?" Andrea's eyebrows knitted together. "Who are you? Jack the Ripper?" Her question was meant as a joke, and she smiled faintly to help it along. Seeing that Gage did not respond, she stated, "No, I'm not always trusting. There are many people I don't trust." Len Daggett came immediately to her mind. "But—" a wisp of fondness played across her features "—you just don't happen to be one of them."

Gage planted a quick kiss on her cheek. "Thanks for the compliment. I needed that after today." He leaned back in his chair again and looked down at the club floor.

When the silence that lingered between them finally became oppressive, Andrea said, "Okay, so you own this club. What do you do when you're not here? I mean, what are you?"

Suspicion and distrust skipped across his face but were dismissed with a shrug of his broad shoulders. "Entrepreneur is probably the best way to describe me. I'm one of those lucky people born to money and blessed enough to have the time to play with it."

"In other words, you're filthy rich?" Andrea's amazement was barely hidden.

Gage laughed good-naturedly. "That's another way of putting it."

She had known he had money—but wealthy? "Chris would love you."

"Who's Chris?" Gage finished his drink and signaled for a refill.

"My kid sister. She has the taste for the good life and not the means to indulge herself." Andrea sighed. "Our parents were killed a few years ago. What little insurance money there was went to pay off my father's debts—he liked to gamble. So I have supported us. There were Chris's enormous hospital bills from the accident—still are, for that matter. And now that Chris is in college—going to UCLA, no less—it's been rough. She can't have what she once enjoyed.''

"Nor can you, from the sound of it.''

Andrea was surprised by his astute comment. "It's not the same for me,'' she protested.

The dark eyes narrowed. "Why not?''

"It's just different, that's all. We're very different people. I've been on my own since I was sixteen. I'm independent; she's not. My family didn't have any money until after I left home, when my father had a good streak going for a while. Chris became a bit spoiled. Then, like all compulsive gamblers, my father lost everything he had won during the good-luck streak, and more besides.''

"So his elder daughter has been paying for his vices ever since.''

Andrea noted the strange expression on his face. "I love my sister dearly. I would do anything for her. I'm just happy that she's all right now. For a long time...'' Her voice trailed off as she remembered the first two months after the accident, when Christine had lain in the hospital in a deep coma, not expected to live. Then one day the miracle had happened. Christine had awakened, disoriented and in pain. When her frisky, rebellious nature had returned a few weeks later, her complete recovery was only a matter of time and therapy.

Andrea's smile was rueful. "Because she's not like me, I do tend to watch out for her. I don't want to see her hurt or end up in a lot of trouble she can't handle. And she does tend to get into things that she shouldn't.''

Gage sipped at his drink, then commented, "Perhaps you should let her grow up. Have you ever thought that you may be spoiling her yourself?"

"Don't lecture me, please." Andrea frowned at his knowing grin. "I do spoil her. Not all the time, but on occasion, yes, I do." A little giggle caught in her throat. "Right now she thinks I'm depriving her because I won't approve of her going off on some archaeological dig in the middle of New Mexico this summer."

"I don't know about that. You sound like a good sister to have." A teasing glimmer lit his eyes and found its way into his sincere smile.

Responding to that smile, she murmured, "Thank you. I'm glad someone thinks so."

Andrea tasted her wine, then carefully balanced the stemware between her hands. Would a question of a more personal nature spark his sharp reaction of the night before? She decided to risk it. "What about your family? Any brothers or sisters?"

His grin was mischievous. "Unlike most wealthy people, my parents had a large brood. There were five of us— I'm the middle child. I've a sister who's a sister, a nun in New Jersey. I've a brother who's a photojournalist, one of those guys who likes living in the hot spots of the world. My younger sister married an artist and now resides somewhere on the Left Bank. And my younger brother shares something in common with your sister—he likes to dig holes in the ground, too."

"An archaeologist?"

"Yes. Last I heard of him, he was excavating some Inca temple in Peru. That was over a year ago."

Andrea's smile sparkled in her eyes. "So you are the strong, upright, walk-in-Dad's-footsteps child—the nightclub owner."

His answer was evasive, bearing the previous evening's reserve. "Among other things."

In for a penny... Andrea thought. "What are some of the other things?"

Gage studied her over the top of his raised glass. "Why so curious?"

Andrea shrugged her slender shoulders. "Why so secretive? You know, I'm getting the feeling you are definitely trying to hide something from me." She lowered her voice to a conspiratorial whisper. "Now, tell me, just what are the skeletons in your closet?" Merriment skipped over her face as she waited for Gage's answer.

Setting his glass down and twirling it slowly on its edge, he cautioned, "I think you have as much propensity for getting into trouble as your sister. You don't realize it, though."

"What makes you say that?" Andrea leaned back in her chair and watched him closely.

He ignored her question. "This job of yours. Do you like it?"

He was changing the subject again. Had she really thought he would be open with her? Andrea bit her lower lip a moment, then nodded her head vaguely. "It's like any job. It has its good points and its bad."

"Such as?"

Why had that unsettling darkness flared in his eyes again? Curious, and feeling challenged, Andrea answered with a touch of pride in her voice. "The pay is a good point. It's very profitable." *So you needn't feel I'm after your money*, she added silently.

"What are the bad points?"

There, he had her. Andrea couldn't honestly admit the bad points herself, let alone to this man whose opinion unfortunately meant something to her. Damn, why did she care what Gage would think of her? After all, wasn't he the one who was hiding things? She was beginning to think that his refusal to open up wasn't just an attempt to hide a possible family back in Los Angeles. That curious, penetrating glare that kept sneaking back into his eyes was concealing something else. For all she knew, Gage could be a modern-day Jack the Ripper. *And,* she thought, watching him watch her, *I'm the Wicked Witch of the East.*

As she tried to swallow the titter that rose to her lips, Gage frowned, a look of perplexity cutting into the rugged lines of his face. When Andrea's hearty laugh followed the failed suppression, Gage asked, "What's so funny?"

She raised a hand to her mouth and laughed harder. "Oh, it's...it's nothing." She reached for her glass of water and drank deeply. "Tell me about your parents. Are they living?"

He hesitated at the change of subject, then said, "Lord, yes. And they will probably outlive all of us children." He finished his drink, then explained drolly, "They got fed up with the lot of us—rightfully so—and gave each of us our inheritance early. Then they washed their hands of the entire family and moved to Miami to save their sanity and lower their blood pressure."

The waiter appeared with their dinner, placing fragrant, steaming china bowls before them, followed by a huge bread basket filled with chunks of sourdough bread that smelled freshly baked. Andrea peered at the spicy Creole stew, thick with chunks of sausage, veal, ham, chicken and shellfish. While the waiter opened the wine bottle and poured a half glass for Gage's approval, the band members started filtering back to the stage. Gage nodded. "That's fine, Bob." When he and Andrea were alone again, he raised his glass. "I propose a toast."

"Okay." Andrea raised hers. "What shall we drink to?"

The strange look that she found so confusing was absent from his eyes; now they held a warmth and gentleness that bordered on seduction. As Gage leaned close, he said softly, "Let's drink to the everyday folk who stumble along and make the world work. Let's drink to us."

Nearly mesmerized by the expression that said more than his words would, Andrea whispered, "To us."

Their glasses touched, a high-pitched bell tone ringing between them, which neither heard.

HOURS LATER, long after closing, Andrea and Gage sat at a table to one side of the stage. The pianist and tenor saxophonist remained, jamming, playing requests from the club personnel and the owner. As the final blues wail from the sax faded in the smoke-heavy air, Gage tapped Andrea's forearm with his finger. "Are you still awake? Or did you just nod off?"

She blinked. "I'm still awake, but it's no wonder you have circles under your eyes. I would, too, if I did this every night." She sipped at her third cup of café au lait.

"Not every night. I'm lucky if it's once a month now. I'm not in Seattle very much anymore."

"Who tends the store when you aren't here?"

"My partner." Gage jerked his thumb over his shoulder. "He's the nervous guy over behind the bar."

Andrea swiveled in her chair and strained her eyes to see the two men counting cash at the register. "The man with the red hair?" It was the same man who had met Gage at SeaTac terminal.

"Yeah, that's him. He's also my lawyer." At Andrea's doubtful countenance, Gage said, "Don't let his looks deceive you. Dan's a shrewd operator. Money seems to multiply right in his hands."

"Legally, I hope," she joked.

Gage roared with laughter. "If Danny had a crooked bone in his body, he'd be governor! No, president! As it is, he's an honest lawyer who's going no further than his practice and this club. Dan likes to jam with the band. He plays a mean trumpet."

Her smile was tender. "You really like this, don't you? The club, the crowd, the music?"

"It's the way I relax. It gets my mind off things." Gage idly stroked the back of her wrist with his thumb. The easygoing calm that Andrea was beginning to suspect was often only self-control had been replaced by a serenity that she found magnetic and enchanting. They moved toward each other, their lips only a kiss apart. Then their intimacy was interrupted.

"Well, Gage, we had a good night, a good take." Dan clapped Gage soundly on the back while his ice-blue eyes quickly appraised the situation.

Gage muttered, "Damn!" and sat back in his chair. Andrea clasped her hands together and fought the giggle that rose in her throat.

A slow, neutral smile spread over Dan's freckled face. "Gage, old buddy, you haven't introduced this lovely lady to anyone all night. You can't bring her here and keep her all to yourself."

Gage glared up at his partner and said grudgingly, "Danny, meet a friend of mine, Andrea. Andrea, this is Dan Joachim—friend, partner and attorney."

More leisurely now, the man's pale blue eyes studied Andrea; they obviously approved of what they saw. Dan extended his hand and grasped Andrea's in a firm but gentle handshake. "It's a pleasure, Andrea. How are you this evening?"

"Fine, thank you." She smiled politely at the short, wiry man. Dress in worn jeans and a baggy sweater, he looked like a leftover from the beatnik era. But the impeccably styled red hair and the wristwatch he wore labeled him a successful businessman of the 1980s.

Dan flashed her a cap-toothed grin and gestured around the club with a wave of his hand. "Well, what do you think of our venture?"

"It seems you have a winner. Good food, good music and an appreciative audience."

"Where did you find this jewel, Gage?" Dan winked at her. "Okay, you've got the job. You start on our advertising committee next Monday morning at eight sharp. With you as our spokesperson, we'll be expanding in no time."

Gage interrupted him, amusement lighting his eyes. "Don't pay any attention to Dan, Andrea. He keeps forgetting that he can play in only one band at a time—and that this is Seattle, not New York or New Orleans." Turning to his friend, Gage added, "This city can't support two jazz clubs. So forget it, Danny."

"That is precisely why we are in business here and not some other city," Dan explained to her. "Got to take care of that business now. Nice meeting you, Andrea. Come back and see us again."

As he strode off, hailing the maitre d' and pulling the man through the kitchen door, Andrea shook her head in bewilderment. "Is he always that way?"

"Wired for action?"

"Yes."

"You bet." Gage laughed. "I don't know where Danny gets all his energy. I'm a few years younger than he, and I can't keep up with him. I used to think he had to live on amphetamines to go the way he does—but he doesn't. Don't think he's ever taken a pill in his life. He's just naturally hyper."

"I'd hate to have been his mother!"

"From what I hear, she's worse than Danny. I feel sorry for his wife, though. But you should see him in court. All that scattered energy is pulled in, compressed, channeled. Absolutely intimidating. He's the top corporate trial lawyer in the state, if not on the West Coast. I'm lucky to have him on my side."

Hearing the firmness in Gage's voice, Andrea asked, "Why? Are you suing someone?"

The black eyes darted to hers. His answer was terse. "Will be."

"Oh, I see." She looked at her coffee cup for a moment, then sipped from it slowly. "What about you? Why did you buy into a jazz club? Do you play with the band?"

"No. I play around on the piano, but I'm not a professional."

"Is Dan?"

"Could be—if he wanted to be." Gage shrugged. "But musicians don't make much money playing in clubs like this. Being a lawyer supports his trumpet playing."

"He's right about that." Dan had appeared at their table again, stopping at Andrea's elbow. "Has he played for you?"

"No." She glanced at Gage long enough to see him shaking his head at Dan, his lips compressed into a thin line. Meeting Dan's eyes, she asked, "Does he play well?"

"Play well? He's the best blues pianist on the coast!"

"Really?" Andrea flashed a grin in Gage's direction and received a withering glare in return. "I'd love to hear you play something."

"Dan, stuff it."

"Play for the girl, Gage. You can't bring her to your club and not play for her." Dan turned and called out to the pianist, "Steve, let your boss have the bench. And lower the spotlight." Then he confided to Andrea, "Gage gets shy under the lights."

Gage mumbled something explosive under his breath and stood up, shoving his chair back in irritation. He headed for the stage floor.

Dan slid into the vacated seat. "He's so modest about his abilities. The big-time chairman of the board gets a royal case of nerves when he's sitting at the keyboard. But he's good. If it hadn't been for his sense of responsibility, I think he'd earn his money sitting before the ivories, not on the board of directors."

"Responsibility?" she said.

"I take it you two haven't known each other long." Andrea shook her head. "He's the only levelheaded one in his family. He inherited management of all the family businesses when his father was forced to retire early— heart trouble. None of his flaky siblings could handle the responsibility involved. But under that executive facade lies the heart of a musician who'd rather be playing the piano than saving a company." Dan sipped at the mug in his hand. "Just how long have you known Gage?"

"Two days," she replied, meeting his steady, examining gaze. "We met on the plane from Los Angeles." When Dan remained silent, Andrea raised an eyebrow in curiosity. "What are you thinking?"

"That you seem such a sweet, young innocent to get tangled up with him."

"Why do you say that? Is there something about him that I ought to know?" Andrea's tone was jesting, but her question was serious.

Dan's eyes flicked to the stage, then back to her face. His smile wasn't completely reassuring. "Not a thing."

As Andrea watched Gage seat himself at the piano and rest his hands on the keyboard, Dan's words echoed through her mind. The man she was so attracted to was turning out to be quite a complex person. And he was becoming more fascinating by the hour.

Gage picked out the opening bass notes and called out, "Danny, I owe you for this!"

Dan snorted into his mug and slouched his lank frame into the chair.

After the first notes of the introduction had blended into the melody, Andrea leaned forward, crossed her arms on the tabletop and stared at Gage. The air of remoteness that she experienced so often had settled over him again. The man she had seen so far was now transformed into the musician. As she listened, Andrea could hear the emotion that he put into the music, the sounds of melancholy that he brought from the strings of the instrument. For the next few minutes, she was caught up in the mood of the song, her heart tight in her chest, aching with a pain that she felt in the music.

As the closing chord was swallowed by the walls of the club, a round of applause broke out among the employees, who had stopped their clean-up activities to listen to him play. Andrea joined in, blinking back a tear or two.

Dan, always observant, caught the fond expression that softened her gentle smile even more. Sipping at the mug, he studied her a moment, then said casually, "Gage hasn't played that well in a long time. You have a good effect on him. Are you going to stick around for a while?"

Surprised by his question, Andrea asked, "What do you mean?" then flashed a tight smile as Gage eased into the chair across from her.

"Nothing." Dan inclined his head a moment. "Well, Gage, you've done it again. Got to close up. Catch you later." He virtually sprinted out of his chair toward the kitchen.

"What was that all about?" Gage raised an eyebrow as he watched Dan depart.

"You tell me. He's your friend." Andrea thought she knew what Dan had been saying, but she would not divulge that information.

"If I read the look on his face correctly, he was doing a bit of matchmaking. Am I right?"

"Maybe."

He chuckled. "Danny likes you. He wouldn't do it otherwise." After a long pause, Gage said, "He's also a firm believer in the institution of marriage."

The subject had finally come up. "What about you?" Andrea asked.

His sly, slightly bemused smile was slow in coming. "With the right person at the right time, it's probably not a bad arrangement."

"I take it you aren't married." Andrea wasn't totally successful at hiding her interest. Her voice held just a hint of hope.

Gage raked a hand through his unruly hair and shook his head gratefully. "No, I'm not married."

"But the way you say that it sounds as if you have been." She leaned back in her chair and swiveled slowly from side to side.

"Yeah, I married young—impetuously—and it didn't work out."

"What happened?"

"She left me for a calmer, older man."

"Calmer?" Andrea's blue eyes sparked with disbelief. "What did she do, marry a stone? I can't imagine *anyone* being much calmer than you, unless he was dead!"

Gage stared at her a long moment, then leaned toward her, putting his elbows on his knees and clasping his hands. "Thank you, Andrea. That was a very sweet thing to say. But...the fact is, I've changed since those days. I wasn't always the nicest guy to live with."

"You mean you haven't always been a 'pleasant cuss'?" she teased.

"No, I haven't."

"Oh. Then I'm glad I met you now." Andrea circled the rim of her empty coffee cup with her finger. After a moment, she said quietly, "Your song was lovely. You play beautifully."

The words "thank you" were spoken self-consciously, and his sudden wave of modesty charmed her.

A long silence fell between them, each thinking their own thoughts and obviously not wanting to share them. Finally, their eyes met, carefully devoid of expression.

Gage cleared his throat. "Well, my lady, it's nearly four. The sun will be up shortly."

"Behind all those clouds."

"That's true." He stifled a yawn. "I don't know about you, but I'm tired."

"Now you're playing my tune!" she exclaimed.

Gage retrieved their coats, helped Andrea into hers, then guided her to the main door. The maitre d' bade them good night and locked the double doors behind them.

The cold night air was a damp slap in the face after the hours they had spent in the warm, smoky nightclub. The rain had stopped, but the sidewalk and street were still wet, their surfaces glistening under the streetlights. The crisp wind stung Andrea's legs. Huddling in her coat, she shivered and said, "Why don't we go back inside where it's warm?"

"Come here." Gage pulled her tightly to his side, slipping an arm around her waist. "The car's this way."

He steered her down the sidewalk, and Andrea pressed close to him as they walked through the dark, empty streets to the multilevel parking structure. The elevator moving down its shaft sent a hum into the still night air. Outside the garage, the sound of a street sweeper sloshing through the city seemed very far away.

Gage smiled tenderly and tucked a strand of hair that had strayed loose behind her ear. "I'm glad you decided to see me tonight. Or rather, this morning. I've enjoyed it tremendously." He traced a finger down the line of her jaw to her chin while he searched her face longingly. "Tell me, is there anyone special back in L.A.?"

Her "no" was lost on the wind. And as Gage bent over her, his finger tipping her chin up, Andrea closed her eyes to meet his kiss.

His moist lips grazed hers lovingly, his restraint reflected in the tenderness of his kiss. It was the tenderness that Andrea responded to, an emotion that stirred all the feelings she possessed; it touched and healed all the wounds of the past. The desire that she had managed to control throughout the evening, despite all the little things that Gage had done consciously or unconsciously to stoke the flickering flame, burst into an all-consuming fever. Andrea slipped her arms around his neck, clasping her hands together and catching locks of his wavy hair between her fingers. Gage straightened slightly, his movement drawing her up on her toes. As her relaxed body arched against the tense length of his, he moaned softly, the deep sound rumbling in his throat.

The elevator clunked to a stop beside them, its doors sliding open noisily in the night's stillness. While the machine waited patiently for its passengers, Andrea was determined not to let the moment escape. She responded to the passion she felt behind Gage's kiss with a telling rejoinder of her own.

As his mouth left hers to burn nipping kisses over her throat, he murmured, "If this is a mistake, don't tell me."

It had to be a mistake, feeling the way she was feeling. Giddy. Warm. Happy. Safe. Safe in his arms, his embrace. Not wanting to leave it, ever. Opening her eyes, Andrea looked deep into his. Whirling in the darkness there, she could see the conflict, the heat of desire fighting the coldness of...what?

Gage's lips brushed across her frown-furrowed forehead and whispered against her bangs. "Why do I keep making that mistake with you?"

Andrea loosened her hold on his neck, her hands sliding down to rest on his broad chest, and leaned her forehead against the smooth poplin of his trench coat. The coolness of the fabric next to her skin only deepened her awareness of the fire within her body. A soft moan of frustration escaped from her.

His hands were in her hair, his fingers caressing and tantalizing. He sighed deeply, then buried his face in her hair. His voice was just a hoarse whisper in her ear when he said, "Woman, if you only knew...."

Andrea turned her head so that her burning cheek lay against his chest. Through the heavy layers of his clothing, she could hear the thudding heartbeat that was no slower than her own. Yet the cold, rain-freshened air that Gage was breathing in deeply was having its sure effect.

Her words were barely audible in the silence of the garage. "What is it about me that makes you pull away?"

She tilted her head back, looking up into the tension-lined face so close to hers. "What is it that you don't want to tell me?"

The conflict that had been so obvious in his eyes moments before vanished. The expression on his face, normally so warm and alive, was impassive. As she started to speak, Gage laid a finger on her lips. "Hush, little one. Not now." The familiar crooked smile was slow in coming. But when it reached his lips, the feelings it reflected made Andrea's heart race a bit more.

Perhaps it was not a mistake.

Slipping his arm possessively about her shoulders, Gage drew her into the waiting elevator. He punched a button and pulled the keys to the rental car from his trouser pocket, jangling them in his hand. Unsure of what was between them, of what was to happen when they returned to the hotel, Andrea leaned against the elevator wall and watched the floor-indicator lights change while she tried to still her thumping heart.

"You know," she said, glad that her voice sounded calm to her ears, "one thing I don't understand is why, when you own a business up here and come to Seattle so often, you stay in hotels."

The seductive huskiness had not left Gage's voice. "I used to have a home on Bainbridge Island. But I put it on the market last spring." The elevator doors slid open, and he grasped her elbow to guide her through the dimly lit parking lot. "This is my first trip up here since the house closed escrow during the fall."

Andrea studied the lines of exhaustion and strain etched into his features. Strain from what, she wondered. "Will you buy another house here?"

"Not a house. Don't need one. Perhaps a condo. Something that doesn't require upkeep. I'm waiting until after the first of the year to decide."

Andrea assumed that this statement meant something significant, but she decided not to pursue the subject. While she was curious about what had happened to cause the sale of his home on Bainbridge, she wasn't up to raising his hostility or suspicion. She didn't want anything to interfere with the time they had left together. It would be so brief, and she wanted to savor every last minute of it.

Their silence was tension-filled as Gage drove back to the North Winds. The sky was already beginning to lighten as they walked the long way around the hotel from the parking level to the main doors. The wind had subsided, leaving a crisp morning air to invigorate the city. Unsure of what was ahead, Andrea nevertheless felt secure within the circle of his arm around her shoulders. After a hesitant moment's deliberation, she put her arm about his waist, and their bodies retained the close contact that had become such a pleasing familiarity. Stifling a yawn, she lay her head against his shoulder.

"I think tonight was too much for you." He smiled tiredly as she looked up at him, frowning at the faint circles under his eyes.

"Me? What about you? You look as if you could sleep for twenty-four hours straight!"

Gage pulled the heavy glass lobby door open. "I told you before—it was the three-martini lunch."

Andrea laughed and shook her head. "Right."

The lobby was empty except for the two clerks on desk duty. The elevator whisked them nonstop to the twenty-second floor, and they strolled arm in arm down the hallway. Her pulse and breathing quickened as she unlocked her door and turned to Gage.

His easygoing smile slowly faded as her brilliant blue eyes focused on him. He sighed, then spoke quietly, his voice unusually even. "Andrea, I've made some mistakes—several with you. I don't want to make any more."

Swallowing hard, Andrea whispered, "Other than kissing me, what mistakes have you made?" As she watched him, waiting for his answer, she wavered under the assault of her aroused emotions. She had always sensed he would be a difficult man to know; she hadn't realized that it could be so easy to like him so much.

His finger stroked her cheek, its touch featherlight, precise, as precise as the growing response of his emotions to hers. But the answer he gave her was vague and evasive.

"My number-one mistake was not doing as I had intended."

Chapter Seven

The shrill ringing of the telephone nudged through her sleep. Andrea stirred, moaning softly. Her pouncing hand eventually found the receiver. With eyes still closed, she murmured, "Hello?" and rolled onto her left side.

A crisp, feminine voice greeted her. "This is your morning wake-up call. It's six o'clock."

"Um. Thank you." She peeked through her lashes to make certain that she got the receiver back into its cradle, then rolled over onto her right side. Her sleep-filled eyes stared across the cool hotel room to the rain-streaked, dawn-lit window. As she tried mentally to shake the cobwebs from her mind, Andrea contemplated the night before, the early hours of that same morning.

Gage had departed abruptly as they had stood outside her door less than two hours ago. The sudden cooling of his manner had clashed strongly with the desire she had felt in his kisses. Through the long hours of the night, he had stirred her own emotions to a point that she didn't want to acknowledge, and she had sensed the same excitement deep within him. But when she could have been so easily persuaded to share her bed with him, Gage had made that oblique remark. Reluctance and a touch of regret dwelled in his eyes as he had turned slowly away.

Pulling the pillow from under her head, Andrea punched it into a new shape and moved it back under her cheek. Just what was going on with that man? He had her totally confused. He wasn't married, was obviously not committed. They shared a mutual interest and an attraction that couldn't be ignored. Yet his designing seductive moves alternated with intriguing, well-guarded suspicion. Suspicion. Andrea bit her lip and frowned. Yes, "suspicion" was the right word. But why would Gage be suspicious of her? He honestly couldn't think she was a gold digger, could he? As her eyes began to close, Andrea granted that a wealthy man would have to be suspicious of any woman who might be interested in him. And, she thought dreamily, there's no denying it. I am very interested.

The telephone rang again, shrilly, bringing her back to wakefulness. She snatched up the receiver. "Hello?"

"Are you ready to go to work?" Len Daggett's cool, impersonal voice sounded well rested.

"Oh, uh..." Andrea blinked. "What time is it?"

"Seven."

She moaned and rolled onto her back. "I must have fallen asleep after my wake-up call." Rubbing a hand across her sore, bloodshot eyes, she sighed. "When do you want to get together?"

"Why don't you come down to my room when you're ready? We'll get some breakfast and work while we eat."

"Good idea." Andrea pushed herself up on an elbow and squinted at the travel alarm. "Give me forty-five minutes. Okay?"

"Right. See you at a quarter of eight." The line went dead.

After hanging up the receiver, Andrea flopped back on the pillows and groaned aloud. "This staying up all night has got to cease!'' In a gentler, almost wistful tone of voice, she said, ''Gage, why did I have to meet you?''

There was no answer to that question. Fearing she'd fall asleep again, she tossed the bedcovers off and crawled out of bed.

Feeling far from her best, Andrea settled for a cold shower and a change into clean underwear, jeans, T-shirt and running shoes. The few strokes of makeup took only a minute to apply, and she decided to let her hair hang damply about her shoulders instead of fussing with the blow dryer for twenty minutes. Staring at her reflection in the bathroom mirror, she wondered if Gage would continue to be interested in her if she started looking like a haggard Witch of the East. She made an ugly face at the mirror and flipped off the light switch.

The sound of her footsteps was absorbed by the thick carpet as she strolled down the hallway to Len's room. She was early for their meeting but doubted that the efficient man would mind. He had probably been up and about for hours. He had certainly sounded ready to get to work when he had called. Reading the room numbers as she passed the closed doors, Andrea spotted Len's on her left. She paused outside his door, her hand raised in the act of knocking, when the sound of Len's voice caused her to freeze.

If she had ever thought the man was unemotional, that assumption was now destroyed. His words were muffled but still distinct enough to be clearly understood. Even if she had not been able to catch each word, Andrea would have known that the calm, urbane engineer was in a state of panic.

Len's voice rose. ''Cal, I'm telling you he's on to us! He knows!''

Andrea slowly lowered her hand and leaned close to the door.

"Let's cut our losses and get out." There was a short pause while Len evidently listened to Cal speaking on the other end of the long-distance connection. When he spoke again, Len was defensive. "I know the man. He's not someone to mess with. We're only asking for trouble.... I know you like trouble," Len commented sarcastically, "but you've never messed with him before. I'm telling you, he'll draw and quarter us and hang us up for the vultures! It's one thing to steal from him, it's another when you start putting lives on the line. That was a goddamn stupid thing to do, Cal. I won't go along with it!"

Andrea felt herself go pale and her knees tremble. She leaned against the door for support and prayed that no one would enter the hall and see her listening at the door.

Len was silent for a long minute. Cal must have been delivering one of his diatribes. When Len finally spoke, his voice was apprehensive. "He *has* to know it's us. Someone's been tailing me since I left Los Angeles. The girl's room was searched.... She told me." At this, Andrea pressed her ear hard against the wood. "She said her room was burglarized the day before I arrived. Nothing had been stolen, but the papers had been looked through. What does that sound like to you?" Len snarled.

During the next few silent seconds, the memory of that afternoon spun in her mind: the relief she had felt when she found her jewelry was safe; her amusement at trying to imagine the burglar's perplexity while flipping through the recruiting cards and company directories; and Len's not seeing the humor in the situation when she had told him. Andrea trembled and strained to hear the engineer's next words.

"Cal, I'm telling you, McLaren is a man you do not want to tangle with. I know him. He's unpredictable. He can play by the rules one minute, then have a bomb planted in your car the next. He's volatile. What's more, he's dangerous. We should get out now—*before* he gets too much on us!"

The sound of the elevator doors sliding open jerked Andrea back from the door. As an elderly couple stepped into the hallway, she began to pat her pockets, pretending to be looking for a room key. When the couple stopped in front of a door only a few rooms away, they glanced at her almost without regard. Andrea went through her pockets again, a deep frown cutting her forehead. Her frown was very real. The unconcerned couple let themselves into their room and quietly closed the door.

Quickly Andrea pressed her ear against Len's door again. His voice was quieter now, almost resigned. He was saying, "All right. I'll see this through. But I swear to God, you pull another stunt like that, and I'm washing my hands of you!"

His next words were unintelligible. His self-control was returning. Andrea listened for a few more seconds before realizing that Len must have hung up the phone. She backed away from the door slowly. The alarm she felt had weakened the muscles in her body; she seemed to be moving in place. Then as the enormity of what she had overheard struck her, fear gave purpose to her movement. She spun on her heel and sprinted silently down the hallway to the stairs.

ONCE AGAIN, the rainstorm had abated by evening, leaving fresh, forest-scented air hanging over the city. But as Andrea and Gage sat at a redwood picnic table eating smoked salmon, Dungeness crab and chips, the pungent

His next words took Andrea by surprise. "Do I remind you of him?"

She studied the contours of his ruggedly handsome face as if for the first time. Of course, Gage did not physically resemble David at all—they were practically opposites. Yet there were similarities. After all, it was because of his gentleness, his warmth, that Andrea had been attracted to Gage in the first place—apart from his obvious sexual appeal. But it was his boyish, unfeigned manner that had won her over.

"In some ways," she stated quietly.

Gage caught up her mittened hand in his two bare ones. The sincerity in his husky voice stirred her more than she could have imagined. "Perhaps someday I can be as open and honest with you as you'd like me to be. Until then, can we be friends?"

A feeling as deep and mysterious as Andrea had ever known swept over her as she stared into the dark, still pools of Gage's eyes. She whispered, "I'd like that very much."

They leaned across the table toward each other until their lips met. Their kiss was as sweet as it was brief. With only a breath between them, Andrea murmured, "I meant what I said last night, at the club. I think you are the gentlest man I've ever known."

"I would never hurt you." Gage's eyes burned into hers with an intensity that was calmly reassuring. "Not intentionally."

Just before her lips touched his again, Andrea said, "I know."

After another long, sweet kiss, Gage cleared his throat and suggested, "Why don't we move along? There are some good shops across from Colman Dock to check out before they close."

Andrea was tickled by his unabashed and sudden nervousness. "Whatever you say," she answered happily.

As they strolled past a big freighter moored to one of the old piers, Andrea paused in the center of the waterside sidewalk and stared up at it, looming above them like a ghostly figure in the night. She put her head on his shoulder and said, "Do you ever get the urge to jump on one of these ships and sail off to some unknown destination?"

"Would you believe me if I told you I suffer from motion sickness?"

"No."

Gage snorted unappreciatively. "Disagreeable wench. Well, I suppose hopping a boat is preferable to jumping on a plane."

"Don't tell me." Andrea's gaze slid sideways. "You aren't afraid of water, are you?"

"Like a fish." Gage juggled the paper sacks. "Come along, there's shopping to finish."

"Sometimes when I'm in an airport, I feel like buying a ticket—any ticket—getting on the plane and not even asking where we'll be landing."

"Why?" He grasped her elbow and steered her toward the footbridge crossing the Alaskan Way. "Things that bad?"

"What?" She frowned a moment, wondering what he meant. Then she smiled. "Oh, no. It's simply that life tends to be rather predictable. It would be interesting to get tossed into a totally unknown situation."

"Don't you get enough of that with these business trips?" he asked, motioning her up the steps. "I should think you run into nothing but unknowns."

"Hardly. These trips are terribly dull and totally predictable." At least they had been until this one, Andrea thought with a start. At the second-story landing, she paused, turning to Gage.

He stopped three steps below her and met her bright blue gaze with a mischievous wink. "Is this trip turning out that way?"

Andrea shrugged and replied nonchalantly, "No more than any other trip where I've met a tall, dark, handsome and frightfully sexy man who would love to make love to me." The glitter in her eyes was dangerous as she smiled demurely.

The elderly couple who had just exited the shop behind her glanced at Andrea as they passed, their stares obviously nonapproving. She blushed darkly, and Gage, every bit the gentleman, focused his attention on the concrete underside of the viaduct. While the oldsters tottered down the flight of stairs, Andrea giggled and said under her breath, "You could have warned me that they were there!"

Gage bounded up the last steps and hugged her tightly, his lips brushing her cheek. "Now, why would I ruin such an admission? So you have a man in every town, huh? What am I to do about that?"

Andrea stared up at him. "What would you like to do?"

Outside the cluttered and inviting curio shop window, with the Alaskan Way traffic noise below and above them, Gage bent and whispered in her ear.

When he straightened, Andrea opened her eyes wide and exclaimed, "You wouldn't!" While her shock was pretense, Gage's idea wasn't all bad, she thought, hiding her amusement.

He caught her hand in his and dragged her through the shop doorway. "Of course I would. And wouldn't you love it!"

Andrea laughed heartily. "The man thinks too much of himself!" Then she took in her surroundings with a sweeping glance. "Oh, Gage, look at that basket!" She rushed over to the side wall and pointed at the dishpan-sized Tlingit Indian piece that was displayed among many other smaller Alaskan and Indian wares. "Isn't it exquisite? Chris would love it!"

Gage nodded his agreement and murmured into her ear, "I think you'll find the price is exquisite also."

"Too much so?"

"Well..." He peered at the tiny tag that was stuck to the tan-and-rust basket's uppermost edge. After relaying the price, he added, "I'm no authority on Indian goods, but the shop carries only first-rate merchandise. That's why I come here."

Andrea bit her lower lip, trying to remember how much Chris had spent the summer before on the small Papago basket she had found during their trip through Arizona. If Andrea remembered correctly, the small yellow-and-willow-green piece had been costly. Chris had explained that the hand-woven items were worth every penny, since their value only appreciated. She turned to Gage. "What do you think? I'm not a good judge of art—native or otherwise."

He peered at the basket again and shrugged his shoulders. Leaning a hip against the counter, he said bluntly, "I wouldn't worry about the quality—the shop's renowned. The question is can you afford it?"

"You do have a way of cutting to the heart of things." Andrea sighed deeply and turned her back to the wall display. "Well, I did tell you that Chris's tastes outcost our pocketbook."

Gage raised a questioning eyebrow. "Chris's or yours?"

Andrea glared at him and marched over to another counter. "I don't collect art," she tossed over her shoulder.

Gage sauntered in her wake. "No, you collect boyfriends."

She turned at his chagrined tone and caught the devilment in his eyes the moment before it vanished behind a mask of nonchalance. Teasing him, she purred, "I do think you're jealous."

"Not in the least." He bent over the glass case and studied the hand-carved walrus tusks. "That free-form statue is interesting."

Andrea came back to his side and looked over his shoulder. "Um." Whispering in his ear, she added, "Not as interesting as what I'm thinking!"

"You're incorrigible."

"The master of incorrigibility speaks!"

Gage laughed and planted a swift kiss on her lips.

Andrea smiled and whirled on her heel, returning to the glass case under the Tlingit basket she had admired.

When they left the shop at closing time, Gage had added a walrus tusk carving to his collection of purchases, and Andrea had settled on a smaller, less expensive Tlingit basket for Chris.

The satisfaction of a profitable shopping trip and a relaxing, enjoyable evening had settled them into a companionable silence during the walk back to the car, which was parked under the viaduct. While Andrea juggled their packages in her lap, Gage swung the Oldsmobile onto Madison and climbed the hill back to the downtown area. The drive was equally silent, yet the tension of the previous night was missing. He idly hummed a Christmas carol, and she thought of Christmases past.

It was after the car was parked in the hotel's underground lot and its engine turned off that Gage turned to Andrea. In the dim light, his eyes caressed her face for a long minute; then he leaned across the seat and whispered, "Have I told you that you're wonderful?"

As his lips hovered over hers, Andrea sighed. "Not nearly enough."

Chapter Eight

The recruiting and interview-setup session with Len Daggett went badly Thursday morning. Bone-tired from lack of sleep, giddy from the feelings Gage had aroused in her, and fearful of what Cal and Len were involved in, Andrea managed to function through the long morning hours and past lunchtime only by consuming numerous cups of strong coffee. Len watched her silently, chain-smoking his cigarettes and keeping all speculation from his eyes. For once, Andrea was thankful Len was the type of man he was. She would not have been able to hold her scattered emotions under tight control if he had attempted to pry into the reasons for her difficulty in concentrating on the work.

After a late, half-eaten lunch in her room, Len suggested that, since they would be busy that evening with the Tectron interviews, they should take the remainder of the afternoon off and rest up. Cal had told him about the recruiting meeting that would follow the last interviews. He assumed it would be a late night, and Andrea confirmed his suspicion. The meeting would go on until midnight or one in the morning.

Len shoved his cigarettes and lighter into the pocket of his sport jacket and stood up. Andrea began to sort the recruiting cards on the table before her. At his continuing silence, she glanced up. For a long moment she thought he was going to say something, perhaps ask her why she was so distracted or if she knew anything about his special interest in Stratcom and its president, Edward McLaren. But Daggett seemed to think better of whatever was on his mind and merely nodded, then strode to the door. He did not look back as he left the room wordlessly.

After taking care of some details for the upcoming night's work, Andrea curled up on the bed, tucking a pillow under her cheek. While sleep flirted with her senses, she was once again on the dock at the waterfront, feeling the security of Gage's embrace. The heat that emanated from his body warmed her; his scent aroused her. Sleep muffled her mind, and as she drifted in its comfort, she yearned to be with Gage.

She slept for the greater part of the afternoon, although her rest was broken periodically by dreams. Most of them were about Gage, but in several of them, he and David became interchangeable.

When the five o'clock wake-up call came, Andrea felt relieved. She tried to concentrate on what lay ahead. Room service was prompt with the light supper she had ordered before taking her nap. She forced herself to eat some of the meal, then took a long, hot shower and dressed for the evening.

As she finished a second cup of coffee, she studied her reflection in the mirror over the desk and was thankful for the invention of makeup. She had creamed away the circles of exhaustion under her eyes, given her cheeks high color and cleaned away the redness from her eyes with eyedrops. Her navy wool blazer suit, white crepe blouse and navy pumps certified that she was the capable recruiter/liaison woman. After she twisted her hair into a bun and fastened it with a few inconspicuous combs, she put a smile on her lips. The expression of goodwill she saw in the mirror did nothing to cheer her.

The next hour was busy with all the preparations she made on these trips for the customers. Earlier that morning she had requested that the four Tectron engineers be given rooms on separate floors, all lower than the tenth floor, all near the elevator. This allowed applicants to be whisked from floor to floor as needed to talk to the suitable interviewers.

The staggered interviewing times would help keep each applicant anonymous to all others, never catching glimpses of one another. This was important, since the aerospace engineering community in the city was small. Many of the applicants came from the same company; in fact, from the same projects and departments. An applicant could find himself in an embarrassing situation if he bumped into his office colleague—or worse, his boss—at the hotel. It was one of Andrea's functions to prevent that from happening.

She checked out each room, making certain it was suitable. Some hotel rooms could be incredibly small and provided an unsuitable environment for a casual job interview. She stocked each room with extra glasses, filled ice buckets, a selection of canned sodas and a large carafe of hot coffee.

As she finished with the fourth room, the one assigned to Kipp Cross, Andrea stood back and surveyed it. It was small, but since the sheriffs' convention had been booked months in advance and her own raiding trip had been a spur-of-the-moment idea, Kipp's room would have to do. In the morning Andrea would see that the bed was removed to give additional space and freedom to the environment. She glanced at her wristwatch. It was 6:45 P.M.

The Tectron crew should have been in their rooms by now. The first interview was scheduled for seven.

Andrea hurried back to the twenty-second floor. Apprehension knotted her stomach, and all the fears associated with these trips suddenly welled up inside her. So many things could go wrong—and any given handful usually did. She went into her room and called down to the main desk, to be told that, no, the Tectron party had not arrived yet. As she hung up the receiver, the phone rang, jarring her already keyed-up nerves. She answered in her most capable headhunter voice.

"This is Mike MacKenzie. I have a seven o'clock appointment with Ed Rees."

Andrea rolled her eyes toward the ceiling. "Yes, Mike." She knew what he was about to say; she had heard it hundreds of times. Yet her voice remained friendly. "What's up?"

"I just called to tell you that I can't make it." The twenty-seven-year-old whiz kid of Stratcom's guidance analysis section was canceling out.

"Well, what time can you make it tomorrow? I can juggle Ed's schedule to free up some time. He's very interested in talking to you, Mike."

"Yeah, but I'm pushing a deadline here, and I can't afford to take the time right now to talk to him. Maybe next time."

Yes, and maybe hell will freeze over, Andrea thought. She thanked him for calling, wished him luck in meeting his deadline—if one even existed—and hung up. Less than a minute later, the phone rang again. The seven-fifteen appointment was canceling. After Andrea said good-bye to the second caller, she mumbled under her breath, took the receiver off the hook so that her line would be busy to more calls, grabbed her room key and headed for the elevator.

The first Tectron man Andrea saw was Kipp Cross, who stood at the very end of the registration desk. Farther down the busy counter was Sean Parker, an unexpected booking for the trip. Andrea had heard only that morning from Cal that Sean was being added to the crew. He had been at Tectron barely two months and was already revamping his entire department—therefore this trip to Seattle. Next to Sean stood Cal Slattery.

Andrea paused in midstride in the center of the lobby. Cal had said nothing to her that morning about his coming to Seattle. She quickly searched the crowd at the desk for Tectron's personnel recruiter, George Nazareth. She didn't see him. Gathering her fortitude about her, she continued across the lobby to greet the men.

Cal signed the registration card and turned to speak to Sean. His eye caught Andrea approaching them, a strained look on her otherwise composed face. He saved his usual boisterous greeting and nodded to her instead. His voice was low when he asked, "How's everything going?"

"We've lost the seven and seven-fifteen appointments, which is just as well, since you're all so late."

"The flight was a real bitch. We're lucky to be here at all. The turbulence practically flipped us to Hawaii. Who's got the first interview, then?"

"Kipp, at seven forty-five. Ed, at eight. And someone I think Sean should talk to is coming at eight-thirty. We're scheduled through to eleven."

"Good. What about tomorrow?" Cal picked up his suitcase and moved toward the elevators.

Andrea and the others followed in his wake. "We're scheduled straight through to noon, beginning at seven-thirty in the morning."

Kipp flashed a glad-to-see-you grin at Andrea. "Who's the lucky stiff who pulled that interview?"

"You did."

The men laughed at the young engineer. The frown that settled on Kipp's fleshy face brought another laugh.

Andrea turned back to her boss. "What happened to George?"

"He had an emergency this morning and had to leave the plant. I'm filling in for him." Cal held the elevator door open at his floor. "Come to my room with me, Andi."

Andrea trailed behind his fast-paced stride and closed the hotel room door after her. Moving hurriedly, Cal unpacked his attaché case and set up a self-contained slide presentation. Andrea had already noticed that he was wearing a Tectron identification badge. The other men, actual Tectron employees, wore them as well. But instead of identifying him as Calvin Slattery, his badge read "Calvin Baker, Personnel Department."

Cal gave her a rundown on his position here while he finished setting up the projector. She was to refer all applicants to him, Cal Baker, for screening. He would handle them from that point on, giving each engineer the Tectron introduction and then passing him on to the Tectron man who should interview him.

Andrea had already established an interview schedule and assigned each applicant to the Tectron man who was appropriate to interview him. A junior programmer or analyst would see Kipp Cross. Someone with a more general background that could be used in Parker's area would see Sean. A more senior-level applicant would see Rees.

That was the way it had always been done before—and the method had proved successful.

Cal assured her that most of the engineers would see the man they had been told they would be speaking with, but there might be some changes. Nothing to rock the boat and upset the show. He flashed her his "trust me" smile.

Andrea felt even more leery.

Cal eyed her closely. "Where's Len hiding out? In your room?"

"No. I've no idea where he's disappeared to. I haven't seen him since early this afternoon. I tried ringing his room an hour ago and got no answer, so I assume he's having dinner."

"When you see him, have him call me." At Andrea's nod, he added, "That's it. Go back to your room and keep everything running smoothly—like always."

Andrea felt herself nodding in the vague manner that Len Daggett had; she even backed out of the room without a departing word. As she rode the elevator up to her floor, she was more convinced than ever that something was very wrong. Perhaps it was only lack of sleep and emotional upset that made her internal alarm go off. Still, she had been troubled about this trip from the beginning. Overhearing Len's phone call had confirmed it. And with Cal in Seattle, she was certain that his plan—whatever it was—was in action.

Over the next few hours, Andrea was too busy to give any thought to the scheme that she knew she must be unwittingly involved in, or even to Gage. All the usual mixups happened. People came early for their appointments, or they came late. Co-workers greeted one another in the lobby. Superiors ran into subordinates. Sean Parker's appointment was with one of those who arrived nearly a half hour early, and Sean was nowhere to be found. Andrea had him paged in the lobby, restaurants and cocktail lounges, but he did not respond. Then, right on schedule at 8:27 P.M., Sean ambled up to his door as Andrea trotted down the stairway to his floor. He smelled of bourbon, and his normally jocund personality was even more spirited. Andrea returned to her room to fetch the engineer she had stored there for the past twenty-five minutes, hoping that the applicant wasn't a devout teetotaler.

At eleven-thirty she rang room service and ordered a variety of sandwiches to be delivered to her room at midnight, along with a carafe of coffee and a pot of hot tea. The men would be filtering in there shortly, and this was the first breather she'd had all evening.

As she flopped into one of the armchairs, Andrea realized that she had never gotten in touch with Len. She called the desk and asked to be connected to his room. His line was busy. Slipping her shoes back onto her aching feet, she decided to go up to the twenty-third floor and let him know that the midnight meeting would be in her room.

After trudging down the hall and up the flight of stairs, Andrea stepped into the corridor in time to see Stratcom engineer Darrell Smith exiting a room. She slowed her pace, her curiosity instantly aroused. As Smith, a rescheduled appointment for Ed Rees, disappeared into the elevator, Andrea paused outside Len's room, the same one Smith had just left. Since his appointment had been at ten-fifteen, Andrea figured he must be a hot prospect to have spent nearly two hours interviewing with different Tectron engineers. But what had he been doing in Len Daggett's room?

She had to assume that the two men were friends. After all, the aerospace community was close-knit. Then she remembered with a jolt that Darrell Smith was the man Len had insisted she set up for an interview with Tectron. Len didn't know him. Then what...? Her thoughts trailed off to a conclusion she did not like.

After lingering outside Len's door for a few more minutes thinking, Andrea knocked softly.

Daggett opened the door a crack and peered out at her. Was there a flash of surprise in those otherwise expressionless eyes? Andrea smiled her public-relations smile. "Couldn't get through to you. Guess your phone's off the hook. Just dropped by to tell you that if you're planning on attending the reviewing meeting, it's in my room and will start in about fifteen minutes."

"Thank you, but no, I think I'll pass on this one. I was getting ready for bed." Len opened the door wider. His shirt was unbuttoned, and a towel hung around his neck.

Andrea blinked, biting back the words that had sprung to her lips. "Oh—sorry to have bothered you. Guess I'll see you at breakfast, then."

"Right." Len favored her with a smile. "Good night, Andrea."

"'Night." She backed away slowly before turning toward the elevator. Behind her, Len's door closed quietly. As she returned to her room, several different possible explanations tripped through her mind, but she could accept none of them.

Kipp Cross was waiting for her outside her door, lounging against the wall. The big teddy bear of a man said, "I hope you have food inside, because I haven't had a bite since lunch. Every engineer must have passed through my room tonight. I'm starved!"

The rattle of a service cart echoed out of an elevator. Andrea smiled. "You get first choice."

After the waiter had left, she settled onto the corner of the bed with a cup of hot tea. Kipp eased himself into a chair and took a big bite out of the corned-beef sandwich in his fist.

"What did you think of Darrell Smith?" she asked nonchalantly.

"Who?"

"Darrell Smith, a communications analyst with Stratcom. Medium height, medium size, nondescript features. Just the type of man you'd imagine having worked for the CIA."

Kipp cracked the pop-top on a can of soda and took a swig to wash down his sandwich. "Didn't talk to him. In fact, never heard of him. Who was he supposed to see?"

A warning bell clanged wildly in her mind. Andrea paused, a puzzled look settling over her features. "You know, I think he was the one who canceled. I've been so busy that I've had trouble keeping everyone straight. I even had to stash a guy in here when he showed early for his appointment. Couldn't find Sean Parker anywhere."

Kipp spoke around the hunk of food in his mouth. "Did you try the nearest bar?"

Andrea laughed, then glanced up as Ed Rees and Cal knocked on the door she had left ajar. A moment later Sean Parker arrived. For the next ten minutes, the men concentrated on their food. Andrea remained seated on the bed, sipping at her cup of tea, staying out of the men's circle and the order of things. If Cal had not made the trip, she would have been an active participant in the discussion of which applicants were the most logical candidates for follow-up interviews at the plant in California, which ones might accept job offers, which ones they should not spend any more time on. But since Cal was the senior representative of ComSearch and had met with each applicant, he was automatically filling Andrea's position at the meeting.

She listened closely to the engineers' comments on their interviews and the applicants. Before the meeting was half over, she noticed a glaring omission. Prudent, she kept her silence until the meeting ended shortly after one.

Ed, the senior member of Tectron, stayed to talk to Cal after Kipp and Sean had left. Then, as Cal and Ed moved toward the door, Andrea stood up and asked, "Cal, could I speak with you before you leave? It will only take a minute."

"Sure, Andi. Ed, we can finish this tomorrow morning." Cal remained at the partially open door. "What's up?"

"I think you will want the door closed, Cal." Andrea's tone was quietly professional.

He shut the door and returned to the table and sat down. Picking up his half-finished bottle of mineral water, he peered at her from under his shaggy eyebrows. "You sound displeased."

"I am. You've lied to me again."

"In what way?"

Andrea remained standing, arms crossed, head tilted defiantly. "I went to Len's room more than an hour ago to tell him about the meeting we've just finished here. He had said that he wanted to attend it. But he told me he was getting ready for bed and wouldn't make it." Andrea remembered him standing in the doorway, his shirt unbuttoned to his waist, his tanned chest smooth under the fabric. "Indeed, he was apparently washing up."

"So?" Cal's glare was appraising.

"Well, just a minute before I knocked on his door, I saw Darrell Smith come out of his room."

Cal's face was so carefully guarded, Andrea couldn't tell what he was thinking.

She plunged into the murky waters of suspicion. "I think Len, you and I are the only people to have seen the two Stratcom engineers tonight. I asked Kipp what he thought of Smith, and he hadn't heard of him. In fact, his name never came up in the meeting, nor did the other fellow's."

The taut muscles in Cal's jawline worked in spasms. The silence that hung between them was dangerous and explosive. Andrea felt herself go pale, and a small tremor shook her hand. She crossed her arms more firmly and said, "George Nazareth suddenly couldn't make the trip, so you fill in as a Tectron recruiter when they have other people who could have come. Len Daggett, an unemployed engineer whose qualifications are obviously outstanding—good enough to get him around the F40A stigma—is trying to learn the headhunting business. But he lacks the killer attitude and seems to be interested in only one thing: Stratcom engineers. And then—voilà!—Stratcom engineers are finding their way to his room. I'll bet that Ed Rees would like to know about that, because I'm sure he doesn't."

Cal's voice was icy. "Remember who you work for."

"Oh, I do. But I don't like being lied to or used, and you know it. I'm tired of your game, Cal. So, before I go have an early morning chat with Ed, why don't you tell me who Len Daggett is and what he's doing here?"

Cal stood up suddenly, looming over Andrea, trying to intimidate her. "I'm warning you. Don't threaten me, Andrea. You're not strong enough to threaten me. Remember, I don't like being threatened."

"This isn't a threat. I will tell Rees unless you explain it to me." She ignored the wave of fear that urged her to put space between herself and the man. "I've had it with being used and set up by you. I'm not as stupid as you think, Cal. I know when I'm being set up to be the fall guy if one of your slightly illegal maneuvers backfires in your face."

Cal was the one to step away, turning to study her from a distance as if she were a stranger. "All right." He paused a long moment. "All right. You want to know the truth, I'll tell you. And if you leak it, I'll know where it came from, and I will ruin you. Absolutely, totally ruin you. Do you understand?"

"Perfectly." Andrea waited nervously but patiently while he decided the best approach to the problem she had presented him with.

When he spoke again, his anger was under control, but his voice was still chilling. "Len Daggett and I are co-owners of NavCom Electronics in Carson. But I am a silent owner. You can imagine what my aerospace customers for ComSearch would say if they knew I owned fifty-one percent of a competing software engineering firm."

Andrea's expression was dour. "Indeed I do. There would be no ComSearch if they found out."

"That's right. Not one of my customers would keep our contracts. I might even find myself involved in several sticky lawsuits."

"So NavCom wants analysts and why not slip a few crumbs from Tectron's recruiting table? Save yourself a lot of money while doing it, since Tectron foots the bills for the trips. Keep NavCom's name out of circulation up here, because the only engineers to hear it are the ones you hand-pick." As Cal nodded, Andrea fought another quiver of fear. Her voice was cold. "You're more Machiavellian than I had previously thought."

She had to admit that Cal had as much guts as he had brains. She wondered when he would get caught playing one of his little games. When that happened, as it must, she hoped she would not be a player. But she was a player in this game, and so was Stratcom's president. Her only consolation was that if McLaren decided to take action against NavCom Electronics, at least Len and Cal were in Seattle. No matter how much a man hated headhunters, he wouldn't bother with a mere recruiter if he could tangle with ComSearch's owner.

"Now that you know the truth, what are you going to do?"

Andrea moved slowly to the door, put her hand on the knob and turned to face him. "Nothing. I just wanted to know the truth. I think you're forgetting that I have thousands riding on this trip, more money coming from the trip to Atlanta. I expect to get placements out of these raids. And I don't anticipate not collecting those commissions."

Cal paused halfway through the doorway. "You'd better be careful, Andrea. You don't fight dirty enough. Someone will come along and squash you flat." The penetrating hazel eyes flicked over her. He nodded. A nasty leer colored his words. "Yeah, you just don't play dirty enough."

Andrea closed the door and leaned against it, trying to calm her trembling nerves. If she could have afforded to quit, she would have done so before Cal had left her room. But with Christine's university expenses, the hospital bills, the regular monthly expenses and her own long, dry spell of no placements, Andrea simply couldn't afford to quit her job. She had four engineers who had given starting dates at the end of January. Those commissions, combined with any job placements from the Atlanta and Seattle trips, would see her bank account in a much healthier condition. As much as she wanted to leave ComSearch, she couldn't. The timing was all wrong. She would have to ride out this spell of bad weather with Cal as best she could before giving notice.

But she couldn't forget his comments about playing dirty and getting squashed. He had never threatened her in that manner before, and she was frightened, very frightened.

Choking back a sob, she glanced at the travel clock on the nightstand. It was nearly one-thirty, but she had promised to call Gage after the meeting. She pushed herself away from the door and crossed to the bed hesitantly.

Gage's telephone rang five times before he answered it.

"This is Andrea. Did I wake you?" Despite her attempt to sound calm, her voice was strained with anxiety.

There was a yawn on the other end of the line. "Yeah. I gave up on you. Do you know what time it is?"

"Yes."

Another yawn. But when he spoke again, Gage sounded alert. "What's wrong?"

Andrea traced the pattern of the bedspread's print with her finger. "Nothing."

"Don't 'nothing' me," Gage ordered. "I can hear it in your voice. Come on, Andrea, talk to me." She remained silent except for a sniff as she fought back tears. Gage said tenderly, "If you won't talk to me over the phone, will you come down to my room and talk to me? I'd come up to yours, but I'm not dressed. What do you say, honey?"

Andrea answered softly, "I'll come down."

Chapter Nine

Gage answered Andrea's tap on his door promptly. His unruly auburn hair was tousled, and exhaustion cut deep lines into his face. He wore only a short brown-and-tan kimono and held a half-full glass of amber liquid in his hand. As Andrea stepped inside, he offered her the glass. "Here. You sounded like you could use a drink." The sleepy dark eyes caressed her blue-jeans-and-T-shirt-clad figure, then followed the swing of blond curls upon her shoulders as she nodded vaguely.

Andrea accepted the glass and sipped at the scotch. Her gaze followed Gage while he moved back to sit on the side of the bed. As she studied the hard muscles of the long runner's legs, Andrea felt desire flicker within her, despite her tiredness and emotional upset.

"Well, are you going to talk to me or just stand there giving me the once-over?" A weary smile touched the corners of his mouth, but his eyes were full of concern.

Andrea sighed deeply and shook her head. "I don't really know what I'm doing here."

"You're here because you're upset and need a friend. Come on, honey, talk to me."

"It's all so stupid!" she burst out. Unshed tears made her eyes bright. "It's just a game! And I hate it!"

Perplexed, Gage said, "Excuse me, but you left me at the gate. What's a game? Us?"

She was startled by his question and stared at him blankly for a moment. "Us? No. I'm talking about my job."

"That's what I thought you were referring to, but I wasn't sure." Gage seemed relieved and his nod was encouraging. "Okay. Go on. What's so stupid about it? I gather your boss has been upsetting you again."

Andrea stormed across the room to the table and slammed her nearly untouched glass down, sloshing whisky onto the tabletop. "He's such a vile man."

"Why does he upset you so much?"

"He's a crook."

"Why do you think he's a crook?"

"I don't think he is. I know he is." Her voice quavered a moment. She crossed her arms in front of her, trying to hide the tremble of fear, and tears edged her eyes. "And he's going to take me to jail right along with him."

Gage stared at her, then asked, "Do you normally tend toward melodrama, or is there a reason for real concern here?"

Andrea met his scrutinizing look. "I am not a hysterical female," she declared.

"I didn't mean to insinuate that you are. But I think you're as exhausted as I am, and things get blown out of perspective when you're too tired to think straight."

As if his words had released them, tears spilled onto her flushed cheeks unchecked. "Not in this case!" Sobbing, she turned her back to him and hid her face in her hands. "Oh, damn! I hate women who cry."

Gage crossed the room in quick strides, grasped her shoulders gently and turned her to him. As she buried her face in the mat of his chest hair, he gathered her in his arms and hugged her tightly. "But I don't." His hand smoothed her hair with tender strokes. "Go ahead, babe. Have a good cry."

Andrea clung to him and tried unsuccessfully to stop her tears. "This is so stupid.... You must think I'm a ninny."

He kissed her forehead. "Not at all. I think you're a beautiful, sexy young woman—even when you're crying."

She sniffed and looked up, her reddened eyes searching his face. Sniffing again, she whispered, "And I think you are a very special man."

His kiss was solicitous but unhurried. Andrea clasped her hands behind his head, burying her fingers in his hair. Gage's lips left hers to plant warm caresses on her tear-stained cheeks, closed eyelids, the hollow behind her ear. He murmured, "I'm glad your boss upset you."

Andrea sighed. "Let's not talk about him. I'd rather talk about us."

"I don't think we can talk about us until you relax." His fingers, as if commanding a piano keyboard, gently began to massage the tense muscles of her shoulders. "You're wound up tighter than a jack-in-the-box that is about to spring."

"Warfare tends to do that to me." Andrea tried to roll her head to the side and discovered that her bunched-up neck muscles wouldn't respond.

Gage pointed to the bed. "Lie down. I'll give you a back rub and see if we can't work some of those knots out."

Andrea started to protest, but stopped when she saw the obstinate expression lurking in his eyes. She turned silently and picked up the tumbler she had set on the table. Sipping at the scotch, she crossed to the bed. "I don't imagine you'd rather make love to me, would you?"

She stretched out on her stomach on top of the rumpled sheets, and Gage chuckled. "Of course I would. But I'd be afraid of breaking something, seeing how tense you are."

"Why don't you let me worry about that?" she grumbled, punching a pillow under her cheek.

Gage sat beside her on the edge of the bed. His hand smoothed her hair over her shoulder, then skimmed along the back of her neck, the featherlight touch of his fingers sending a tingle down her spine. "Maybe later."

Andrea willed herself to relax, but the unpleasantness with Cal kept flashing through her mind, disrupting any mental progress she was making. Soon, however, the warmth and gentle manipulation of Gage's hands began to work on her. Several silent minutes passed as he continued massaging the tension away.

With her eyes closed, Andrea sighed contentedly. "You are a multitalented man."

"So they say," he maintained huskily.

"Is there anything you can't do?"

"Yeah. Fly a plane."

Andrea giggled into the pillow a moment, then rolled onto her back. A delighted smile erased the strain on her face, but the brilliant blue eyes studied Gage soberly. "You look done in." After pausing a moment, she continued quietly. "I guess you haven't gotten much sleep lately."

A conceding smile touched a corner of the mouth she loved to kiss. "Some say I've been seeing too much of a certain lady."

Andrea whispered, "Anyone I know?"

"Maybe." He cupped her face tenderly in his hands. "Now. What's happening with your boss that makes you so uptight and sends you into tears?"

Her smile faded. "I told you I really don't want to talk about him."

"Why not? Don't you trust me? You said you did." Gage picked up his empty glass on the nightstand and refilled it from a silver hip flask.

Andrea shoved two pillows behind her and sat up against the headboard. She twisted the corner of the top sheet around her finger. "It's not that I don't trust you," she said hesitantly.

"Just what is it, then?" he demanded, his eyes burning into hers.

Andrea's temper flared a moment, then subsided as she realized both of them were tired and edgy. "It's a matter of fighting my own battles. I guess, coming from a background like yours, you can't understand what I mean."

Gage glared at her over the top of his raised glass. "Don't sell me short, Andrea. You might be surprised."

Pulling her knees up to her chin, Andrea wrapped her arms around her legs and rested her chin on her knees. Carefully, she focused her eyes on the pattern of the rumpled sheets. "Okay, maybe you do understand. Well, it's simply the fact that I've come a long way since the day I ran away from home. I've gotten where I am all on my own—with no one to help me."

"You mean no meal tickets."

Andrea glanced up. "Yes, that's precisely what I mean. And despite what people think where I work now, I'm still earning my living honestly and by my own hard efforts. My boss isn't my sugar daddy, and I've put a sizable sum into his coffers."

"Yet you said a few minutes ago that he's a crook headed for jail and he's taking you along for the ride."

Andrea's look was glum. "It's his damn Machiavellian games. He's going to get caught playing one. And if it's not this one, I'd be surprised."

Gage slowly hitched himself farther over on the bed, closer to Andrea. "What is it about this game that makes it more dangerous than any other?" He paused a moment, looking at the sheet that was twisted in Andrea's grip. "I don't know anything about the talent scout business. Danny hires the musicians for the club."

Andrea met his curious gaze and thought of the first time she'd seen those expressive dark eyes. Had it only been four days earlier? It seemed a lifetime ago. She felt so comfortable in his presence, his embrace, but this conversation reminded her that they were practically strangers.

Yes, she had led him to believe she was a talent scout, a form of which she was. But Andrea did not want to take the time to explain her job accurately so Gage would comprehend what she did for a living, especially since all she really wanted was for him to take her in his arms and love her. And she certainly did not want to explain her confrontation with Cal.

Her answer was slow in coming. "Don't misunderstand me, please, but I feel that if I tell you what happened this evening, I would be disloyal to my company. You know, like airing the dirty laundry in public." Andrea watched her bare toes pushing under the bedcovers. "It's not something I can share."

Gage studied the woman huddled against the pillows, chin on knees, thick blond hair half hiding her face. He said quietly, "I imagine most of the people in prison today on bum raps share your philosophy of loyalty."

Andrea tilted her head to the side. "You think I'm a fool."

"I don't think anything." Gage leaned closer to her, and she felt his warm breath on the backs of her wrists. "You aren't giving me enough information to make any type of decision. So I can't even advise you—other than to say be careful." He sighed, then added, "But I wish you would trust me. It sounds like you're involved in something that is way over your head. I think you need help."

A wan smile touched her lips. "You're probably right, but..."

Gage shrugged, a dispassionate look clouding his eyes. Then he let out a long, sad sigh. "Andrea, too many mistakes are being made."

Her smile was gentle as she sought to assure him that everything would be all right. "Don't worry about me, Gage. I'll be careful. I may be loyal—but I'm not stupid."

He slipped his hand into her hair and fondled the back of her neck. "I think you could easily be misguided, but I'd never think of you as being stupid. Quite the contrary."

Andrea watched him through half-closed eyes. She murmured softly, "Am I being misguided now?"

His lips were only a breath away from hers. "Misguided by me?"

"Uh-huh."

"Never. A friend wouldn't misguide you."

"Uh, I don't like the sound of that."

"Has anything changed since last night?"

As Andrea's lips touched his, she whispered, "You tell me."

His kiss was the familiar warm caress that was so gentle, so claiming. Yet, as she slowly pulled away and watched him through her thick eyelashes, Gage smiled. "Honestly? Do you want me to be honest?"

"Oh, Lord, I knew I'd regret saying that." Andrea moved back against the pillows and opened her eyes wide. "Yes, please, be honest."

"I think it's best if we keep things as they are."

Restraint, desire and something else alternately found their way onto Gage's face. Watching the battle of his emotions, Andrea couldn't ignore her own. She reached out and touched the side of his face. Running her fingers over the prickling stubble of his beard, she said quietly, "I—I'd like to stay with you tonight.... I need to be with you."

Gage clasped her hand in his, turned it over and kissed her palm. Andrea uncoiled from her defensive position and leaned into the circle of his arm. That strong arm pulled her to him, into his lap. She slipped her arms around his waist and placed her cheek against the hard muscle of his chest. The steady beat of his heart beneath her ear was strangely reassuring, strangely home to her soul. As the heat from his body warmed her, she relaxed, feeling protected from all possible harm in his embrace, wanting never to be apart from his touch.

Gage drew her to him tightly. Then, slowly, he lowered her onto her back and stretched out beside her. His hand brushed her tousled hair from her face, and his fingers strayed over her cheek to her lips. His eyes were so close, yet seemed so far away. Andrea lay secure in his embrace and watched the pupils dilate until his eyes were nearly black. The lips that she loved to kiss so much gradually formed into a tender smile. His words were spoken gently, teasingly, but he had understood her fears.

"You're safe here, Andrea."

His fingers rested against her lips. She kissed them and whispered, "Thank you."

IN THE DEEP RECESSES of her mind, Andrea tried to identify the annoying sound. As she roused herself nearer to wakefulness, she realized it was the telephone ringing incessantly. Raising herself up on an elbow and slitting her eyes open, she saw that Gage was sleeping despite the loud noise. She shook his shoulder and mumbled, "Wake up," then reached across him to pull the receiver off the cradle by its curled cord. "Hello?" she said into the phone.

There was a split-second pause while the caller assessed the situation. Then a familiar masculine voice said, "Sorry to wake you. I'd like to speak to Gage."

Andrea stifled a yawn and blinked her eyes, trying to spot a clock in the dimly lit room. Gray daylight was showing at the window. "What time is it?"

"Ten of six."

"Oh. Just a moment." Andrea peered over Gage's shoulder. He looked so peaceful she was reluctant to wake him. "May I tell him who's calling?"

"Dan Joachim."

Andrea clamped one hand over the receiver and shook Gage's shoulder vigorously with the other. "Wake up, Gage. It's Danny."

Gage moaned and held out a hand. With eyes still closed, he grumbled into the phone, "This had better be important. God, what time is it?"

Andrea could hear Dan's laugh clearly as he answered. His next words were barely audible. "Ol' buddy, you aren't going to like what I have to tell you."

Gage's eyes flashed open and flicked to Andrea's quizzical face. Placing his hand over the receiver a moment, he said, "Hey, babe, would you get me a drink of water? I'm parched." While she padded barefoot across the carpet, she heard Gage stir in the bed and mumble, "Go on."

The cold bathroom floor jarred her warm feet, and she hurriedly filled a glass with tap water, took a sip and turned back to Gage.

He was swearing under his breath. "Don't let him out of the plant! I'll meet you there. Make it seven. And get the troops together. I'm going to stop them this time." He slammed the phone down and rolled off the bed, straightening his robe.

Andrea remained in the bathroom doorway, glass in hand forgotten. "Is something wrong?"

Pulling underwear from a bureau drawer, Gage snapped, "No."

"Right. You always greet mornings with a curse."

"Don't, Andrea. I'm not up to it." He took the glass from her hand and, stepping into the bathroom, turned on the shower.

Andrea moved back to the bed and sat where Gage had lain only moments before. The sheets were warm and smelled faintly of his scent. "What's going on?" she asked.

Gage stuck his head around the doorway, a towel wrapped about his hips and his dark eyes flashing with suppressed anger. "You tell me."

"What do you mean?"

While anger and suspicion hardened the line of his jaw, Gage held his breath a moment, only to let it out in a long sigh. "Never mind."

She was upset, but did not want to leave, especially with Gage acting this way. "Shall I order up some coffee?" she suggested.

His temper relented slightly. "Please," he said, then closed the bathroom door.

Uncomfortable with his anger, Andrea tried to sort through her jumbled feelings while Gage showered. He had admitted to not always being pleasant in the past; she guessed she was seeing that side of him now. But the vehemence he displayed was unnerving. It was so incongrous with the man she knew. Or thought she knew.

She had finished a cup of coffee before the bathroom door opened. Meeting her worried eyes, Gage seemed surprised to see her still there. Andrea poured a cup of coffee and held it out. "Do you want to talk about it now?"

"No."

"Okay."

Every time the subject of his work had come up, Gage had reacted with varying degrees of moodiness. This time his anger had been surprising and frightening. Andrea didn't understand, yet she wanted to. But since she would not talk about her problems with Cal, Gage would not share with her. Thinking about it, Andrea realized that Gage knew more about her work than she knew about his. She was certain that this immediate problem—whatever it was—did not involve the club; he had been willing, even eager, to share that aspect of his life with her.

Gage disappeared back into the bathroom to dress. Andrea twisted the edge of the sheet around her hand and thought how different Gage and David were, and how similar. Gage seemed truly to care about her and was concerned with her welfare. David had been insufferably self-centered. But Gage's reticence about his work was an echo of David's absorption in his acting career. With David, Andrea had always been a distant second in importance. And as Gage continued dressing in silence, virtually ignoring her, Andrea realized that, once again, she had become involved with a man whose own interests came before love. After the pain she had endured with David, she had no desire to repeat the experience.

Gage stepped back into the room and shrugged into his suit coat. Finishing his coffee, he poured another cup. As he sipped the hot brew, the dark eyes that had been so loving only hours earlier scrutinized the woman who sat cross-legged on top of the bed in her wrinkled top and jeans. The brilliant winter sun streaming through the window lighted her profile and glistened on the tousled locks that rested on her shoulders. Andrea met his gaze coolly, his own distance reflected in her expression.

Gage set his cup on the table. "I have to go."

"Right."

Pulling his overcoat from a hanger, he said, "Look, I'm sorry about this." As he faced her, he added, "But it's important."

"I understand." From her tone of voice and the hurt she was trying to disguise, it was obvious that Andrea did not understand.

He crossed the room to stand in front of her. His hand tenderly stroked the side of her face while he said, "I'll call you later this morning."

"You may not be able to reach me."

"I'll leave a message."

A smile found its way to her lips. "Okay," she said softly. "Remember, I fly out this afternoon."

Gage bent and kissed her forehead. "I won't forget. Talk to you later."

Andrea remained sitting on the bed after he had left. She'd longed to jump up and rush into his arms, to kiss his lips over and over and not allow him to leave. But she had forced herself to sit still and watch the door close behind him.

Alone in a hotel room that was not hers, Andrea turned her face to the window, closing her eyes against the bright sunlight. Memories from the past and fear of the future

pushed tears through her lashes. Why did life and rela-
tionships have to be so difficult? *Because people are involved,* Andrea reminded herself. *And people have a real
knack for making things harder than they already are.
Gage and I are prime examples.* Blinking the tears away,
she sighed and crawled off the bed in search of her room
key.

THE HASSLE AND HURRY of the morning's business kept
Andrea's mind occupied as she handled her end of the final interviews. All the usual problems repeated themselves, and it seemed as if she'd spent the entire morning
in the hotel lobby. Among the frustrations she had to deal
with was the return of Darrell Smith to talk to Len Daggett. The young Stratcom engineer was open to negotia-
tions. Trying to remain cool and nonflustered while
speaking to the communications analyst in the middle of
the convention traffic, Andrea thought that she saw Gage
in the crowd. When she did a double take and looked
again, beyond Darrell's slightly paranoid countenance,
Andrea guessed that she had been wrong. Gage was not
in the lobby. Evidently her worried subconscious was
making itself known.

It was after noon, and the Tectron engineers were re-
porting to Cal's room one by one as they each finished
their last morning appointment. Andrea had ordered
lunch delivered for the roundup meeting, and now, as she
finished packing for the flight home, she realized just how
hungry she was. There had been no time for breakfast,
only a quick shower, before she had greeted the first
interviewee.

In a few minutes she would check out and join the others in Cal's room for the meeting. She and her boss had
spoken little to each other that morning. Andrea wished

to continue avoiding him, but she knew she would eventually be faced with their discussion of the night before. She wondered how he felt about it now that he'd had time to reevaluate the situation. His threats would probably be much worse.

Folding her travel bag in half and securing the straps, Andrea reluctantly allowed herself to think of Gage. She wondered if there was a message from him at the main desk. Her initial hesitation to call downstairs was justified: there was no message from Gage. As she hung up the receiver, Andrea glanced at her watch. It was almost one o'clock. He had promised to call during the morning, and her plane was leaving at 3:20 P.M. A twinge of desire and a stab of remorse gave her no other option. She picked up the receiver again and dialed the main desk.

The meeting in Cal's room was in full swing by the time Andrea tapped on the door. The men had left her a can of soda and a ham and cheese on rye, which she ate as she listened to the discussion and avoided Cal's eyes. When the meeting was over and the Tectron crew was picking up their attaché cases, Andrea stood up, dusted crumbs from her skirt and announced that she had changed her travel plans. Withstanding Cal's questioning glare, Andrea said casually that she wanted to visit a friend while she was in Seattle and that she'd be returning home on the red-eye.

After storing her luggage in the hotel manager's office, Andrea tucked her clutch under her arm and pushed her way through the heavy hotel lobby doors into the brilliant sunshine. As an even more chilling wind whipped her coat around her legs, she was thankful that she had changed into slacks and a heavy sweater. Pulling her knit cap farther down over her ears, she squinted against the sunlight, shoved her mittened hands into her coat pockets and turned toward the Westlake Mall Monorail platform.

The daylight ride revealed that downtown Seattle was as crowded and pulsating as any busy city during a work-week. At Seattle Center, Andrea disembarked and strolled past the Space Needle, deep in restless thought. Gage's club didn't open until five o'clock, and with three free hours, she needed to spend the time in a familiar setting. The Center was as familiar to her as anything else in Seattle; besides, it had been the site of some very happy and comfortable moments with Gage. As she wandered through the park, oblivious to her surroundings, she thought of home, Christine, headhunting, Cal and Gage.

Slowly, Christmas music reached past her worried musing and pulled her back to reality. She had no idea how long she had been standing in front of the International Fountain, but the late-afternoon shadows were long, and the sunlight had faded into a soft winter glow behind the encroaching fog bank.

As she watched the light shimmer on the millions of water droplets spraying upward in the fountain's sun-flower shape, Andrea remembered the night she and Gage had stood there, his arms around her, his body shielding her from the frigid wind. She remembered the warming sound of his gentle laugh and the peace she had felt in their companionable silence. It had been a world she had not wanted to leave that night. It was a world she still wanted desperately.

Yet Andrea knew that if their budding relationship was to survive, the effort involved would be enormous. But what she and Gage had shared was too natural, too right, to be lost to outside influences and difficulties. After her coolness toward him that morning, she knew it was her move.

Andrea drew in several deep breaths of cold air and
turned back toward the quad and the towering Space
Needle behind the museum buildings.

When she reached the hotel, there were no messages
waiting for her, nor was there an answer to her call to
Gage's room. After collecting her luggage, Andrea hailed
a cab and gave the driver the club's address in Pioneer
Square.

A half hour after it had opened, the club was doing a
light business, with most of its clientele enjoying happy-
hour drinks and hors d'oeuvres. Andrea stood in the foyer
and glanced around the dimly lit room. The pianist who
had relinquished his instrument to Gage the other night
was entertaining the after-work crowd with jazzy rendi-
tions of current hits.

The maitre d' approached Andrea, smiling politely and
obviously remembering her from before. "Good evening, miss. May I help you?"

Andrea set her luggage down. "Yes. I'm looking for..."
She suddenly remembered that she didn't know Gage's
last name. How had they become so close and still did not
know a simple thing like each other's last name? But was
knowing someone's last name really that important?
Wasn't it the emotions they shared that counted the most?

As the man waited patiently, Andrea said, "I'm looking for Gage."

"I'm sorry, but he'd not expected this evening."

Andrea's hopes sank at this announcement. Still, she
smiled sweetly and asked, "Is Mr. Joachim here?"

"Yes. May I tell him who's calling?"

"Andrea."

The maitre d' stepped to a phone and dialed a digit.
After speaking inaudibly for a moment, he hung up the

receiver and picked up Andrea's travel bag and attaché case. "This way, please."

As her luggage and coat were being checked, Dan Joachim bounded up to Andrea's elbow, startling her with his sudden appearance. Andrea gasped, but then, recognizing him, she smiled warmly. "Hi, Danny."

The redheaded man beamed a wide grin at her and patted her shoulder. "Sorry. Didn't mean to frighten the wits out of you." His ice-blue eyes flicked over her, then warmed with the same expression that lit his freckled face. "How are you? This is a pleasant surprise." Grasping her elbow lightly, Dan guided her to a secluded table. "Can I get you a drink?"

Andrea sank into the comfortable chair. "Please."

"Hard? Soft? Coffee?"

"Coffee would be great. Black, please."

As Dan strode to the kitchen, Andrea leaned back in the chair and closed her eyes, listening to the music. She supposed it was silly, but she could almost feel Gage's presence in the club. The sound of a cup being set on the table in front of her drew her attention to Dan. He settled into the chair across from her and studied her through the steam rising from his own mug of coffee.

Andrea picked up the large stoneware mug, which was nonregulation tableware. The coffee was freshly brewed and strong. "Delicious. I needed this after a cold afternoon outdoors." She sipped again at the warming liquid.

Dan set his mug down and pulled a pack of cigarettes from the pocket of his dark blue suit coat. "I didn't think we'd be seeing you again so soon," he said, lighting a cigarette.

Andrea watched the lawyer exhale a thin stream of smoke. She asked nonchalantly, "Any particular reason for thinking that?"

A wily grin creased his thin face. "You're a sharp cookie, aren't you?"

As Andrea met his penetrating gaze, she decided she didn't want to get into a fencing match with him. "I had the impression the other night that you think I should stay away from Gage—or vice versa."

Her directness didn't faze Dan. A slow smile crept across his features. "And the lady shoots straight from the hip."

"And the lawyer likes to play games."

Dan roared with laughter. "You know, Andrea, I like you. Very few people are as honest and direct as you are." He leaned forward, resting his elbows on the table and clasping his hands together. Smoke from the cigarette curled upward. A sober look settled over him, and Andrea knew she was seeing the corporate lawyer image. "Don't read me wrong. I've nothing against you, Andrea."

"Then what is it?"

Dan sucked on the cigarette. "I don't want you to get hurt."

Andrea placed her mug on the table with a gesture of defiance. "Why should you care whether I get hurt or not? You don't know me. I should think that you'd actually be more concerned about Gage."

Dan shook his head. "Gage I know. I don't need to worry about his getting hurt. He's tough and can ride with the punches. You—you're another story. Under that cool professional exterior lies, I sense, a heart of butter that can be cut very easily."

Andrea swiveled slightly from side to side in the barrel chair. Her eyes remained fixed on Dan's face. "Why wouldn't Gage get hurt?"

"His priorities won't allow it."

Andrea stopped swiveling. "What?"

Dan leaned back in his chair and took several drags of his cigarette. The pale eyes watched her closely through the smoke. "As long as his priorities remain what they are, you can't hurt him."

"What you mean is that I can't get close to him."

Dan rubbed out his cigarette in a ceramic ashtray and picked up his coffee mug again. "I didn't say that. In fact, it's my guess that you've gotten much closer to him than he intended. He's not going to let himself get hurt, though. You can bruise him, but you can't wound him."

Andrea's voice rose slightly in dismay. "Why on earth do you think I'd want to hurt Gage? What have I done to give you the impression that I'm trying to hurt him?"

Dan studied the pained expression on her face for a long, silent minute. When he spoke, his tone was matter-of-fact. "You don't know, do you?"

"Know what?"

The lawyer lit another cigarette, evidently using the stall to weigh things in his mind. "I think this is something you had better square with Gage. I'm not going to step out of bounds here. Sorry, Andrea." There was nothing in his voice to give her any more information than his answer had.

For several moments, Dan and Andrea stared silently at each other. Finally, she faltered under his unyielding eyes and looked down at the half-empty mug. Running her finger over the handle, she said quietly, "It's all been very confusing. I wasn't expecting to find myself feeling this way."

Dan reached across the table and placed his hand on her arm. "Do any of us expect to find love when we aren't looking for it?"

Andrea's head jerked up, her eyes studying the man's serious, thin face. Her thoughts were racing. She had never used the word "love" when thinking about Gage. Was it possible? No, she couldn't be in love with Gage—she had known him for only six days! They were practically strangers. No. She was not in love with him. It was impossible. She felt merely a certain fondness for him, a fondness that she couldn't deny.

Dan leaned back in his chair and shook his head in wonder. There was a note of amusement in his voice when he said, "This is going to be interesting."

"Why do you say that?" she demanded.

Merriment danced in the ice-blue eyes, and his grin was ear-to-ear. "You had better save all that energy for the battle ahead. You'll need it."

Bristling under Dan's laughing eyes, Andrea was still feeling confused. "Battle? What battle?"

Dan's gaze moved from her face to somewhere past her right shoulder, and she turned in her seat. The rush of excitement that warmed her blood was replaced by a deadening chill as her eyes met Gage's.

Gage stepped to Dan's side and stood there, towering over his friend, who lounged in the chair. A stony expression molded Gage's rugged features. Undaunted, Dan grinned and waved a hand at the chair that remained empty between him and Andrea. "What'll you have to drink? Coffee or scotch?"

"Neither," Gage snapped, easing into the empty chair.

Dan glanced at Andrea and saw the emotions that warred on her face. He unfolded his wiry frame and said, "Well, the dinner crowd will be here soon. Guess I'll go and see how things are cooking in the kitchen." Stepping around Gage, Dan paused at Andrea's side and touched her arm lightly. "Be sure to say good-bye before you leave."

The warmth in his eyes was unmistakable, and Andrea felt encouraged by it. She smiled timorously. "I will. And...thanks, Danny."

He gave her arm a squeeze, then marched toward the kitchen.

Gage stared at Dan's departing back. "I was surprised to hear that you had come here."

"Dan called you?"

He swiveled his chair to face her. "Yes. So what are you doing here?"

Andrea gripped her mug with both hands and sipped at the cold coffee. She said quietly, "You didn't call me."

"I'm sorry about that." His usually warm tone was icy. "Things got hectic this morning."

"And you forgot."

His eyes, bloodshot now, met her reserved gaze unflinchingly. "Yes, I forgot. I had a lot of important things to take care of."

"More important than us?" she asked softly.

He ran his hand over the tabletop as if dusting crumbs from the cloth. His answer was succinct. "Yes."

"I'm glad you respect me enough not to lie to me. But I thought that what we had was important to each of us." She looked at him, waiting for an answer. Gage sat immobile in his chair, watching his fingers drum lightly on the table. When he continued to remain silent, Andrea said, "After this morning, I felt we needed to talk—that there were things that had to be said."

"Like what?" he asked casually, signaling a waiter.

Anger flared in her and she snapped, "Oh, don't bother playing the aloof cold-blooded playboy with me. It won't wash."

After ordering a drink, Gage asked, "Why not?"

"Because I've known enough playboys to be able to spot one. And one thing you are *not* is a calculating, uncaring playboy."

Gage met her clouded eyes. "It sounds like you've been hurt by one of those men."

"The past has nothing to do with this."

"Why not? As angry as you sound, I'd say you're reacting to someone else, not to me." Gage sipped at his drink, eyeing her over the rim of the glass.

"Don't psychoanalyze me, Gage. The problem isn't in the past." She tapped the table as she said, "It's right here." Her blue eyes flashed fire, daring him to argue with her.

Gage sighed. "Look, I've had a miserable day and I'm beat. I don't want to fight with you, Andrea. It's obvious that the past few days have meant more to you than to me." His eyes, carefully masked, flicked over her face, then down to the glass in his hand.

Andrea stared at him for a long minute, the background sounds of the club unheard in the silence between them. Her voice was heavy with pain. "I don't believe that. I can't."

Resignation tinged his words. "Think what you wish."

Only the people sitting so near them kept her from screaming at him. "Quit playing the role of a callous and cruel man to the hilt. Please," she pleaded, "be honest with me."

Exasperation flooded his voice as Gage's temper snapped. "For God's sake, what do you want me to say, Andrea? That it was wonderful? And that I wished it didn't have to end?"

Shaken by his hostility, she gave a weak smile nevertheless. "That would be a start."

He stared at her a long moment, then ran his hands through his hair and sighed deeply. "All right. It was wonderful. I admit it. But it has to end."

"Why?" she whispered.

Gage leaned toward her, laying his hand on hers. "Because it won't work. It's that simple."

Andrea's hand trembled under his, and she pulled it free of his grasp. "Is there another woman?" she asked quietly.

As she withdrew from him, Gage settled back in his chair and crossed a booted ankle onto a knee. "No. There isn't another woman."

Her voice was a soft wail. "Then tell me what I've done to...to change the way you feel about me."

A muscle twitched in the square stubborn jaw. "Just forget us, Andrea."

"Why? Why should I forget us? Why won't it work?" Her eyes burned bright with unshed tears.

"Because this was all one huge mistake." The coldness in his voice faded minutely as Gage added, "Let's not perpetuate it."

Biting her lower lip, Andrea thought a moment. "You keep mentioning mistakes." She shrugged, shaking her head sadly. "But what's the mistake? Is it a mistake to meet someone you like and then care about? Is that such a terrible thing?"

Gage's eyes dropped to the tabletop. His voice was hard to hear over the background sounds of conversation and tinkling ice. "No, it's not. It's what I've done that is the mistake. I should never have gotten involved with you. I had a wild idea, but I didn't have the guts to follow it through." Troubled eyes met hers only for a moment. "Forgive me, Andrea."

As her heart thudded dully in her chest, Andrea said, "I don't understand."

Gage spoke more to himself than to her. "No, I don't think you do. But you will—someday." After a poignant pause, he said softly, "I'm sorry, Andrea."

She rose, pushing her chair back roughly. Her body was stiff with pain and dismay. "Not nearly as sorry as I am." She snatched up her clutch purse and threaded her way quickly between the now-crowded tables.

After asking the maitre d' to call her a taxi, Andrea retrieved her luggage and coat. As she tried to pull her coat on in jerky tugs, Dan appeared and took it from her. "Here let me help you." She turned her back and ducked her head, trying to hide the tears that edged her lashes. While she fumbled with the buttons on her coat, Dan said, "So it didn't go well."

Andrea mumbled, "No," and sniffed.

Dan picked up her travel bag and attaché case and slipped his other arm around her shoulders. As a group of noisy patrons entered the foyer, he guided her around them and outside, saying, "Let me give you a lift to the airport."

Under the dim pool of light from the fog-shrouded streetlight, Andrea turned to Dan with a faint smile. "Thanks for the offer, but no, thanks. A cab is on its way right now."

"You're sure?" He set her luggage on the sidewalk and stepped back.

"I'm sure." Watching him shiver in the brittle wind, she added, "It's freezing out here. You go back inside. I'll be okay until the cab comes."

"No way. I'll not have people accusing us of abandoning innocents on doorsteps." Dan grinned a moment; then his expression sobered. "Too bad things had to work out this way. Just bad timing. Gage can't handle both what's happening to his company and the problems related to a romance right now. Things might have been different at another time."

Andrea murmured, "You don't have to apologize for him, Danny."

The lawyer shrugged. "I'm not. I'm merely trying to explain the situation to you—which I'm sure he didn't—without betraying my loyalty and position. Ah, here's your taxi."

He helped her into the taxicab while the driver loaded her luggage into the front seat. As she settled back, Dan said cautiously, "Andrea, things are going to get rough." He pulled a business card from the breast pocket of his suit coat. "If you ever need anything, call me. Okay?"

Her eyes darted from the card in her hand to the steady eyes that watched her so intently. "I don't understand."

"You will soon enough." Dan straightened, preparing to close the car door. "Take care of yourself, Andrea." He shut the door and stepped back to the center of the sidewalk.

Although she was perturbed by his cryptic remarks, she tried to smile. Realizing he wouldn't be able to see her face in the darkness, she merely waved good-bye as the driver pulled the cab away from the curb. The slight figure on the sidewalk returned her wave for a moment, then shoved his hands into his pockets. Dan was still standing there, watching the taxi drive off, when Andrea slowly turned in her seat to face front.

The trip to Seattle had proved to be worse than she had ever anticipated, in ways she had never dreamed of. Now she wanted only to escape and leave the pain behind in this cold, rainy city, with the quiet, complex man who had made her feel completely alive and loved, if only for a few days.

As the taxi rolled onto a freeway entrance ramp for the ride south to SeaTac Airport, Andrea knew she wouldn't forget Seattle, Danny or Gage. But life had to return to normal. There was no room for rainy-day romances in Los Angeles. L.A. was home, and Andrea needed to be home more than ever now where she was free and on her own, independent and needing no one.

Chapter Ten

Andrea laid the paperback novel on the velvet arm of the
swivel rocker and uncurled her legs, stretching her toes to
a point under the heavy hand-knit afghan. Moments earlier the back door had slammed shut, and now she heard
Christine's footsteps padding in the hallway. Her sister
stepped into the cream painted and carpeted living room,
a bag of groceries perched on each hip. Andrea smiled. "I
hope you didn't forget the clams for tomorrow night's
dinner."

"Of course not." Christine stomped into the kitchen
with her load.

Vaguely amused by her sister, Andrea hoped that
Christine would change from the perpetual uniform of
faded jeans, torn sweatshirt and scuffed cowboy boots to
something more suitable for pre-Christmas entertaining.
Her gaze swept around the older Santa Monica apartment, sparsely but beautifully furnished in the pastel-
colored, original Art Deco pieces their parents had owned
and that Andrea had managed to keep from the creditors
after the accident.

Christine had done a good job of cleaning the apartment. It was the first time in nearly two months that her
sister had done more than the dishes, Andrea noted

dourly. She had known in Seattle, during her phone call home, that something special must be happening to motivate Christine to do any housecleaning. Her sister had invited a young man to dinner the next evening, explaining to Andrea that he needed a good meal or two during the Christmas vacation from campus meals.

In the corner of the small living room stood the six-foot-tall Douglas fir Christmas tree they had bought the evening before, on Andrea's first night back home.

Andrea tossed the afghan off and padded across the carpet in her bare feet. She ran her hands lightly over the tree limbs, its needles pricking against the palms of her hands. Its scent reminded her of the smell of Seattle on a rain-freshened night.

"Are you going to spend all weekend moping?" Christine flopped on the thirties-style stuffed sofa. Her mood was quarrelsome, and Andrea didn't want to get into an argument with her again that day.

"Chris, you know I'm tired. I had two rough trips back to back. Lay off."

"Just because some guy did a song and dance and dumped you is no reason to get so depressed." Christine ran a freckled hand through her curly brown hair.

"I'm not depressed. I'm tired. And I'm sorry that I even told you about him." Not that she had told her everything about Gage or the unsettled feelings he had left in her.

Christine said grumpily, "I think we need a diversion." She jumped up from the sofa and dove into a hall closet to pull out two large paper bags full of Christmas ornaments. "Let's hop to it and get this tree decorated. Maybe that will help the holiday blues."

"Holiday blues? Who's had time even to think about Christmas?" While Christine unpacked the bags of or-

naments and lights, Andrea moved the tree out from the
wall to make decorating easier. "I know what we need—
some music to set the mood. Where are the Christmas
albums?"

"In my room."

"I think I'll make hot chocolate, too."

"Lace mine with brandy!"

After a mug of spiked cocoa apiece, they were feeling
jovial and were definitely getting into the spirit of the season. By dusk, the tree was trimmed and set back in its corner. Andrea did the honors and plugged in the lights.

From the kitchen doorway, Christine breathed, "It's
lovely!"

Andrea took the refilled mug Christine held out. "It is,
isn't it?" Settling into the rocker, she studied their han-
diwork. The soft strains of an Andy Williams Christmas
album filtered through the oversized stereo speakers in the
corners of the room, and for the first time in more than
two weeks, Andrea felt relaxed. If she had one more cup
of hot chocolate, she thought, she might not even worry
about facing Cal when she went in to work the next morning. She knew that more conversation about her knowledge of NavCom Electronics, Len Daggett and Cal's role
in both NCE and ComSearch was upcoming.

Christine disappeared down the hallway but returned
a minute later with a gaily wrapped box in her hand. "The
first for the tree," she announced, putting the small,
professionally wrapped package under the tree.

"Who's it for?"

A giggle caught in her sister's throat, and Andrea
watched a blush color Christine's face. "It's for me."

"Oh?" Andrea wondered why her sister was blushing;
it was so unlike her. "Who's it from?"

"A friend." Christine eased down onto the plush ivory carpet in front of the tree and wrapped her arms around her knees.

"Christine!"

"Oh, all right. His name is Roger."

"The boy who's coming to dinner tomorrow night?"

"One and the same."

"Oh." Andrea didn't like the happy little sound of hopefulness in her sister's voice.

Christine stared over her shoulder at her sister, who sat huddled in the rocker. "You aren't going to grill him like you did the last guy I brought home, are you?"

"I didn't grill Jim."

"Like hell—heck you didn't. I never saw him again. He disappeared as if I had the plague."

"Then he wasn't for you, was he?" Andrea pulled the afghan into her lap. Remembering the case of instant creeps the young man—and he was a man, not a teenaged boy—had given her, she said bluntly, "I didn't like him."

"No kidding? I would never have guessed," Christine griped sarcastically. "Just because the guy had motorcycle grease under his nails and made a pass at you—"

"Didn't that make you mad?" Andrea interrupted.

"No."

"Oh, Christine, be honest. The guy was a creep. I wouldn't be surprised if he wasn't another Hillside Strangler."

"That's your opinion—and warped it is, too."

Andrea smiled at the English inflection that occasionally slipped into her sister's speech. Christine's mother had been English and had never lost her accent while living in the United States. Christine had picked up the inflections; Andrea had not. "You might be right."

"You know I am."

"I just think that any guy who makes passes at your older sister probably has rather suspicious motives."

Christine grinned. "Not if he makes passes at every female he meets, young or old."

Not understanding her sister's choice of friends, Andrea shook her head and reached for the mug sitting on the angular, gray-lacquered lamp table beside the rocker. "Just who is Roger?"

"A guy from my department."

An archaeology student. Andrea groaned slightly. "Why don't you invite a girlfriend and make it a foursome?"

"Oh, I can't do that." Christine's grin was devious. "This is special."

"Chris, I hardly think that your young friend will want your nearly over the hill sister at your dinner. He'll think I'm here chaperoning you. And you know I stopped that a year ago."

"You aren't over the hill. You have two more years before you're thirty."

"One and a half, but who's counting?" Andrea stood up, mug in hand, and headed for the kitchen.

"But I want you to be there. I think you'll like Roger. He's really a neat guy."

"Neat?" She paused in the doorway. "I doubt that. If he's an archaeology student, he'll show up in torn jeans, stained T-shirt and with dirt under his nails."

Christine smiled slyly. "Roger's not like that."

The expression that was dancing in her sister's eyes was more than a little naughty, Andrea thought. Perhaps she should stay around. She drew in a deep breath, then spoke carefully. "Well, I had planned on starting my Christmas shopping tomorrow night, but I guess it can wait until

Tuesday. Besides, I love the way you cook clams bordelaise.''

EARLY THE NEXT MORNING Cal called the office and said he was feeling under the weather and would not be in. With his absence, Andrea's day was more pleasant. Any possible confrontation had been postponed at least twenty-four hours. Forcing her mind off the conflict in Seattle, she spent the day filling in all of the recruiting staff on the outcome of the Seattle raid and the prospects for hires at Tectron. In her few spare moments, she wondered about dinner; Christine could be so conniving.

When Andrea returned home from work that evening, the apartment was virtually spotless, with everything in its place. There were even cut flowers on the dining table. Christine was in the kitchen whistling ''Deck the Halls'' and chopping parsley. She looked up from the cutting board as Andrea moved toward the refrigerator. ''Well, what do you think?''

''I'm impressed. I think the young man will be also.'' Andrea leaned a hip against the counter and crossed her arms. ''Chris, why don't you tell me what's up?''

Christine wiped her hands on the festive apron that covered her white mohair sweater and red gabardine jeans. ''Why must you think something's up?''

''Because you never dress up and cook a fancy meal unless you're up to something.''

Christine stated matter-of-factly, ''Clams bordelaise is not fancy.''

''It's not a Big Mac and fries, either. I'll go change.'' Andrea turned in the doorway. ''When do you expect him?''

''In ten minutes, and Roger's always punctual. So hurry!''

Roger was a few minutes early. He arrived before Andrea had finished dressing. She could hear the muted chatter of Christine's clear tomboy tones and a slightly lower, more mellow voice. Andrea slipped into black slacks and a short-sleeved gray cashmere pullover. If she was meeting a possibly serious suitor of Christine's, she wanted to look as matronly as possible. If this Roger was a clone of the motorcycle masher, she wanted to look intimidating. She pulled her hair into a bun at the nape of her neck and slipped a hand-crocheted snood over it. Changing her sterling-silver hoop earrings for the black pearl studs, she slicked on a glimmer of lip gloss before switching off her bedroom light.

Roger stood with his back to her as she entered the living room, but Christine quickly diverted his attention from herself to her sister, "Andi, come her so I can introduce you!"

As Andrea moved to her sister's side, her appraising glance flicked over the young man.

"Andi, this is Roger. Roger, this is my big sister, Andrea."

Suppressing a smile at Christine's reference to her age, Andrea held out her hand. The sandy-haired, twenty-year-old student, dressed in pressed designer jeans and a striped velour sweatshirt, took her hand and returned her firm handshake. Andrea mirrored his friendly smile and decided that she liked his looks. "Nice to meet you, Roger."

"Likewise, ma'am."

Andrea blinked, wondering where Christine had met this polite, well-scrubbed young man, who looked and sounded as if he had just deserted the family farm somewhere in the Midwest. "Please, call me Andrea."

Roger smiled again. "Yes, ma'am."

Christine's hazel eyes darted between Andrea and Roger. As her eyebrows disappeared under her long, frizzy bangs, she said, "Well, dinner's almost ready. Why don't you two sit down and relax, and I'll get the wine." To Roger, she added, "Andi will let minors have one drink. But don't push it after that—house rules."

Andrea settled into the rocker. Roger perched himself on the edge of the sofa. He looked ill at ease, and she wondered why. "Is something wrong?" she asked.

"No, ma'am, uh, Andrea."

Christine handed him a glass of white wine, and he flashed a row of even white teeth at her. "Thanks, Chris."

Andrea sipped at the glass in her hand and watched the boy watch her sister disappear into the kitchen, behind the swinging café doors. No doubt about it, Roger had a crush on Christine. And judging from the anxiety Christine was displaying the crush was mutual. *Ah, young love,* Andrea thought with a sigh.

Roger sat up even straighter and said, "Look, uh, Andrea, I don't like this, but, uh, I think there's something you should know."

His nervousness made Andrea leery. "What's that, Roger?

"I'm supposed to do a number on you to make you more agreeable to letting Chris go on the Chaco Canyon dig this summer."

"No!" Andrea's temper flared. "I've said no and I mean it!"

Roger shrugged. "That's exactly what Chris said your attitude would be. That's why I'm here. Although I did tell her I thought it was useless—why should you listen to me? But she wanted me to try."

Andrea had to admire the young man's honesty and earnestness. Reining in her temper, she asked, "Is that the extent of this conversation?"

His sunny grin was completely disarming. "No, there's a whole sales pitch I'm supposed to go through."

"Oh." She had been right; this dinner was part of a scheme to win her over to Chris's way of thinking.

"You will let me go through it, won't you? I don't want Chris to think I chickened out."

Sighing, Andrea said, "You'll be wasting your time, I'm afraid."

Christine pushed the café doors open and carried a laden tray to the table. "Soup's on!"

Roger stood up and smiled at Andrea in a manner that she thought was too old for his years; it revealed how intelligent and mature he really was. As he stood aside for her, he murmured, "We'll see."

Christine was setting out steaming bowls of clams, broth and rice. Roger pulled out a chair for Andrea. While he slid her chair in, she gave him a warning look and prepared herself for warfare.

But dinner, despite the trend of the conversation, was a pleasant experience. Andrea thought it was nice to have a man sitting at their dining table, moderating the fighting between the sisters, lending a calm, levelheaded presence to the proceedings. And she definitely liked his style, although it would be a few more years before the maturity he exhibited would remain constant. But as Roger brought arguments to an end with a reasonable, quick witticism and corrected Christine for being too harsh on her sister, Andrea decided that Christine had finally found a winner.

Apparently Christine thought the same. Her hazel eyes sparkled with a liveliness Andrea had not seen since before the accident. The fact that the girl was obviously devoted to Roger disturbed her, but there was something about him that made Andrea believe that the situation would not get out of hand. Whatever developed would be their choice, a mutual choice. And as long as they cared for each other the way they appeared to now, Andrea knew everything would be fine.

Watching the two bicker good-naturedly across the table, she felt a profound sadness come over her. If things could only have been difference with Gage! He had made her feel the way she imagined her sister felt—safe, loved, wanted. These were the things that a person needed in life to feel whole. What had she done, or failed to do, that had made Gage so decisive? The memory of their last conversation was a painful wound. Each of the many times that Andrea had looked back and tried to discover her mistake, she could come up with only one answer. There was something in their relationship so powerful, yet so negative, that all the gentle words and feelings between them counted for nothing. What that something was consistently eluded Andrea, and her tired, befuddled mind was beginning to rebel against the task she had assigned it.

Laying her dessert spoon down, she leaned back in the bentwood chair and closed her eyes against the tears that threatened to spill over at such an inopportune time. *Oh, Gage, why couldn't you tell me what's wrong?* she moaned silently. *I feel like I'm looking for a needle in a whole field of haystacks!*

Fighting the tears back and breathing deeply, Andrea resolved that she would discover what that destructive thing was. And, if it were ever possible, she would try to heal the wounds that she was sure both of them suffered from. If she didn't do it for love, she could at least do it for friendship.

And there was no doubt in her mind that they were friends.

DESPITE ROGER'S ATTEMPT to interject some common sense and reason into the conflict over the Chaco Canyon dig, the battle continued. Christine was furious that Andrea would not change her mind, no matter how stridently she and Roger had tried. Coming home Tuesday after work, Andrea felt as if she were walking into a mine field. Christine had obviously decided to make this summer trip to New Mexico the *cause célèbre*. Bitter and angry words flowed the entire evening.

The next morning, Andrea swung her classic Mustang into the parking lot behind the house that had been remodeled into the ComSearch office building, located three blocks north of the mid-Wilshire district of Los Angeles. While she pulled her shoulder bag and attaché case from the backseat, she yawned broadly. then sneezed. Locking the car, she thought miserably, *If I don't get some rest, I'll catch the flu bug that's going around, for sure.*

She had some trouble fitting her key into the kitchen-door lock. She fussed with it for several long seconds before the old tumblers finally worked properly. As she stepped into the modernized kitchen, Andrea called out, "Anybody here?"

She glanced at her watch. It was eight twenty-seven and only Wednesday. If the interview board for the next week was filled—as it was this morning for the short holiday workweek—the ComSearch staff wandered in late. Laying her belongings on the kitchen table, she checked the thirty-cup coffeepot. It was cold and still held the grounds from the previous afternoon's brew. Wrinkling her nose, she dumped the filter and its contents into the trash.

It was nearly nine o'clock when, as Andrea poured her first cup of coffee, three members of the staff appeared. A few moments later, Cal's lemon-yellow Lotus roared into the parking lot below the kitchen window. Andrea gathered up her things, exchanged greetings and strolled, coffee cup in hand, through the large two-story house to her upstairs office.

She set everything down in the center of her desk, since that was the only cleared-off spot. Piles of recruiting cards, group sheets, aerospace company telephone directories and assorted notes lined the edges of the desktop in an orderly manner. The five-button telephone sat on the left corner of the desk, and within moments, Andrea could find any piece of paper she needed. She pulled up the venetian blinds to let in the dazzling December sunlight streaming through the leaf-bare tree limbs outside.

Downstairs, the furnace creaked to life; that meant her office partner had arrived. Larry was the only one who thought to turn the heat on in the morning.

As Andrea leaned back in her desk chair, sipping at the steaming coffee, Larry bounced into the office. He grinned at her and immediately turned on the portable radio they used to liven the deadness of slow mornings. After propping his ragged-sneakered feet on top of his desk, he flipped through the *Daily Racing Form* looking for the day's best picks.

While Larry phoned his bookie, Andrea pulled out the recruiting cards for those people she hoped to set up to see Tectron and her other customers in two weeks' time. She went through the piles of cards twice, then looked over at Larry. "Hey, Larry, did you or Cal use any of my cards yesterday after I left?"

"No. In fact, we were out of here only a few minutes after you departed. We were the last ones out, too. Why?"

"I can't find some of my paperwork."

"You probably misplaced it." Larry plopped his feet on his clean desk again and went back to studying the racing sheet.

Andrea flipped through everything a third time. "It's not here," she grumbled under her breath. She then buzzed all the other offices on the com line, asking if anyone had picked up some of her paperwork. As she hung up the receiver, Andrea shook her head in disbelief. Slowly, she went through the drawers in her desk. After she had slammed the last drawer shut, she jumped up and trotted down the stairs, calling, "Cal! Cal!"

Cal sat behind his desk, already on the telephone with Ed Rees. He waved an impatient hand, motioning her to be quiet. Andrea glanced around his office, then surveyed the top of his antique oak desk, looking for familiar items that were always there.

"Cal, I think you'd better hang up. Something's wrong. Very wrong." At her words, he dropped the receiver noisily into its cradle and swiveled to face her. "I'm missing paperwork—a lot of paperwork. I'm also missing the company directories I was pulling names and phone numbers out of yesterday afternoon."

Cal glared at her with ill-concealed irritability, as he had done every time they'd spoken since that morning in Seattle. "One of the other guys probably has them."

Andrea ignored his anger. "Nobody has them. And I don't see all the books that are usually on your desk, either."

Larry stepped into the doorway behind Andrea, a scowl on his plump face. "Say, Cal, I'm missing that organization chart for Tectron—the one you gave me last night right before we left. I put it in the center drawer of my desk, but it's gone. Andrea's missing papers, too."

Cal surged out of his chair, striding urgently to the upstairs room they used to store supplies and files. His key fought the lock for a moment before it turned. The trio stepped into the office and looked around. The room was as neat and tidy as usual—except that the three-shelf bookcase that normally stored the company telephone directories not in current use at the recruiters' desks was empty.

There was fear on his face as a frantic Cal began to unlock the five-drawer steel filing cabinets. All nine cabinets held fifteen years' worth of recruiting files. Cal barked, "You two, go through these and see if you can spot any missing files. I'm going to check the other offices." As he rushed from the room, Andrea and Larry exchanged nervous glances and yanked drawers open.

A half hour later, the twenty ComSearch staff members lounged around the kitchen anxiously. They sat at the table or stood against the empty cabinets, chain-smoking or drinking the strong coffee that none of their nerves needed at the moment. Andrea sagged into a chair and sat with her elbows on the tabletop, her chin resting on her clasped hands.

Cal stormed into the kitchen and stopped abruptly, folding his arms across his muscular chest. Like his employees, he was dressed casually in jeans and a polo shirt. But, unlike them, he was in a cold rage. He studied each employee shrewdly. Finally his suspicious gaze rested on Andrea. She didn't see his glance stop when it flicked in her direction. She didn't have to. She could feel his eyes boring into her.

His anger barely controlled, Cal said, "Okay. Someone's hit us. Whoever did it took all of our key applicants' paperwork and cleaned us out of resources. Does anyone have an idea who might have done this?"

There was a long, tension-filled silence. Andrea thought that if anyone did know anything about the burglary, he— or, in her case, she—would be a fool to admit it. For the past hour, Cal had not seemed above violence. Andrea kept her eyes on the scratched Formica tabletop.

Finally Larry spoke. "Do you think whoever did it was trying to put us out of business?"

"No," Cal answered confidently. "If they had meant us to be out of business, they would have burned us out. No, they mean to make it hard—*very* hard—for us to do our jobs. Does anyone have any idea why?"

Andrea felt Cal's eyes burning their focus into the top of her bowed head. Fear kept her own eyes on the tabletop.

When no one had answered Cal's question, Larry asked, "Why don't we call the cops?"

"No!" Cal roared immediately, then continued in a more controlled voice, "Our loss is undeterminable. No insurance company could pay us for losses. Besides, how do we explain to the police that most of what was stolen was in our possession illegally? All of your initials are in those company directories—besides every name you've ever called and recruited. Remember, as far as most of the industry is concerned, we are operating on the fringe of legality and are tolerated only because we're a necessary evil. While most engineers and companies look down their noses at us, we provide a service that makes their lives a little easier. But remember, if anyone ever took us to court, your initials in those phone books would implicate you." Cal paused for effect. "No, we'll change the locks, and only I and the managers will have keys to the building and the offices. So I want all of you to turn your keys in to me by the end of the morning. That's it."

As Andrea rose to follow the shuffling pairs of feet out of the kitchen, Cal snapped, "I'd like to see you in my office, Andi."

Once inside his office, Andrea eased herself into the leather softness of the enormous sofa and faced the over-sized desk. Cal closed and locked the door, then walked slowly around the desk. Andrea watched the seconds tick off on her wristwatch.

Sitting down in the leather swivel chair, he steepled his fingers under his chin and stared pointedly at his star recruiter. Andrea's face wore a cool, slightly defiant expression, but her blue eyes held a trace of fear. She met his direct gaze and waited silently. Finally Cal asked in a smooth, curious tone, "Who do you think did this?"

She blinked innocently and said, "I have no idea. Why? Should I?"

"I can think of a few reasons."

"Let's hear them." Andrea's gaze didn't falter. "I would be interested in knowing why you think I might know something about this."

"You know more about my operation than anyone here," he reminded her. When she didn't answer, he continued grimly, "Papers dealing with NavCom Electronics were stolen from my desk last night. My desk was locked, and there is no sign that the lock had been forced. Only the manager and you have keys to my desk. Only you would know the importance of those papers."

Cal was probably correct on that point, Andrea mused. Of all the staff, she was probably the only one who knew of his connection with the Carson company. That kind of information was not something that more than one or two people would know. Still...

Andrea asked quietly, "Have you forgotten the word 'loyalty'?"

He stared back at her, his expression incredulous. She knew that loyalty meant nothing to a Machiavellian man. To him, it didn't exist. Yet he recognized that other people believed in such a trait.

Cal changed tack. "Well, if you think of anything, let me know immediately. Even if it's in the middle of the night."

"I will." Andrea rose. "Is that all?"

"No, it's not. The main reason I called you in is that I have a special job for you to work on today." He reached into the leather briefcase that lay open on the credenza. Sliding a sheet of paper across the desktop, he said, "I want you to call that group today—every name on the list. I want you to recruit each one as you would any other recruit, but I also want you to work in the questions scribbled down in the corner. I want the answers to those questions from each person you talk to. Each question. Every person."

Andrea felt cold. Cal was up to his dirty tricks again with another illegal activity. And, once again, she was the central figure. Pretending naïveté, she asked, "What's this for?"

"Tectron is having problems delivering the software package on the NSG program. Grant International has the same contract with the government. If they deliver the system ahead of Tectron, our customer will lose the second-phase contract bidding." Cal leered at her. "We're going to find out how Grant is doing, what their timing is, if they're having any problems."

"I assume that you're using 'we' editorially," Andrea snapped.

"That's right. You are going to call those Grant engineers and do a little industrial espionage for our customer.'' The owner of ComSearch and co-owner of NavCom Electronics waited for her response.

Andrea knew she couldn't flatly refuse to do it. She had done this type of calling before, although she always had serious conflicts with her conscience about the ethics of this work. If she refused now, Cal would have more reason to suspect that she knew something about the break-in. She needed a stall.

''Cal, I've got so much work to catch up on—those trips to Atlanta and Seattle threw me off schedule in working my interviews and offers on the board right now. I just don't have the time.''

His voice was brittle. ''Make it.''

Andrea bit back the words she wanted to hurl at him. Picking up the sheet of paper and glancing at it, she said as calmly as she could, ''You're the boss.''

''You'd better remember that, Andrea.'' Cal leaned back in his chair again and smiled smugly.

She turned toward the door. Cal was playing yet another game, and he had involved her in it. This was a dangerous one, and she had to be careful. If she didn't handle the questioning of the Grant engineers just right, if the tone of her voice said that she was doing more than simple headhunting, she could land ComSearch and herself in trouble. If that happened, Cal, of course, would declare his innocence, claiming that she had acted on her own. There would be no files to support her stance; the paper in her hands was even in an unknown person's handwriting. Situations like this had happened to others. It could happen to her so easily.

As Andrea grasped the doorknob, Cal spoke again. ''By the way, Andi, I trust you remember our conversation in Seattle.''

She glanced over her shoulder in his direction, squinting against the sun backlighting the man through the window behind him.

"Remember, you mention our little secret to anyone—and you'll have to deal with me, I don't think you'd like what I have in mind for solving that type of problem. In fact, I'm sure you wouldn't like it."

Knowing that Cal felt he had her cowering again, Andrea nodded and left the office wordlessly. As she slowly climbed the stairs to her office, she sank into a deep state of depression and bitterly wished that she could afford to quit that moment.

Was there anything she could do? She doubted it. Yet...

Memories of the Seattle raid had been plaguing her ever since her return: Cal's revelation about his involvement with NavCom Electronics; Len Daggett's interviewing of the Stratcom engineers; the telephone conversation she had overheard between Len and Cal in regard to Stratcom's president and the dangerous situation that Len wanted out of. Her hotel room had been searched, and Len had believed the man named McLaren was behind it. ComSearch had been burglarized, and by someone who knew exactly what to look for and to steal. She had to assume that McLaren was behind this break-in also. Something Len had said about him niggled at her brain.

Andrea wandered into her office, oblivious to Larry's questioning stare. Sinking into her chair, she replayed a mental tape recording of the overheard conversation. Len had said that McLaren was unpredictable, dangerous. Lord, she thought, a burglary like this was certainly an unpredictable way to retaliate against the small raid on his company. If the man hated headhunters to the degree that he'd order something like this done, what else was he capable of? Andrea frowned. Len had also said that Mc-

Laren was volatile. And she would be extending offers to two of the Stratcom engineers next week. What would the head of that company do when he heard about that? She didn't think she wanted to know.

Nevertheless, Andrea decided that the only prudent course of action was to learn all she could about Edward McLaren. She reached for the telephone.

THE DECEMBER SUN was blood-red on the horizon as Andrea walked toward it on the Santa Monica pier early that evening. A gentle, unseasonably warm breeze swirled her hair into her face. Above her, a single gull called out, its screech a lonely warning. Stepping to the side of the pier, she rested her arms on the old wood railing and looked down at the easy-rolling surf that was washing up onto the beach below. The two-foot breakers were no challenge to the local surfers, but red riptide warning flags were posted up and down the beach. Gazing northward through the light of dusk along the beach, she saw no one in the water, but hundreds of late-afternoon sunbathers were still camped out on the sand.

With sundown, the temperature began its usual plummet, and Andrea zipped up her lightweight parka. Turning back toward the fish-and-chip shop, she pushed her hands into her jeans pockets and searched for coins among her keys. Another gull circled over her head, its wings spread, soaring on the air currents. Andrea stopped and craned her head back. Her eyes followed the large white-and-gray bird. For one moment, she wished she were that bird, free to fly away as it desired, to roost where it wanted. As the gull finally flapped its wings and went higher, Andrea sighed and looked down at the worn boardwalk under her jogging shoes. She wasn't free and she had to remain here. The sound of the carousel starting up, its music jubilantly floating on the evening air, lifted her spirits a bit. She continued toward the food stand, where she was to keep her appointment.

The crowd was light that night. Andrea assumed that most people were out Christmas shopping; the holiday was less than a week away. Still, there was a carnival atmosphere under the pier's garish neon lighting. The pier was one of Andrea's favorite places, one of the reasons she lived in Santa Monica. She always came to it when she was feeling down.

At the fish-and-chip shop, she bought a cup of coffee and asked for the time. Hopefully, the traffic going north from the South Bay wouldn't be the usual horrendous rush-hour jam. She wanted to learn what she needed to learn and then go home, lock herself in her bedroom and think.

She heard her name called out and turned. Kipp Cross lumbered up, a white motorcycle helmet in his hand and a friendly grin on his face. Unzipping his black leather jacket, he joked, "Can you spare a buddy a dime?"

"Sure. It's the least I can do after you rode all the way up here." Andrea turned back to the girl behind the counter. "What do you want, Kipp?"

"Coffee." He ran an hand through his shaggy mop of light brown hair. "That robber down in the parking lot took all my change. When did the rates go up?"

"Make that a large coffee, please." Andrea turned back to Kipp after placing the money on the counter. "Last month. Isn't it awful? I'm glad I live close enough to walk here. I certainly wouldn't want to have to pay to park. The price of these beach lots is getting steep."

Kipp stirred cream into the thick black coffee. "Just what was it you wanted to talk about but wouldn't discuss on the phone?"

Andrea motioned to a bench by the railing, out of the surrounding pools of light. "Let's sit down."

Watching Kipp settle his bulk onto the wooden bench and cross a size-thirteen motorcycle boot onto a knee, Andrea smiled. "Right off, I want to thank you for agreeing to meet me."

"How could I resist?" Kipp's laugh was infectious. "You sounded so mysterious on the phone. I thought I'd just landed a part in a new James Bond film."

She looked into her coffee and, responding to Kipp's cheerful manner, mused, "Maybe you have." During the long pause that followed, she gathered all her mental fortitude together and decided that she had to plunge into it. Meeting Kipp's curious gaze, she said, "You're the only person in the aerospace industry I know I can trust."

"This sounds heavy." Kipp raised his Styrofoam cup. "Is this the place where I get the option of turning the assignment down?"

"If you wish."

"What are the risks?"

"None to you—that I know of. You might know the risks better than I."

Kipp took a large gulp of the steaming coffee. "Okay, lay it on me. What is it you want to talk about?"

Andrea leaned toward him, her expression suddenly serious. "I want you to tell me everything you know about the Seattle firm—Stratcom Limited."

Kipp choked on his coffee and coughed a moment. Tilting his head back, he stared at the eager woman beside him. "God, you're not messing around with that company, are you?"

Surprised by his reaction, Andrea said, "What if I am?"

His joker image vanished. "Get out—while you can."

"Why?"

"What do you know about Stratcom? Were you recruiting them in Seattle?"

"Yes, I was. You know that. I asked you about Darrell Smith."

"I was hoping you were mixed up, got the name wrong—or something."

"Well, I didn't." Andrea took a sip of her coffee. "Kipp, I'm serious. Something funny is going on."

"You got that right." He laid an arm across the back of the bench. "This is between you and me and this bench. Right?" At Andrea's nod, he took a deep breath and said, "Well, let's start at the beginning. Stratcom was founded about fifteen years ago by three Massachusetts Institute of Technology graduates. It's a think tank of scientists and engineers. As you probably know already, most of their work is in space communications." As Andrea nodded, Kipp continued, "Two of the founders, Chang and Perlstein, are the smartest guys ever to get doctorates from MIT. The other guy, McLaren, isn't in the same class—don't get me wrong, he's brilliant—but he was the one who had the money and the brains to oversee all the technical, cerebral types."

A gust of wind blew her hair into her eyes. Andrea pushed it back with an impatient shove of her hand. "This McLaren—what's he like?"

"Like?" Kipp snorted. "God, the man is practically a legend at UCLA. He's one of those guys who picked up a bachelor of science degree and a master's degree in electrical engineering at UCLA by the time he was eighteen. He's renowned in the Department of Engineering there for both his intellect and his formidable temper. He got his doctorate at MIT by the time he was twenty."

A frown creased Andrea's forehead. "Doesn't sound like someone you'd want to be mad at you."

"He's not." Kipp finished his coffee and tossed the cup into a nearby trash can. "To give you an idea, he was the one who came up with the concept for Stratcom. The government was immediately interested in the talent he was pulling together. And—get this—since its founding, Stratcom's main source of funding has been from federal contracts for research and development of space communications systems. with most of those projects highly classified. A really unusual feat for such a young company."

"Why do you think that is?"

"Well, most of McLaren's employees are ex-CIA analysts. Rumor has it that not all of them have cut their CIA ties. McLaren knows this but leaves well enough alone. After all, his money is coming from the government. He may not be one of the richest men in the country, but in the aerospace industry, he's one of the most powerful. He knows which wheels to grease, and he does it very well."

Andrea tried to sound nonchalant. "I hear he's a volatile man, perhaps even dangerous."

Kipp's eyes narrowed, and he fidgeted on the hard bench. "Well, they say he's mellowed with age. However, with a track record like his, I wouldn't want to gamble on it. Stratcom had a rocky first decade under his management. Seems his temper made it a pretty erratic company. But he's a man who knows his weaknesses and hires the right people to cover for them. He brought in a lawyer several years ago who balances things out. I'd bet the guy owns a large percentage of Stratcom by now."

Andrea ignored the growing uneasy feeling in the pit of her stomach. "So what's happening with Stratcom right now?"

Kipp's laugh was chilling. "Well, with all those CIA types around, Stratcom is always a hotbed of rampant paranoia. But lately, the paranoia level has been running triple its usual high level."

"Why?"

"It's my guess the paranoia is coming down from management." Kipp paused and looked around at the people near them. Continuing in a low voice, he said, "I've heard rumors that someone in the aerospace industry is trying to put Stratcom out of business."

Andrea shivered, and she knew it wasn't from the cold. She also knew the answer to her next question before she asked it. "How?"

"Basically by hiring away all the key people at outrageous salaries. Someone is paying through the nose to get them, too. Of course, McLaren's got the money to make a counteroffer and keep any and all employees, but he isn't doing that. And the most peculiar thing about it is that no one in the industry seems to know where these people are going. It's got to be the best-kept secret of the year."

Except that Andrea knew the answer to the secret. She would stake her reputation as an instinctive headhunter that NavCom Electronics was the new employer for departing Stratcom employees. No wonder McLaren hated headhunters! Andrea wrapped her arms around herself. But who had recruited the employees Len Daggett had bought away?

She was concentrating so hard on this puzzle that she barely heard Kipp's last comment. Turning her attention back to him, she asked, "What was that you just said?"

"What? Oh, the other rumor. Well, according to the grapevine, there's also been sabotage at the plant. That's what's supposed to have McLaren gearing up for war. And, man, I wouldn't want to be around when he unleashes that lawyer of his. If you're working Stratcom recruits, Andrea—I'd quit. He'll be going after everyone he can.''

Andrea shook her head and sighed. "Kipp, I can't quit. It would ruin me financially."

The engineer fidgeted again, stretching his legs out in front of him on the boardwalk. Shoving his hands into his jacket pockets, he said, ''Look, I've heard about some of the things Cal Slattery has done at Tectron. The man has a vicious reputation. It wouldn't surprise me if he has done worse things elsewhere. And don't tell me if you know of any of them,'' Kipp cautioned. When she remained silent, he added gravely, ''It's better to be poor than in prison. Or worse.''

Andrea tried to laugh. ''Oh, come on, Kipp. I'm just a little fish. Why would Edward McLaren want to bother me? Wouldn't he rather spend his time going after the big guys?''

Kipp stared at her for a long moment, then chuckled. ''I don't think anyone's called McLaren by his first name in years. At least not anyone who's a friend.''

Andrea tried to remember exactly how the Stratcom telephone directory had listed the president's name. ''What do his friends call him?''

''Gage.''

''Oh, no!'' she exclaimed, staring at the engineer. *Gage. Gage McLaren. Stratcom.*

Her heart skipped a beat as she realized with a paralyzing sickness what had happened in Seattle, what Gage McLaren must have known.

Watching his friend's pale, anguished face, Kipp shook her shoulder gently. ''Andrea, what's wrong?''

Her blue eyes swiveled to meet his. Tears lined her lashes, and she tried to blink them back, unsuccessfully. As they spilled down her cheeks, she cried, "Oh, God, I have been such a fool!"

Chapter Eleven

Andrea maneuvered her Mustang through the Friday night rush-hour traffic into the exiting lanes for the northbound Harbor Freeway. Swinging into the left lane and heading for Pasadena, she again wondered how she had missed all the little clues that had been there, pointing to Gage's identity as Stratcom's principal owner. While he hadn't been honest enough to say, "I'm Gage McLaren and you're raiding my company," he had dropped enough hints and signs that she should have noticed. For such a perceptive woman, she had been completely blind. But wasn't love supposed to be blind?

Gage. A sad little smile played at the edges of her lips. For a brief, flirting moment, she could feel his strong arms around her, smell the light, earthy cologne he wore, hear the warming sound of his husky laugh. For that moment, Andrea felt at peace. However, as she braked for a backup in the traffic, the security she had felt dissolved; in its place was an overpowering sense of poignancy. Unshed tears threatened to cloud her vision, and she shook her head angrily.

That she could have fallen in love with Gage in such a short time was almost beyond her comprehension. After all, hadn't she always taken her time when making important decisions? She never jumped into things. Every move was made after careful, even cautious, deliberation. She had spent the past two days agonizing over what was the correct thing to do about this Stratcom affair. It had been late that afternoon before she had finally called Danny, in an attempt to locate Gage.

Yet hadn't she—in a way—carefully weighed her feelings, carefully assessed the situation, before becoming involved with Gage? Hadn't she? At times she thought so. She had always sensed he'd be a difficult person to know. But despite his reserve, she had found the man behind it captivating, easy to know, easy to love.

Dismayed by the intensity of her feelings for Gage, Andrea tried to turn her thoughts to a different topic. The events of the past three days immediately came to mind. Cal's cold rage at the unknown perpetrator of the burglary was still being felt around the office, and she was receiving more than her share of sidelong glances from the staff. At first she had thought that a recently fired employee was responsible for the break-in, but what she had learned Wednesday night from Kipp made her certain that Gage was behind it.

As she drove through the unfamiliar streets of Pasadena to the exclusive community of San Marino, Andrea wondered if what she was about to do was more foolish than her previous actions. What had started out to be a complex, sticky situation involving her knowledge of NavCom Electronics and Cal's connection with the company had now escalated into a surrealistic escapade of crossed paths, ignorance, deceit and deception. Andrea wasn't certain whom she feared most—a wronged lover or a suspicous employer. But she did know whom she trusted.

She turned into Huntington Drive, San Marino's main thoroughfare, and drove along it until she had reached her destination. A jungle of potted plants greeted her on the gaslit, red-brick patio at the front of the sprawling, two-story Spanish-style house.

Reaching for the doorbell, Andrea paused, again wondering if, perhaps, the most intelligent way of dealing with the situation wasn't to disappear from the surface of the earth. As Kipp had said, she was in an undeniably precarious position. With what was probably an extreme example of gross stupidity, Andrea pushed her fears aside and pressed the doorbell. Waiting for her world to end with an explosion of righteous and justified indignation, she straightened the skirt of her navy suit, studied a white azalea at her toe and fought the butterflies of nervousness.

Gage McLaren pulled the ornately carved door open. When he saw her standing there, his dark eyes narrowed speculatively. Still, the familiar gentleness and warmth was in his voice. "Of all places, I never expected to find you on my doorstep."

Andrea's smile quivered. "You aren't the only one, I assure you."

Despite his coldness at their bitter parting in Seattle, Gage didn't look completely displeased to see her. "Come on in."

Andrea stepped into the white-walled, Spanish-tiled foyer and held her clutch purse with both hands. Gage led the way down a long, dimly lit hallway. After passing several closed rooms, he pushed open a pair of louvered doors, flipped a light switch on and motioned Andrea inside. She gazed around her at the French and English antique furniture, the walls lined with Impressionistic paintings, the exquisite Persian carpet and the small Austrian chandelier.

Gage strode to the wet bar. "What would you like to drink?"

"Nothing, thank you." Andrea forced her voice to sound confident. She sank into a Queen Anne chair and clasped her hands together tightly over her purse.

Gage strolled across the room and settled into a chair facing her. "Then what may I do for you?"

Dressed in faded jeans, moccasins and a Yosemite T-shirt that emphasized his muscular chest, he was the consummate casual man, totally out of place in the formal room. Andrea glanced around her again, then met his guarded gaze. "I never pictured you being into Victorian and Provençal antiques. You seem to be so much the rugged, contemporary type."

Her comment appeared to take him by surprise. Gage blinked a moment; then a corner of his mouth turned up. "I'm not. This is my parents' house. All of us siblings use it as home base when we're in Los Angeles."

Andrea nodded vaguely and looked away from him. Her eye was caught by a free-form jade carving on the lamp table, and she got up to examine it. As her fingers traced the curves of the statue, she fought to control her rebellious nerves and desires. Most likely, she would become involved in warfare with Gage, and she needed her wits about her to hold her ground. Andrea knew her chances of winning her case with the headstrong, sometimes volatile man were next to nothing, but she, too, hated to lose. Defeat was certain if she allowed herself to be ruled by her aroused emotions.

She felt Gage's hands rest lightly on her shoulders as he came to stand behind her. She focused her attention on the carving until she heard the seductive voice she loved so much murmur, "Does this visit have anything to do with Seattle?"

Would her throat loosen up so that she could speak? "Yes, I'm afraid so."

His strong hand smoothed her hair back over her shoulder while his lips caressed the hollow behind her ear. Unconsciously, Andrea tilted her head back, inviting his kisses to skim across her neck. As his breath warmed her ear, Gage whispered, "Is it good news or bad?"

"Bad."

He turned her gently by the shoulders to face him, took the jade carving from her and placed it back on the table. Cupping her face in his hands, his thumbs stroking her cheeks, Gage asked, "Well, then, what's the bad news?" He didn't give her a chance to answer before he said, "Seattle seems a lifetime ago."

Andrea nodded in agreement and, unable to curb her desire, closed her eyes. As his lips teased hers to respond, Gage slipped his arms around her and drew her to him. She relaxed in his embrace, feeling the strength of his closeness and the sense of security it gave her. But it was a false security, and that reality gnawed at her mind. She pushed weakly against his chest.

Gage's mouth left hers reluctantly to brush a kiss across her forehead before yielding completely to her unspoken request. "Lady, you do have a hold on me."

"Purely unintentional, I assure you." Andrea moved away slightly, trying to collect her thoughts. "I'm sorry. That came out wrong. I care for you very much. But I have to talk to you, and I can't talk to you when you're kissing me."

Gage shoved his hands into the hip pockets of his jeans. "What's the matter?"

"Everything." Andrea went back to her chair and sat down. "It must be evident, from the fact that I've found out where you live, that I've also learned much more about you than I knew in Seattle.''

Gage's loving manner faded abruptly, replaced by a tense aloofness. ''What have you discovered?''

Andrea breathed deeply and stared down at her purse, which she had picked up again. Plunging into the murky waters of dread, she said as calmly as she could, ''For starters, that you own Stratcom Limited.'' Then, without looking at him, she related what she had learned from Kipp. Not until she had finished speaking did she dare to meet his eyes.

The tension that had been reflected in Gage's rigid stance was now forced behind a mask of polite gentility. ''You certainly have learned practically everything there is to know about my business affairs.'' He went over to the wet bar and splashed some whisky from a decanter into a crystal tumbler. ''What puzzles me is why. I assume this is some sort of a shakedown. You'll tell me who—for a price.''

Andrea surged out of her chair, slamming her purse onto the lamp table. ''How dare you assume such a thing!'' She made an effort to rein her temper in, then said, ''I wasn't lying when I said that I care for you.''

Gage sipped at his drink. ''Go on.''

''You aren't making this easy for me.''

''I have no intention of doing so.''

Andrea stared at him over the expanse of Persian carpet. For a moment she thought of the man who had played the piano with the emotion of a true artist, not with the analytical mind of a distinguished engineer. ''It's because I care for you that I came here to make a confession.''

''I'm not a priest.''

"Will you shut up?" she snapped. At Gage's indifferent shrug, she said, "I do know who's raiding your company—at least right now—and who's hiring your people away."

Gage remained silent, sipping his drink, the rugged lines of his face reflecting his hostility.

"ComSearch is the recruiting firm, and NavCom Electronics is the company that is buying."

Slowly, cautiously, Gage set his half-empty glass on the mirror surface of the bar. She could barely hear him ask, "How do you know that?"

"I'm the headhunter who was raiding your company a week ago. And I'm the one who is working upcoming offers for your employees right now. But of course, you knew who I was in Seattle."

For a single, eternally long moment, a deadly silence hung between them.

Andrea made a move toward Gage, but stopped when his dark eyes flashed at her. "Please. Hear me out." The feelings she was trying to ignore softened her next words. "It's not exactly the way you think. Please believe me." She took Gage's silence as permission to continue. "I found out only two nights ago that you own Stratcom. In fact, all the time I was in Seattle I knew nothing about the company. I was simply told to recruit its software communications analysts. Then Len Daggett showed up."

The look of hatred in Gage's eyes when he heard Len's name was unmistakable. Andrea rushed on, explaining how the trip had come about, Len's arrival and her lack of knowledge of the real purpose for his being in Seattle. She ended by detailing the confrontation with Cal that had driven her into Gage's arms.

Gage listened to her story intently, standing immobile behind the bar. After a long silence, he said, "I think I remember that night best."

Andrea crossed the distance between them and placed her hands on top of the bar. "Believe me, I would never have deceived you. If I had known in Seattle, I would have told you."

"Sure you would." His mood was glacial. "There's a saying: 'Never believe a headhunter.' After all, who's going to take the word of an engineer's pimp?"

Andrea had heard that line before—that engineers were prostitutes and that recruiters were their procurers. It was a radical viewpoint, yet not an uncommon one. And knowing Gage's reputation for hating headhunters, she was not shocked by his attitude, but she was hurt. She had hoped he would think differently about her. "I wish you would believe me."

"I don't tend to believe people who play games."

"What are you talking about?"

"You're a master games player. You may have won the first round, Andrea, but I'll win the next."

Frustrated, she demanded, "What *are* you talking about?"

His anger was barely controlled, showing plainly in his savage look and sardonic voice. "When you mess with my company, lady, you are asking for big trouble."

"You sound as if I'm responsible for all the personnel losses that Stratcom's sustained. I am not."

He glared at her. "Do you expect me to believe that?"

"No, I don't." Andrea tossed her head back. "Not now. But I'm sure that if you bothered to do some checking around, you'd find out who else has been raiding your company. I'm positive it wasn't ComSearch. And you would certainly discover that I have nothing to do with your troubles.''

Gage's mouth curled into a cynical sneer. ''Never believe a headhunter.''

''The whole industry knows that Stratcom is going under—and fast.''

''Even faster with your help.''

Tears of frustration stung Andrea's eyes, and she whirled away from him. ''You don't believe a thing I've told you!''

''It's impossible to believe anyone who is as good at game playing as you.''

She turned to face him, pale and shaken, fighting to keep her pain from her voice. ''I'm not playing games.''

''Like hell you aren't!''

His accusations and disbelief ignited her temper once more. ''You are impossible! How do you ever manage to run a company when you're as closed-minded as you are? It's no wonder you're losing Stratcom to Len Daggett!''

As soon as she had said it, Andrea regretted it.

Gage's rugged features hardened into those of a menacing stranger. When he spoke, his tone was full of fury. ''That's the other reason why I don't believe you. Anyone who works for Daggett can't be trusted—*or* believed.''

''I don't work for Daggett! You know that. Damn it, you know everything!'' Her dismay etched itself into her voice, her face.

''It's a great act, Andrea, but I don't buy it.''

She gulped several deep breaths of air. ''Here I was, thinking you're just stubborn. You aren't stubborn. You're pigheaded!''

''I've been called that before.''

''Whoever said it was right!'' Andrea whirled away from him.

"Len knew what he was doing by hiring you. You do your job very well."

Andrea forced herself to turn around and look at him. "It would be very easy for me to learn to hate you, Gage. So easy. Please don't make me."

"You will hate me if you work any job offers for my personnel." The dark eyes burned into hers.

"Is that a threat?"

"You'd better believe it."

"And just what are you going to do?" Andrea stepped back to the bar and leaned intrepidly toward him. "If Len and NCE want to extend job offers, it's my job to work those offers. That's the way I make my living, and I happen to have a great deal riding on getting a placement or two out of that Seattle trip. If you think you can scare me by threatening me, think again, Gage. I'm not frightened of you or your power. If you want to keep your company—solve your problems with Len Daggett. But leave me out of it. And while we're at it, you are not utterly blameless yourself. You had your own game going. *You* played *me* for an absolute fool!"

Anger flushed her face a rosy pink and turned her eyes a dark blue. Gage returned her stare. Tense moments became even tenser minutes as he studied the emotions that warred on her face. Then he nodded slowly, his movement sparking a curious light in her eyes.

"That might have been my first intention, but it changed," he said quietly.

Andrea's face screwed up in disbelief. *"What?"*

The gentle huskiness returned to his voice. "You're right. I did know who you were from the beginning—even before I saw you with Cal in the airport coffee shop."

The angry contortions on her face smoothed into a perplexed frown as she stared at him in confusion.

Gage laid his hand on top of hers, his thumb idly circling her wrist. He sighed. "It was no coincidence that we were booked on the same flight to Seattle. I've had private detectives working for the past two months to get evidence for my case against Daggett and NCE. It was through them that I learned about Slattery and ComSearch." A wry smile lurked at the corner of his mouth. "There's not much I don't know about everyone involved. Including you."

Andrea's face darkened. "What do you mean?"

"I knew you were in severe financial straits and that, from Slattery's point of view, you would be the easiest person to buy, the easiest to control. The fact that you are exceptionally good at your job made you the likeliest candidate to raid Stratcom. When you were booked on a flight to Seattle, we knew it was coming down to the wire."

Shocked, Andrea asked, "And what was your first intention?"

Gage drew his hand away from hers and ran it along the edge of the bar. He cleared his throat, then stated dryly, "To meet you on what was an apparently casual basis and then seduce you. Depending on what I learned about the degree of your involvement in my loss of personnel, I would have bought your information. Or had you prosecuted along with Daggett and Slattery."

Observing the stillness in the dark eyes that waited for her reaction, Andrea squared her shoulders. "Well, I guess you are giving me the honesty that I asked for in Seattle." Her voice wavered, and she paused a moment before saying, "I gave you ample opportunity to seduce me. Why didn't you take it?"

"I couldn't." He shook his head. "Not after I got to know you."

Her words were a whisper. "Why not?"

A tender smile eased the tension on his face. "You were too sweet, too open. I started out thinking you were a major participant in what's been happening these past few months, but I soon realized how ridiculous a notion that was. I thought I'd been completely wrong about you—until I saw you talking to Darrell Smith."

With a sudden jolt, Andrea remembered that brief moment when she had thought she glimpsed Gage in the hotel lobby. At the time, she had assumed that her over-active imagination had been playing tricks on her. Slowly, she nodded. "Yes, I thought I'd seen you there."

"My temper got the best of me. I left in a hurry. If I hadn't—well, I'm sure the hotel management would have remembered us for a very long time." He smiled ruefully.

"But we might have straightened all this out then and there." *And we wouldn't have had to live through the hell of the past week,* Andrea thought miserably.

"Perhaps. I guess things could have been different."

"Can't they be now?" she whispered.

Gage frowned, skepticism furrowing his brow. When he spoke, his voice was heavy with emotion. "I don't know. Danny and I are preparing for an all-out war with Daggett. Our plans are to haul him and everyone associated with him into court. And I intend to win."

Listening to the note of vengeance in his voice, Andrea shivered. "Why is Len determined to close Stratcom?"

"Actually, he isn't. He needs Stratcom."

"What?" Andrea stared at him, perplexed by his comment.

"See, NavCom Electronics' current success is based upon my failure in the past to make certain that security was tight enough."

"What did Len do?"

"We were competing for the first phase of an important government contract. My team had finished its research and written the preliminary proposal for the bidding; we were going to get it in well ahead of the competition. Len somehow found out how ahead of schedule we were. He hired two men who had government credentials and sticky fingers. Next thing I knew, we'd lost the bidding and several of our top engineers."

"Len bought them."

"Right. Only at the time, we didn't know where they'd gone. Their stories were that they were going into private contracting."

"And you believed they were becoming job shoppers?"

"Not after the first three left."

Andrea asked in a hushed tone, "What's going on now? Why is Len interviewing your analysts?"

"Phase two bidding for the contract is coming up. I'm not exactly sure what he's trying to pull. But plant security is so tight that even I have a difficult time getting in without the proper ID." His grin was wicked.

"And you have detectives working to see what he's up to."

"Right again. I'm going to stop him this time. Len doesn't know how close Stratcom is to going belly-up, but I can't afford to lose any more employees or contracts. Whatever it takes, I'm determined to stop him. We're almost ready to file suit for industrial espionage and sabotage. I suspect that before the first of the year—with what he's up to now—the list of charges will be longer."

Andrea took his hand in both of hers. "You've got the money to counter all of his offers and keep your people. Why don't you?"

Gage laughed self-derisively. "It's the principle of the thing."

Her head tilted to the side as she studied him. Finally she said, "I don't understand."

"That's all right." Gage leaned across the bar and kissed her cheek. "Most people in the industry don't. I figure if an employee is willing to trade ethics for money, that's his prerogative. But I don't want him on my team." Andrea winced at his explicit phrasing. "So I don't make a counteroffer."

Ignoring her discomfort, she said, "You might want to keep a close watch on Darrell Smith. I have a feeling he's Len's new inside man, if your security is as tight as you claim."

"What makes you think that?" Gage drained his glass of whisky while studying Andrea intently.

"Headhunter's instinct. He just didn't sound like a man who was looking to change companies or positions. He didn't ask the right questions or answer mine in the usual way."

"I'm already on it. Darrell has been under surveillance since I saw him talking to you."

"Did you know that he had interviewed—talked to Len?"

"No. Not until later."

Andrea's smile was sardonic. At least Gage McLaren hadn't always been two steps ahead of them. She brought the fact up cautiously. "You know, ComSearch had a break-in Tuesday night."

"A break-in?" Gage raised an eyebrow in mystification.

"The thought occurred to me that you were behind it. Who else has a reason to hit ComSearch? With the pure intent of making life miserable for us—and recruiting quite difficult—until we manage to replace our resources?"

A slow smile crept across Gage's face and eventually reached his eyes, lighting them with great amusement. "Someone robbed ComSearch?"

"You know someone did," she said defiantly. "And you even know who."

"I hate to disappoint you, Andrea, but I don't. I don't know anything about a break-in at ComSearch. But I'll gladly congratulate whoever's responsible and buy that man a drink." Gage didn't bother to hide his delighted grin. "I wish I'd thought of it."

Andrea glared at him. "I bet."

His eyes danced mischievously over her face while the familiar entrancing smile worked its magic.

Andrea released his hand. Her voice trembled as she said, "So. Now that everything is out in the open, where do we stand?"

"In a house in San Marino."

"Very funny." As her gaze explored the masculine lines of his face anew, she smiled tentatively. "I'll take that drink now."

Gage pulled a tray of ice cubes from a small refrigerator hidden under the bar. "It's still early. Would you care to do something?"

Andrea's hesitant blue eyes met his dark desirous eyes. She wanted so much to be his, to feel his arms around her and his lips against hers. Breathless, she asked, "What did you have in mind?"

A teasing glint flitted through those mesmerizing eyes. "I'm open to suggestions."

She accepted the drink he poured for her, and the touch of her hand on his was electrifying. Both of them took a deep breath, their smiles slightly hesitant but extremely hopeful. Moving back a few steps, Andrea turned on her heel and paced halfway across the room before facing

Gage again. The reluctance she felt was revealed by the strain in her soft voice. "I'm not sure that getting involved again is a good idea."

"Again? What do you mean by 'again'?" Gage came from behind the bar, but halted when he saw the anxiety that darkened her blue eyes.

"It was over when I left Seattle. I didn't know why, but you made it clear that you wanted nothing to do with me."

"That was then, not now." He shoved his hands into the pockets of his jeans. "I...unfortunately, I let my temper get the better of me. I jumped to conclusions."

"They were the logical conclusions, given the circumstances. I don't blame you for that, Gage." She shook her head, pain evident in her voice. "It's just that I don't like getting hurt. And I'm sure that, from your point of view, you got hurt, too. If we're going to go around hurting each other, we'll both suffer."

Gage crossed the distance between them with quick, long strides. Gently placing his hands on her shoulders, he stared down into her wide eyes. "Darling, getting hurt and hurting others is unavoidable. It's a fact of life. We may not mean to—or even want to—but we will." His tone, already mild, softened even more. "All we can do when we hurt each other is to try to fix what's wrong and say we're sorry." His voice throbbed with emotion. "And please believe me when I say I'm sorry that I didn't trust you enough to ask you just what the hell was going on in Seattle. I owed you that much—and more."

Andrea's eyes dropped to the glass that she gripped tightly in both hands. Gage pulled the tumbler from her grasp and set it on the lamp table. Slowly, he slipped his arms around her and drew her close.

She laid her head against his chest and put her arms around his waist, letting out a long, soft sigh. "You're forgiven."

Gage kissed the top of her head. "After the way I treated you in Seattle, it must have been difficult coming here tonight."

Her laugh held no humor in it. "Understatement of the year!" Glancing up at him, she added, "But I was able to come here because I trusted you. Even if you do own Stratcom."

Gage hugged her tightly. "Thank you for trusting a stubborn cuss!"

She smiled shyly. "Anytime."

His voice dropped to a whisper as he tenderly cupped her face in his hands. "I'll hold you to that, darling."

Andrea's heart leapt to her throat. Hesitantly, she murmured, "You know, don't you, that I think I'm in love with you?"

His eyes scanned her features, and he smiled in such a way that the small pilot light deep inside her flared into a consuming blaze. Stroking her cheeks with his thumbs, Gage teased, "I should hope so. Because, lady, I know I'm in love with you."

"You are?" she breathed.

Gage nodded silently.

Andrea closed her eyes and tilted her head back to meet the searching, inviting kiss that claimed her lips. Sighing softly, she clung to him as if to steady herself in the wave of sensations that washed over her like a wave over sand. When Gage's lips left hers, she murmured, "You once accused me of being a tease. I think you're the tease now."

"Is that so?" His dark eyes sparkled with good-natured humor and something else that made her pulse race erratically. He sucked in a ragged breath and whispered huskily, "I have a suggestion."

Intoxicated with desire, Andrea whispered back, "What's stopping you?"

As his lips grazed a burning trail over her throat, Gage growled in mock fierceness, "Absolutely nothing!"

APPARENTLY OBLIVIOUS to the Sunday evening theater crowd around them, Gage placed his hands on Andrea's shoulders and whispered, "Have I told you lately how much I love you?"

Andrea smiled serenely. "Not for at least an hour. We made it through the first act without you so much as breathing a word about it—or anything else," she teased.

Gage tapped one of her dangling silver-and-black pearl earrings, kissed her cheek, then stood back and looked deep into her eyes. "Well, consider yourself told again."

Laughing, Andrea hooked her hand into the crook of his elbow and glanced around at the people milling about the lobby of the Ahmanson Theatre.

"Looks as if they got a good turnout for this benefit performance. I'm surprised, at two hundred dollars a ticket," Gage commented dryly. "Fortunately, the play is first-rate."

Andrea purred, "I think you've fallen for the heroine."

"If I weren't already hooked on someone, I would— what a woman!"

Andrea merely nodded and smiled. Tonight she looked decidedly feminine in a soft blue silk dress that clung to each curve of her slender frame. The expression in her eyes as she gazed at Gage left no doubt about her feelings for him, nor did the happy smile on her lips.

Suddenly, the color left her cheeks and her blue eyes darkened.

Leaning close, Gage inquired, "What's wrong?"

"It's Cal!" she exclaimed.

Gage's eyes followed the line of hers. The crowd near them was parting as if on command, and a fashionably dressed couple stopped a few feet away. Andrea's hand trembled on Gage's arm, but her eyes were glued to the man who stared icily at them. His shrewd hazel eyes studied the couple with barely disguised hostility.

With marked politeness, Gage said, "Good evening."

Cal Slattery stepped closer, leaving his small, blond wife at the edge of the crowd that idly watched the trio with open curiosity. "Good evening, Andrea. Are you enjoying the play?"

Oh, damn Cal, she thought; of all the places for him to show up! And, of course, he had his usual effect on everyone within radius of his abnormally strong vibes. She summoned her voice from the tips of her toes and forced it to be calm, quiet and resonant. "Yes, I am. Are you?"

"Yes, thoroughly. Superb acting." He paused, his glacial expression melting minutely as he extended his hand to Gage. "I don't believe we've met. I'm Cal Slattery." If he had intended to introduce his wife, it was impossible now. Andrea noted that she had disappeared from the scene.

Gage shook the proffered hand. "Gage McLaren." His dark eyes wore that mask of studied neutrality that admitted and denied nothing.

Andrea looked about anxiously, not certain what would happen next between the two men at her side. Cal was barely controlling his anger as his glance flicked between Gage and her. Gage, a study in civility, nevertheless radiated the tension she felt in the muscles of his arm beneath the white dinner jacket he was wearing.

The silent, staring appraisal continued for several long moments as each man estimated the other. Andrea glanced furtively at Gage and was relieved to see the same polite, gentlemanly smile molding his lips, even if it didn't reach his fathomless eyes.

Cal allowed his blistering look to wander to Andrea. His voice was snide when he said, "Well, McLaren, I see you've made the acquaintance of my star recruiter. What do you think of her?"

Gage replied smoothly. "She's quite exceptional. Your business must depend heavily on her talents."

"That it does. I would hate to lose her. She'd be hard to replace."

Gage's snort was humorless. "I'm sure she would be. But I understand that you pay her well. She's particularly devoted to her job; I'm sure the income is a contributing factor in her loyalty."

"Probably is. However, I suspect she'll be receiving job offers that I'll have a hard time countering."

As Cal's hazel eyes stared into hers, Andrea felt a twinge of terror. She had worked for the man for over two years and had thought she had seen him in every conceivable state of rage. She had been wrong, very wrong. That was apparent now.

A wicked smile slowly touched his thin lips. "But no employee is irreplaceable." He looked at the crowd around them. "Intermission is nearly over. Must go find Sharon. See you at work tomorrow, Andrea. McLaren, we'll meet again."

Gage nodded slightly. His voice was brittle. "I'm sure we will."

As Cal barreled his way back through the crowd, Andrea looked questioningly at Gage. "What on earth was that all about? Gage, did you hear me?"

Gage stood with his hands shoved deep into his trouser pockets, watching Cal's retreating back. A look of cold determination molded the lines of his jaw. He glanced absently at Andrea, whose worried eyes were dark in her pale face. Gage hunched his shoulders for a moment. Then, as the chimes began to ring, announcing the end of intermission, he forced a smile to his lips. "Let's return to our seats. Five minutes until act two. Wouldn't want to miss anything."

After they had settled into their seats, Andrea linked her arm through Gage's and laid her head on his shoulder. All her fears were fighting for supremacy; reason was losing the battle. The theater lights dimmed and the curtain rose.

Gage glanced sideways as Andrea raised her head from his shoulder. Their eyes met, and the smile that came to his lips was strained, but the love that darkened his eyes was real. Of that, Andrea was certain.

She leaned close and whispered in his ear, "You know, I love you very, very much." Her lips grazed his slightly beard-stubbled cheek before she sat back in her seat, a telling smile dancing on her face. The tension she had felt in his body began to ease as Gage caught up her hand and laced his fingers through hers. They sat that way through the remainder of the play.

HOURS LATER, they lay locked in each other's embrace. Andrea rubbed her cheek against the damp mat of hair on his chest, feeling it tickle her skin. The faint musky scent of their lovemaking was a heady perfume, one that nearly, but not quite, overpowered the tension she felt between them.

As she ruffled her fingers over his skin, she urged, "Okay, what is it that has you so quiet? Don't you know a girl likes to have sweet nothings whispered in her ear?"

Gage's laugh was a deep rumble in his chest. "I think I ran out of terms of endearment yesterday afternoon in the hot tub."

"A likely story," Andrea mumbled in mock peevishness, smoothing her fingers over his muscular forearm. "You're upset about running into Cal, aren't you?" she asked quietly.

He studied her with unbridled concern. "You said Friday night that you were scared and didn't know what to do. Well, now that I've met him, I'd say you have every right to fear that man. You'd have to be a fool not to." His lips brushed the back of her hand as it rested on his arm. "As to what you should do—there's no question about that. You call in your notice tomorrow and never go back to the office."

"No, I can't quit my job yet. I have too much riding on my commissions. I need them. I must keep working."

An incredulous frown cut across Gage's forehead. "What? Are you crazy?" He propped himself up on an elbow and stared darkly at her. "You stay away from that man. He's dangerous. Let me take care of him."

"And how are you going to do that?"

"By putting him and Len Daggett behind bars. It may take a while, but I'm going to win that lawsuit."

"Oh, sure. And what do I do in the meantime? Sell matchsticks? I've already told you I won't accept your money for Chris's bills."

When Gage spoke again, patience colored his every word. "Cal thinks you were behind the break-in. That was *before* he knew you were involved with me. Now he has to be convinced you had a hand in it."

Andrea jumped from the bed and yanked on Gage's pajama top. "But I didn't!"

"But he knows I did."

As Andrea stared blankly at him, Gage sat up and nodded. "Yes, you were right—I was behind the burglary. The
detectives who have been getting evidence for the lawsuit
did it on my instructions."

"Gage, that makes you as much of a crook as Cal is!
How *could* you?"

"Easily. Those men have cost me millions of dollars and
put the lives of my employees in jeopardy."

Trembling, she asked, "What do you mean?"

His eyes darkened with that now-familiar intensity.
"Their little shenanigans at the plant have put one man in
the hospital already. I'm not about to endanger the rest of
my people. We're very close to getting all the goods on Cal
and Len—and if what I suspect is correct, I won't need to
sue to see them behind bars."

She shook her head. "I don't believe you. Cal may be
a crook, but I don't think he'd hurt anyone. And I certainly can't see the quiet, urbane Len Daggett harming
anyone, either."

Gage stared at her gravely for many seconds before he
finally leaned back against the pillows. "You certainly
have been taken in. Don't let Daggett's polish fool you—
he's a heartless little bastard. As for Cal—you and your
misguided sense of loyalty! You're terrified of the man,
yet you refuse to believe he would resort to whatever it
takes to get what he wants." Gage ran a hand through his
hair. His voice held a note of entreaty. "Andrea, you are
too intelligent to be this...this senseless." As they stared
at each other across the length of the king-size bed, Andrea shrugged her slender shoulders. Her voice was weak
from mixed emotions. "This weekend has been such a
whirlwind.... But I need to be by myself now.... I need
time to think." Turning, she scooped her dress off the

chair it was draped over and hunted for her shoes on the plush brown carpet.

While she padded barefoot toward the bathroom, Gage said, ''Andrea, honey, be reasonable. I don't want to see you get hurt.''

She paused in the doorway and glanced over her shoulder. The dark eyes that had held so much passion and love during the past two days again wore that expression of...of what? Andrea had never been able to label accurately that masked look in Gage's eyes. It wasn't indifference. It wasn't coldness. She hadn't identified it yet, and she wondered if she ever would.

Softly, she said, ''I've got to get home.''

Chapter Twelve

Andrea sat on the sofa in the stillness of early morning, slowly flipping the pages of the photograph album and remembering the past with an ache. The only illumination in the room came from the Christmas tree lights and the bayberry-scented candle on the lamp table by her side. She heard the sound of a bedroom door opening, and moments later Christine appeared.

"When did you get home?" Christine asked, wrapping her robe around her and yawning broadly.

Staring at a memory-laden photo, Andrea replied, "A couple of hours ago."

"Found your note." The teenager flopped into the rocker and swiveled from side to side, her sleepy eyes studying her sister. "Did you have a nice weekend?"

A sorrowful sigh covered the silence of the room. "For the most part."

Christine twisted the end of her tie belt around her finger. "Have you been crying?" she asked, suddenly alert.

Andrea shook her head, closed the album and laid it beside her on the sofa. "No. Just thinking."

"'Bout what?"

"Everything, it seems," she murmured.

A frown knitted Christine's eyebrows together. "You sure you haven't been crying? You sound strange."

Closing her eyes, Andrea leaned her head against the back of the sofa. "To be honest, I feel strange."

"How so?" Worry edged into Christine's voice. "What happened? You've been acting strange ever since you came home Wednesday night."

"Life, it seems, is very unpredictable."

"You're just now finding that out?" Her sister snorted. "I could have told you that!"

Andrea laughed sadly. "If you have any more secrets you'd like to share..." Her voice trailed off.

Christine plucked a miniature chocolate from the candy dish on the coffee table. "It sounds like you've been smitten by the love bug."

Andrea's eyes flicked open, and she watched her sister pop the candy into her mouth. "I guess I have. And been making a fool of myself, too."

"So what else is new?" Seeing her sister's displeasure, Christine added quickly, "No offense intended. It's just that you're never very levelheaded when your emotions are involved. Despite what you think."

Andrea's smile was rueful. "You're probably right."

"Of course I am."

Andrea sensed that now was the time to rectify the differences with Christine. Placing the photo album in her lap, she ran her hands over the leather cover. "You know, I haven't looked at these pictures since Mom and Daddy died."

Christine nodded. "Yeah, I know. I think their deaths bothered you even more than me. You really miss him, don't you?"

"Yes, I do." She opened the album to the last page with photos on it. There was a picture of the sisters with their father and Christine's mother, taken at Thanksgiving, a week before the accident. Afterward, Christine and Andrea had agreed that the informal family portrait would be the last in the album.

Looking at the image of the small, slight man with the receding hairline and the impish smile, Andrea sighed. "For all his faults, Daddy was so loving, so..." She trailed off again, thinking of his compulsive generosity, which had gone hand-in-hand with his gambling habit. He had been a friendly, active man who had cared deeply for his daughters, wanting only the best for them and giving them the freedom they needed to fulfill their dreams.

Christine slouched in the rocker, one leg over the chair arm, as her father had sat so many times in the past. The deceptive stillness that had been harbored in his eyes was reflected now in Christine's.

Searching for the right words, Andrea began to speak slowly. "Until a couple of days ago, I thought we were totally different. But we aren't different in every way, are we?"

A wary look crept into Christine's eyes. "What do you mean?"

"Before you woke up, I was thinking about when I'd left home. I was a year younger than you—only sixteen. And Daddy let me go."

"He didn't understand why you wanted to leave—I remember overhearing him and Momma talking about it."

Andrea nodded absently. "I'm sure he didn't. But it was what I wanted and he let me go. It meant having to work days at low-paying jobs and finishing school at night. Living in dumps. Fighting my own battles. But Daddy let me do it." Andrea stared at her sister, who was reaching for another chocolate. "I haven't given you the freedom that Daddy gave me.'' The same freedom Gage was giving her.

Christine replaced the glass cover cautiously, forgetting the candy in her fingers. The lightness in her voice sounded forced. ''I get the impression you're trying to say something.''

Andrea's laugh was affectionate. ''I guess I am. It's not right for me to deny you something I was so generously given—the right to make my own mistakes and be responsible for them. I've wanted to protect you so much from the pains and aches I've suffered.... Guess I've been a smothering parent. Forgive me?''

The two sisters stared at each other across the small living room furnished with the memories of their childhoods. Christine nodded and said hesitantly, ''Sure.''

Knowing that her sister didn't understand fully what she meant, Andrea added, ''Of course, I still expect you to keep in touch and tell me all about the dig while you're out there in the wilds of New Mexico. They do have mail service, don't they?''

Christine stared at her for a long moment, her mouth half open and disbelief on her face. Then a shriek of joy resounded off the walls of the apartment, and she bounded out of her chair to throw her arms around Andrea's neck. ''Do you really mean it? Really?''

''Yes, really.'' Andrea returned her sister's enthusiastic bear hug and patted her back.

''Oh, Andi, that's the greatest Christmas present you could have given me!'' Christine jumped up and whirled around the room. Then she stopped, staring at Andrea, who watched her with the regretful eyes of a parent who realized that the child was growing up, if not away. Christine popped the half-melted chocolate into her mouth and grinned. ''Of course there's mail service. Miles from the site, I'm sure. But don't worry, I'll be fine and I'll write every day.''

''Once a week will suffice.'' Andrea smiled ruefully, knowing that she would always worry about her sister. But that was all right; it was part of letting go.

Christine clapped her hands together. ''Oh, gosh! I've got to tell Roger. He won't believe it!''

As she sprinted into the hallway, headed for the telephone, Andrea called, ''But it's only six o'clock!''

''That's okay. He's an early riser!''

Andrea flipped the album open again and thumbed through the pages. Staring at her favorite photograph of herself and her father, Andrea murmured, ''Daddy, she's so much your daughter. We aren't alike and never had much in common. That's made it hard for both of us these past couple of years without you and Mom. But it's time to let her live her life, and I'll live mine.''

Closing the album, Andrea set it aside, stood up and moved to the stereo to switch the radio on. She could hear Christine chattering excitedly on the phone. Andrea thought of the changes in her life that were made that morning, and in previous days. Her stable world of work and home had vanished with a single trip, an eventful meeting with a stranger. Her life now was disordered, her future uncertain. Only her emotions were sure. And she was trying desperately to ignore their influence.

Tears edged her lashes, and she shook her head angrily. Damn Gage McLaren! If she had not met him, she would not be going through this pain and turmoil now. She had not heeded the warning bells of that evening, which seemed a lifetime ago but had only been two weeks earlier. They had known each other for such a short time, yet the love they shared was deeper and more real than anything she had ever felt before. Gage's face surfaced in her mind, his dark eyes tender with emotion, his roguish smile endearing beyond belief.

He wanted her to be reasonable. Didn't he realize she was trying to be sensible? She couldn't blithely throw away the little financial security she had, not when she was still responsible for Christine. She couldn't take his money, nor could she let him fight her battles. She had to find her own solutions.

And, damn it, the man was giving her the freedom to do that. Didn't he know that giving her that freedom tied her emotions to him more securely? Didn't he understand she wasn't yet certain that she wanted that bond?

Or did he?

IT HAD BEEN A LONG MONDAY, brightened only by the fact that Cal had not come into the office. Andrea slid the tray of mincemeat cookies into the oven and set the timer. But the confrontation with her boss had been postponed only for a few hours. Cal had telephoned late in the afternoon and asked her to meet him at the office that evening. He had been tied up in software-requirement meetings at Tectron all day. and he wanted to finish off some business before the ComSearch office closed for the long Christmas weekend.

In two hours, Andrea would have to face Cal's justified anger. He probably thought that he had been deceived. Andrea hoped that she could convince him of the truth. All day, Gage's words had echoed incessantly through her mind. Cal was dangerous; of that she had no doubt. But he was dangerous only because he was a master games player, who sought to beat the odds no matter how high they were. He might be unethical, but he wasn't evil.

There was a commotion at the front door. Andrea wiped her hands on a towel and went to stand in the kitchen doorway. Laughing loudly, Christine and Roger stumbled into the apartment, their arms laden with packages and paper bags.

Christine looked around the dimly lit living room and chided her sister. "Sitting in the dark again, I see. Roger, hit the lights! Turn the stereo up! Let's get this place hopping. By the way, put on some of your albums. I'm tired of listening to Andy Williams and the Ray Coniff Singers!" She stomped past Andrea, disappearing into the kitchen.

Andrea turned on a lamp reluctantly; she enjoyed the soft glow of the Christmas tree lights and a few candles. Roger stood in the center of the room, faintly embarrassed and definitely uncomfortable. Taking a sack from his overloaded arms, Andrea said, "It's okay. Remember, she's my sister—I'm used to her. And I guess my choice of music is a bit sedate for her taste. What did you bring?"

Roger pushed gaily wrapped presents under the tree, then rubbed the palms of his hands on the legs of his jeans. "Some country, some rock. I hope you don't mind. Chrissie kinda insisted."

Andrea had never heard anyone call her tomboy sister Chrissie before. She smiled warmly. "Come here and give me a hug. It's the holiday season!"

Grinning, Roger gave her a quick hug and a peck on the cheek. As he stood back, shoving his hands into his pockets, he asked, "Are you sure it's okay if I spend Christmas with you? I mean, a guy with two ladies?"

"Chris said you were alone—something about your folks being in North Dakota and you couldn't go back east?"

"Yeah, they got transferred last month. It's my first Christmas away from my family." Roger's grin faded.

"Chris and I can identify with that. And of course it's okay! That's why we have that sleeper sofa. I just hope you're ready to be stuffed full of Christmas goodies. Chris and I both have been baking up a storm."

Roger laughed and shrugged out of his Windbreaker. "I could tell when we walked in. The apartment smells just like home—cookies, cakes and things."

Andrea took his jacket and turned toward the hall. Pausing in the doorway, she said, "Well, this is home for the next few days, so put your records on and enjoy." Remembering the dinner a week earlier and how much she had liked the boy, Andrea added, "It's good to have you here, Roger."

Roger pushed the hair off his forehead with a shove of his hand. "Thanks." Within moments, while Andrea hung his jacket in the hall closet, strange sounds reverberated off the apartment walls with the opening bars of a hard rock Christmas album.

The evening was lively as the music played on, and Christine and Roger engaged in nonstop bantering. After a light supper of mulled cider, hot dogs and oven-warm cookies, Andrea found herself reluctant to go into the office. Facing Cal's wrath was not her idea of a fun-filled evening, but the event was inevitable. The sooner she talked to him, the sooner the entire incident would be resolved.

After freshening her makeup and pulling a brush through her hair, Andrea put on her down jacket, grabbed up her purse and car keys, and headed for the door. She wasn't certain if her farewell even registered over the crashing guitar chords and thudding drumbeats of the music. While she trotted down the stairwell to the accompaniment of Roger's album, she figured that the staid apartment manager would have a few words with her in the morning.

The drive north to the mid-Wilshire district was made in record time, since the nighttime traffic was very light. The anxiety she had felt all day increased in direct proportion to how close she was to the office. By the time she swung the Mustang into the unlit parking lot, Andrea could no longer ignore Gage's words or the warning bells that were clanging wildly in her mind. The building was dark, the parking lot empty. Evidently Cal had been held up at Tectron longer than he'd anticipated; she had allowed plenty of time for him to reach the office before she did.

She parked her car in the slot nearest the kitchen door, then turned the ignition off and sat there for a few moments, deep in thought.

She had not wanted to admit to herself that Gage had been right, at least to a degree. While headhunting was a lucrative business if one was successful at it, it was not necessarily the best way to make a living. Andrea had always felt slightly ashamed to admit to anyone what she did, and too often she had ignored her guilty conscience when carrying out some of Cal's less-than-ethical assignments. Long ago, she had acknowledged that she was compromising her values for the sake of financial security.

Andrea had planned on staying at ComSearch until Christine's hospital bills were paid off. But considering the events of the past and her new knowledge of both NavCom Electronics and Stratcom, she wasn't certain that she could—or even should—remain at ComSearch. With her need for money so acute, she had hoped to weather what was to come from Cal's indignant fury and the lawsuit Gage would file.

Now, after spending the day thinking about the bleak and stormy future she was facing, Andrea decided that perhaps the prudent course of action would be to ditch her floundering dinghy of a job and find a large, safe vessel in which to ride out the storm. Quitting her job at ComSearch would cost her thousands of dollars in commissions. But, Andrea mused, opening her car door, perhaps money wasn't everything. Perhaps, as Gage had said, it was the principle of the matter that counted.

The office building was still warm and smoky after the day's business. Checking out the refrigerator, Andrea found a can of soda and opted for that instead of brewing coffee. Leaving the kitchen light on, she wandered into the hallway and up the unlit stairway to her office.

Everything was as she had left it at five o'clock that evening. Cards and recruiting sheets were stacked in neat piles around the edges of her desk. The white poinsettia she had bought the previous Christmas and nurtured through the year sat in its red ceramic pot on the corner of her desk, its second-year brackets profuse and spidery. On Larry's desk, the *Racing Form* lay spread open and marked up; he'd had a winning day and had left early to collect from his bookie. On the wall opposite their desks, the large blackboard was filled with Andrea's neat printing and Larry's wild scribbling, indicating interviews, job offers and start dates for the upcoming month.

Sitting behind her desk, Andrea stared at the board and thought of the many pressure-filled weeks and months she had spent trying to fill it with names, dates and times. Two years. It seemed so much longer. She'd watched so many people come and go in the business, headhunters who couldn't make it. Why had she been a success? She honestly didn't know the reason, other than that people trusted her.

Despite Cal's dishonesties, Andrea was proud that she herself had never lied to one of her recruits, beyond stretching the truth to get an engineer to a first interview. Once interest had been created by an interview, she had always been aboveboard and had refused to deceive applicant or client company. For that, and because all the people she had recruited into new positions had benefited their careers, Andrea did not regret her short tenure at ComSearch. She had learned a great deal, but now it was time to move on. And for the first time, she knew that Cal would be thrilled to see her depart.

She gathered her current, in-use paperwork and updated her already precise notes on the standing of each applicant. In the turmoil of her departure, Andrea did not want any of her job offers falling through cracks in red tape when their careers were on the line with a move.

Cal still hadn't arrived by the time she had finished, so she reluctantly started cleaning out her desk. It was surprising that she felt as she did about her decision to quit, especially considering the situation. But she could not deny feeling a stab of uncertainty about the future.

Andrea's gaze traveled slowly to the phone. It seemed appropriate that she should share this decision with Gage, no matter what happened with their relationship in the upcoming days and weeks. Andrea jumped up, peeked between the venetian blind slats and looked out at the parking lot. Her car still sat alone. Returning to her desk, she took her address book from her purse and dialed Gage's number. At the third ring, his answering machine switched on. The warm sound of his recorded voice accelerated her already quick pulse, but Andrea was not ready to leave an impersonal message on the machine. She hung up.

A fleeting movement caught her eye, yet the doorway to her office remained empty. Andrea called out, "Is anyone there?"

Silence greeted her question, and she strained to hear any sounds in the big old house. There were none. Certain that her imagination had not been playing tricks on her, she started to rise from the swivel chair. Just then Cal stepped silently into the doorway.

Her gasp of surprise caught in her throat. Forcing a smile to her quivering lips, she muttered, "Cal! I didn't hear you drive up. You certainly gave me a start!" She sank back into her seat and picked up the files she wanted to turn over to him.

Cal remained framed by the doorway, hunching his shoulders under the bulky corduroy jacket he wore and shoving his hands deep into its pockets. He flicked a calculating glance over the surface of her desk. His normally booming voice was a hiss. "What's all that?"

Andrea looked at the small pile of her personal belongings. "I was cleaning out my desk." Meeting his brittle gaze, she stated in a neutral tone, "Today was my last day, Cal. I'm quitting."

An elusive emotion danced in his cold eyes. "That won't be necessary."

"What?"

"You heard me." Cal unhunched his broad shoulders and took a step toward the desk. "There's no need for you to resign."

Andrea snorted in a stir of anger. "Oh, I see. It's a case of 'you can't quit—you're fired.'"

She didn't like the leer that split his face or the snideness that touched his words. "Not at all. It's more a case of—" Cal withdrew a hand from his coat pocket "—your unfortunately getting caught in your own game."

Andrea was about to ask him what on earth he was talking about when she noticed the snub-nosed revolver held loosely in his hand. Staring into the black hole of the two-inch barrel, she tried to swallow, but her throat muscles wouldn't obey. The words that rattled through her mind like a runaway freight train could not fight their way through the dryness of her mouth. She wished she could disappear into the fabric of her chair. Faced with an anger that could prompt this type of behavior, Andrea was not only speechless but terrified.

"I see you've nothing to say. Just as well. I've no time to spare; I have an appointment to keep for my alibi." The barrel waved in a jerk. "Put your things back."

Hesitating only a moment, Andrea did as she was told, scraping her belongings into a drawer and sliding it shut quietly. Her voice was barely a squeak. "What are you going to do?"

Cal smiled and answered almost pleasantly, "It seems that our burglar was dissatisfied with the damage done last week and returned to complete the job." Possible intentions flooded her mind, but Cal left no doubt as to what he had planned. "I warned you, Andrea, not to mess with me. You played the game and lost. Gage McLaren will learn no more about my operations or NavCom's. There's only one apparent way to put me out of business. And when you play with fire, you can expect to get burned."

Remembering his words and rage of a week earlier, Andrea blanched and whispered hoarsely, "You can't! You can't burn the building down!"

Cal's slow smile was wicked. "I won't. You will. Or it will appear that you did. And, being inexperienced at arson, you died in the fire you set."

Andrea trembled violently and rose unsteadily from her chair, supporting herself by grasping the edge of her desk. Her voice was stronger as she challenged, "You're mad!"

The glittering hazel eyes grew brighter with amusement. "I have a rule—I don't get mad, I get even."

Stepping around the corner of her desk and moving toward him, Andrea drew herself up to her full height and sucked in a deep breath. "But I haven't done anything for you to get even with."

The so-far agreeable voice turned vicious. "You are his witness. McLaren will destroy me with your testimony. Only you can connect me with Daggett's activities at McLaren's plant. Only you know about NavCom. Only you can ruin me!"

As Cal's hand holding the gun tightened its grip until the knuckles whitened, Andrea tried to distract him with conversation, hoping to escape through the doorway that now gaped beside them. "Gage McLaren has other witnesses for Len Daggett's wrongdoings. I'm not the only person who knows about the sabotage and Daggett's other schemes. Besides, being a co-owner doesn't make you responsible for his illegal actions."

"True. But being the mastermind behind Len does." Cal's eyes held hers as she tried not to glance at the doorway. An escape attempt was probably futile, but Andrea wasn't about to let him kill her without giving him a fight.

Trying to judge the distance to the door from the edge of her peripheral vision, Andrea asked, "You mean you were the one behind the sabotage that injured that man?"

Cal's laugh was devilish. "You don't think Len is capable of that type of planning, do you? Oh, he might have started this little war with McLaren, but I will be the one to finish it."

Andrea thought of Gage, and her heart twisted with remorse and pain. She had finally found a man who loved her as deeply as she loved him, and if she had listened to him, she wouldn't be in this predicament. He had warned her that Cal was dangerous, and she had refused to believe him. Now, as she faced the end of the gun barrel only a few feet away, Andrea blinked back tears and fought to keep the fragile control she held over her terror.

"You're going to kill me, is that it?" she whispered.

His coarse cackle filled the room. "Killing you is only the beginning of the end." He shook his head slowly. "No, there's more to follow. You see, I have great plans for NavCom Electronics, plans bigger and bolder than Len Daggett ever dreamed."

Suddenly, escape was the only thought in Andrea's mind. Heedless of the consequences, she bolted for the doorway, seeking the safety of the dark hallway and the stairs to possible freedom. Her abrupt movement caught Cal off guard, and his fraction-of-a-second hesitation was all Andrea needed to reach the beckoning darkness. Her jogging shoes made little sound on the thick carpet as she sprinted for the stairs. Behind her, Cal shouted an angry oath, and she heard his heavy footsteps for a few strides. For some reason, he wasn't following her; and as Andrea raced down the first flight of stairs, she realized why.

Only moments away, the second and last flight of stairs stretched to the first-floor hallway. The kitchen doorway cast a shaft of light across the hall and up the lower stairs. As Andrea glanced over her shoulder, she saw Cal standing at the railing, backlighted by the office light. The gun was extended and held in both his hands. Vaguely, she wondered how good a shot he was. Committed to her flight for freedom, Andrea decided that getting shot in the back was preferable to being burned alive. She began to descend the lighted steps.

As her hand slid smoothly on the waxed banister and steadied her swing off the final step and onto the shining linoleum, Andrea thought for a solitary moment, *I'm going to make it!*

Then, reaching the doorway to the kitchen and freedom, she felt an intense sting of pain. A deafening blast was accompanied by a multitude of fireworks behind her eyes. Confused by the pain, the noise and the inability to see, Andrea stumbled against the doorframe, grasping it for support. She tried to remember what it was she had been doing, but she couldn't. Slowly, she sank to her knees.

The darkness that enveloped her seconds later was a welcome relief.

SHE WAS WRAPPED in his loving embrace, secure, warm and peaceful. Gage's lips caressed her cheek with a disconcerting roughness while his gentle laugh crackled strangely. It was the sound of his voice that jarred her. It wasn't right; it wasn't Gage's husky, mellow baritone.

Andrea tried to ask him why he sounded so odd, yet her own voice was only a whimper. Why wasn't she hearing the words she was speaking? She tried to move away from Gage, to push against the strength of his arms, but she wasn't strong enough to break away from him. She collapsed against him, roughness prickling the side of her face.

Slowly, almost indolently, her senses responded to her surroundings, screaming out their warnings. It was the crackling sound, steadily increasing, that brought her to full consciousness and reality. As she listened with fierce concentration, trying to ignore the stabbing pain in her head, Andrea realized that she was lying on the carpet in the dark. Crawling to her hands and knees, she moaned softly and closed her eyes tightly against the stars of pain. As the tormenting ache subsided minutely, her faculties grew stronger. Despite her confusion, she made the connections in her mind.

With a gasp, Andrea pushed herself to her feet and staggered across the darkened room, to collide with a closed door. As she pressed her face against the wood, the smell of smoke was nearly overpowering, the crackle of the flames beyond the door terrifyingly distinct. The conversation with Cal swept through her mind with the devastation of a tidal wave. Horrified, Andrea sagged against the heated door.

Yet panic remained aloof, and her mind, still reeling from pain, was surprisingly clear. Flicking the light switch, she continued in darkness; either Cal had cut the electricity, or the fire had already burned the wiring. Andrea reached out, attempting to determine her location in the building. Her hands bumped into, then skimmed over, a tall metal surface. She was in the supply room, touching one of the five-drawer file cabinets.

Laying her aching forehead against the cool metal, Andrea tried to maintain her calm against a rising fear. As she began to cough from the smoke that was curling around the door's edges into the small room, she reviewed her situation. Getting outside help was impossible; there was no phone in here. Set back off Wilshire Boulevard, the office building was secluded. Traffic that night had been extremely light. No one would notice the fire until the building was fully engulfed.

Hesitant, Andrea let her gaze swing to the far wall. The security bars over the room's only window were clearly defined by the faint orange glow.

In despair, Andrea cried out, "Oh, God, help me!"

Running to the window, she looked down from her second-story location. Shadowy orange demons danced across the lawn and on the side of the vacant three-story building next door. The entire first floor of the Com-Search building was clearly involved, and as Andrea turned her back to the ghostly terror below, she realized with a sickening fear that the flames were spreading rapidly. The fire's roar was stunning, and smoke now filled the small supply room, making her cough continuously.

How long had she been unconscious? How long had the fire been burning? As she gripped the hot doorknob, Andrea knew it had been only minutes, perhaps even less time. The telling odor of gasoline lingered in the room.

With a surge of panic, Andrea screamed, knowing that her only escape would be through the flames on the other side of the door. Trying to summon her remaining courage, she breathed deeply, renewing a vicious bout of coughing. However, when she tried to turn the heated doorknob with a trembling hand, it failed to respond. Terror took control, and Andrea screamed again.

Over the roar of the flames, she heard a familiar voice anxiously calling her name. The husky baritone that had echoed through her mind as she had lain semiconscious on the floor called out again. "Andrea! Where are you? Tell me!"

Surely she was hallucinating. Gage was somewhere very far away from the conflagration—safe and unaware of her deep love for him. Yet, hearing her name again, Andrea whispered, "Gage?"

Another racking spell of coughing doubled her over and onto her knees. In the one moment that she caught her breath, Andrea screamed, "Gage, I'm here! In the supply room!"

Within moments, the door she was leaning against was forced open a few inches. Smoke boiled inward, and amber light bathed the walls. Andrea staggered to her feet and saw Gage slip into the room. He slammed the door shut, then coughed violently. By the glow at the window, Andrea stared at him, uncertain if he was real or an apparition.

As a wavering smile touched his lips, Gage drew her to his side and wrapped a very real singed wool blanket around them. His husky voice was oddly calming when he joked, "I don't know about you, but I've no intention of being a marshmallow."

Andrea trembled. "I agree!"

"Put the blanket over your head, wrap your arm around my waist and run like hell. We've only seconds before we're trapped."

Throwing his half of the blanket over his head, Gage yanked the door open and pulled Andrea into the hall. The blast of heat took her breath away. She was only vaguely aware of the flames that licked at her shoes and jeans as Gage dragged her down the smoke-filled hallway to the stairs.

At the landing, a funnel of fire and smoke was all she could see. Screaming, she tried to back away but was pulled tightly against Gage's side. He yelled over the inferno, "Come on! It's our only chance!"

Ducking her head under the blanket, Andrea clenched Gage's belt tightly in her fist. After a moment's hesitation, she yelled back, "Okay, let's go!"

Together, they plunged into the hell that had been created expressly for her.

Chapter Thirteen

The chill of the midnight air was being felt now. The all-consuming blaze was dying into smoldering embers beneath the torrents of water from fire-department hoses. Andrea sat on the hood of Gage's Mercedes coupe and stared at the charred skeleton of the two-story building, a specter against the full moon. The burned-out shell of her car still sat in the parking space by the kitchen door. Paramedics were busy packing away their equipment, satisfied that oxygen and minor medical treatment were all that the victims of the fire required.

Whirling red and blue lights from the emergency vehicles cast eerie, pulsating images around the now-crowded parking lot. Gage stood several yards away, talking to police officers. From the backseat of the patrol car, Cal Slattery glared through the window at Andrea with uncamouflaged hatred. She shivered inside her down jacket, but the tremors were from residual terror, not from the cold air.

It was difficult to think, her mind numbed from the assault of horror and the joy of being alive. If it hadn't been for Gage, Andrea knew she would have died in the fire. She closed her eyes against the tears that crept onto her cheeks. The commotion around her faded into a sooth-ing drone as she concentrated on the memory of Gage's arms around her and his tender kiss on the burned and bullet-creased side of her forehead while they had stood alone on the asphalt, watching the flames shoot from the roof into the night sky. Their escape from the building had preceded the collapse of the second floor by mere sec-onds. Yet it wasn't the fear she remembered but the deep gratitude and love she felt for the man who had held her so comfortingly.

Feeling a gentle hand on her shoulder, Andrea opened her eyes slowly. A fond smile dimpled Gage's cheek. "How's the head?"

"Okay." Andrea's hand slid up to the bandage cover-ing her left eyebrow and half of her forehead. "Don't you think the paramedic got carried away with the gauze and tape? It was such a little cut."

Gage snorted. "Not from where I stood." He leaned close and peered at her eyes. "I agree with the paramed-ics—we should take you to the hospital and have you checked over for a concussion."

Andrea protested. "I told you I'm okay. Aspirin will take care of my headache."

"Well, we'll see about that. I promised those guys I wouldn't let you out of my sight for the next twenty-four hours. So consider yourself under observation."

A little giggle caught in her throat. "Being with you will certainly beat lying in an old hospital bed."

Gage grinned. "Behave yourself. You're wounded."

Andrea murmured, "Yes, sir." She asked hesitantly, "What did the police say?"

Gage leaned a hip against the car and tucked a strand of hair behind her ear. "We'll have to go to the station to file a complete report before we can go home. Then we'll probably have to come back tomorrow to talk to some detectives.''

"What did they say about you, ah, collaring Cal?"

While they had listened to approaching sirens responding to the fire, Gage had explained to her why Cal's prone form was sprawled on the pavement nearby. Cal had been hurrying out the kitchen door just as Gage had pulled into the parking lot. Seeing Andrea's boss fleeing the fire-lit building with two five-gallon gas cans in his hands, Gage had cut off Cal's escape route by swinging his car into the man's path and bailing out the door to tackle Cal as he turned and sprinted in the opposite direction.

"Oh, they view it all as a citizen's arrest," Gage told her. "Actually, that bastard should consider himself lucky that I was more concerned about getting you out than retaining him." He shoved his hands into the back pockets of his jeans and stated coldly, "I wanted to bash his brains in."

Andrea slid off the hood of the car and looked up into his angry eyes. "I'm glad you didn't—the police would be arresting you for attempted murder instead of Cal. That wouldn't be a very happy ending to tonight."

Gage slipped his arms around Andrea's waist and drew her to him tenderly. His voice was a husky whisper. "Are we going to have that happy ending?"

Hearing the familiar affection in his voice, Andrea felt her heart leap in her chest, her pulse racing rapidly. As joy and uncertainty fought for control of her emotions, she forced out the question she had been waiting to ask. "Why did you come here tonight?"

"You'd had enough time to think things over. If your decision wasn't the right one, I wasn't going to let you pack up and run away. There's too much between us for me to let you get away without a fight." A slow smile spread over his face. "And believe me, lady, you try to run from me again and you'll discover what a fighter I am!"

Andrea curled her arms around his neck. "Do you fight dirty?"

Gage's answer was a sigh. "Only in the clinches." His warm, moist lips brushed over hers, reminding her of the past and promising an exciting future.

Snuggling close and laying her cheek against his sweater, Andrea murmured, "How wonderful!"

Gage breathed into her hair. "Tell me, would you have run away?"

Listening to the steady beat of his heart beneath her cheek, she said, "Only as far as home." She tipped her head back to look into his eyes and ignored the heavy thudding ache at her temple. "And home is with you."

The look in Gage's eyes told Andrea all she had ever wanted to hear. His kiss was a whisper against her lips, a secret they would always share.

He held her tightly, neither of them moving. They both were oblivious to the clamor around them as the firemen prepared to clean up the area and turn over the scene to the arson investigators and police detectives who were standing by to gather evidence that would be used in upcoming trials.

"Tomorrow's Christmas Eve. What are we going to do?" she asked.

The good humor that Andrea found so captivating returned to Gage's voice. "First, we'll have to invite Chris and her boyfriend—Roger, isn't it?—to the annual McLaren Christmas Eve party. In exchange for all the food and drink you want and a rousing good time, you'll get to help decorate the twelve-foot tree that I managed to wrestle into the house tonight. That way, your family will get to meet the entire outrageous McLaren clan and vice versa.''

Andrea's heart skipped a beat as she looked up at him. The genuine love and tender emotions she saw in his eyes alternated with boyish mischief and yearning desire. A playful smile skipped across her lips. ''And,'' she said, ''what happens after the party?''

While a policeman approached them briskly, Gage bent and whispered in her ear, ''A private celebration that neither of us will forget.''

As Gage released her to turn toward the officer, Andrea murmured with a little giggle, ''Darling, you can count on that!''

ANNE MATHER

Anne Mather, one of Harlequin's leading romance authors, has published more than 100 million copies worldwide, including **Wild Concerto,** a *New York Times* best-seller.

Catherine Loring was an innocent in a South American country beset by civil war. Doctor Armand Alvares was arrogant yet compassionate. They could not ignore the flame of love igniting within them...whatever the cost.

HIDDEN IN THE FLAME